AMBER EVE

The Accidental Impostor

SATURDAY LANE

"Till this moment I never knew myself."

— Jane Austen, Pride and Prejudice

Chapter 1

There's a sheep on the bus.

No, it's not something you see often. I'd have to agree with you there. Not even here in the Highlands of Scotland, where there are probably more sheep than people. Trust me when I tell you, I was just as surprised as you are, and I grew up here, so not a lot surprises me about the place.

The fact remains, though: there is a sheep on the bus, and it stares at me balefully (Is there any other way for sheep to stare, I wonder?) as the bus leaves the outskirts of Fort William and creaks its way up the coast. The sheep's owner — an elderly farmer with an unlit pipe in his mouth — is staring at me too, as are the three teenage girls on the back seat, whose kohl-ringed eyes have been locked on me ever since they got onto the bus.

It's probably because of The Thing.

I mean, it *could* be that I've got lipstick on my teeth, or my skirt tucked into my knickers or something. Both of those things would be very 'on brand' for me; and don't even get me started about the time I nodded off shortly after applying fake tan and woke up with a white hand-print on my bright-orange face.

They could be staring at me for any of those reasons, really. But it's probably because of The Thing.

It's *always* because of The Thing.

The Thing is the reason I left Heather Bay in the first place. It's the reason I swore I would never come back. It's the reason Tam, the bus driver, greeted me by name when I hauled my suitcase up the steps, and it's also the reason he accepted my promise to get my mum to pay him as soon as I got home. Tam knows my mum, you see. Everyone knows my mum. Everyone in Heather Bay knows everyone else, really. Which means everyone knows about *The Thing*; and, pretty soon, everyone will know that Emerald Taylor rocked up to the bus stop in Fort William, saying she had no money, but could she get a lift home, anyway?

Classic Emerald. Just classic.

That's Ben's voice in my head, by the way. He's my ex-boyfriend of — *checks watch* — about 10 hours, and although he'd never been to the Highlands in his life, having been born and raised in Watford, he thought he knew all about the place, because he'd seen *Outlander* a few times, and that tells you everything you need to know, really, doesn't it?

But no. Not really. Well, not *at all*, actually. Or not unless you were to *actually* travel back to the 1800s, obviously, and I'll let you into a secret: the standing stones are *just stones*. Sorry. Don't tell anyone.

Heather Bay itself *is* pretty scenic, though; that much is true. It has a cute little row of pastel-painted cottages that people like to take photos of for Instagram, a picture-postcard harbor, and a small beach, fringed with seafood restaurants. There's even a castle on the cliffside just outside the village, but it's not ruined *or* haunted, and, no, Jamie Fraser doesn't live in it, so it's always been a bit of a disappointment, really.

Non-haunted castles aside, I guess I can see why tourists like the Bay, as it's known locally. I'd probably like it myself if I was one of them. But I'm not, more's the pity. I'm the infamous Emerald Taylor, a.k.a. Heather Bay's Least Wanted person; which is just one of the reasons my current situation is a real bind, really.

The other reasons are all sitting there silently staring at me, as if I'm an exhibit in a museum or something, and it's making me so uncomfortable I really wish my phone was working, so I could pretend to be doing something very busy and important on it, in a bid to avoid the awkwardness.

Sadly for me, though, my phone died somewhere between London and Fort William — at about the same time as my will to live — so, instead, I have to make do with staring out of the grubby window of the bus, secretly waiting for that moment when you crest that final hill just outside Heather Bay, and see the town spread out before you, the pastel colors reflected in the shining sea, and the mountains looming majestically behind it.

I'd deny it if you asked me, but, it *is* pretty.

Beautiful, even, in a wild and rugged kind of way.

But I still don't want to be here, and I'm determined to hate every second of my homecoming.

So there.

I jut out my chin and stare defiantly at the sheep, as if it was the one who dared suggest I might actually enjoy being home again. The sheep stares back as if I've hurt its feelings. The farmer turns around to glare at me accusingly, and, right at that moment, a loud roar drowns out the rattle and creaks of the bus as a bright red sports car goes screeching past us,

3

forcing Tam to steer us right into the ditch at the side of the road.

Silence.

Then a loud, indignant bleat as the sheep, who skidded all the way across the aisle when Tam slammed on the brakes, registers its disappointment with the situation.

"Edna!" splutters the farmer, almost dropping his pipe as he stumbles towards the animal. "Are ye alright, Edna?"

Edna? The sheep's called Edna? Is it... a pet sheep?

"Never mind Edna, Jimmy," says Tam, struggling out of his seat. "It's that Jack Buchanan ye want to get a look at."

"Aye," Jimmy replies, pulling Edna back to her rightful place by his side. "I thought that was his car, right enough. Flashy bugger, so he is."

There's a murmur of excitement from the three girls at the back of the bus, and I follow the direction of their gaze to where the red sports car has stopped a little further along the road. The driver is standing beside it, deep in conversation with yet another farmer, who seems to have jumped off his tractor to see what's going on.

(Not everyone in the Highlands is a farmer, by the way. It just seems like it, sometimes.)

I can't see much of the man's face through the grime on the bus window; what I *can* see of him, however, is enough to tell me that this is obviously not a Heather Bay local. He's wearing a camel overcoat over a navy sweater and dark jeans, and his immaculate suede brogues are going to be absolutely ruined by the mud he's currently standing in. Even from here, I can see that his dark hair has been expensively cut, and his eyes are hidden behind a pair of designer sunglasses.

Nope, definitely not a local.

4

"Isn't he amazing?" one of the girls behind me sighs to her friends, and, for a moment, I forget I'm supposed to be trying to keep a low profile and twist round in my seat to face her.

"Amazing?" I say, before I can stop myself. "The guy who just ran a bus full of people off the road, you mean? That guy?"

Okay, "a bus full of people" might be stretching it slightly. It's six people and a sheep, after all. But even so, now that the initial shock has passed and no real harm has been done, indignation is starting to take over. This guy with his flashy sports car and his stupid suede shoes could have killed us; and trust me, I did not come all this way just to die in a rusty old bus with a sheep.

"'*That guy*' is Jack Buchanan," the girl who'd described him as "amazing" says, as if she expects this to mean something to me. "He's basically the richest man in the country *and* the sexiest. And he's the Laird of this entire area. So, yeah, he *is* pretty amazing, actually."

She stares at me challengingly before popping her gum in my face, and I turn back to face the window, wishing I hadn't spoken. Teenagers scare me — especially the girls. I'd rather face an entire army of vampires, say, than three teenage girls. Vampires can only kill you, after all; teenage girls, on the other hand, can totally *destroy* you. Don't ask me how I know.

"I think Mr. Buchanan's only the *eighth* richest man in Scotland," Jimmy-the-farmer is saying, but whether that's true or not will have to forever remain a mystery, because before he can go on, the bus doors ping open, and a familiar figure steps through them.

McTavish.

Today really is the gift that keeps on giving.

"Jimmy," he says cheerfully, nodding at the farmer. "Edna.

5

Tam."

His bright blue eyes pass over the teenagers before settling on me, and I shrink into my seat in horror as he beams in recognition, his wide smile revealing two black gaps where his front teeth should be.

When we were at school together, McTavish still had his teeth. Everything else about him is more or less the same, though, from his haystack hair to the goofy grin that always seemed to have me as its target.

McTavish was the boy next door, but not in a *Dawson's Creek* kind of way, so if that's what you're thinking, I'm going to stop you right there. For one thing, when I say "next door" I mean the McTavish farm was the closest building to my parents' cottage, so it's not like McTavish and I spent our childhoods chatting over the garden fence or crawling through each other's bedroom windows or anything like that.

The truth is, I tried my best not to see McTavish at all. He, however, was always determined to see *me*, which meant I spent most of my childhood and teenage years with him following me around, like a particularly enthusiastic puppy. My parents' toy poodle has never in his life shown me the level of loyalty McTavish has; not even when he was an *actual* puppy. That's because Jude Paw hates me, though, and McTavish used to make me hand-drawn cards every so often, which he'd give me in person, always at the most public moment possible.

Mortifying.

McTavish was present for every important occasion in my life in Heather Bay, so it figures he'd be here now for my return.

"Emerald, is that really you?" he asks, looking genuinely delighted to find me here.

"Aye, it's her," confirms Tam, before I can speak.

"The very same," nods Jimmy.

"I told you it was her," hisses a voice from behind me.

(Edna says nothing, on account of being a sheep, obviously. But if sheep could talk, she looks like she'd be weighing in on this one, too.)

"She's come back with no money," Tam continues, as if I'm not there. I really wish I wasn't. "Her mam's going to come round and bring me the fare tomorrow, she says."

I swear to God, Edna snorts in disbelief at this. Who knew sheep could be so sassy?

"Och, dinnae worry about that," McTavish says, digging in his pocket and pulling out a handful of change. "Here, that should be right."

"No, don't," I say, springing up from my seat to stop him, but McTavish just waves me away, grinning his toothless grin.

"It's good to see ye again, Emerald," he says shyly, looking at me from under his mop of yellow-blonde hair. "I didnae think ye'd be back here, after... well, ye know."

An awkward silence descends, which Edna breaks by bleating loudly. I thank her silently, while giving McTavish my best attempt at a smile, even though smiling is the very last thing I feel like doing right now.

"Thanks, McTavish," I say. "And thanks for paying the fare. I'll get the money back to you tomorrow, I promise. It's just, my bank card stopped working, and I only had enough cash on me for the train fare, so I—"

"Dinnae mention it," McTavish says cheerfully, holding up a hand to stop me. "Now," he says, turning back to Tam. "If ye sit tight, I'll get my tractor and pull ye out of this ditch. Then I'll see to Mr. Buchanan. It's a good job I was working this field when ye passed."

7

"I'd *love* to see to Mr. Buchanan," giggled the gum-popping girl. This time, I manage to resist the impulse to turn around. The red sports car is still stuck in the mud on the other side of the narrow road, and I suppress a small smirk of satisfaction as I watch the owner — one Jack Buchanan, according to everyone around me — frown as he attempts to wipe the mud from his suede loafers onto the grass.

The shoes look designer, as do the rest of his clothes. His coat alone probably cost more than the rent I pay to Ben every month.

Used to pay to Ben every month.

I won't be paying rent any more, of course, given that he dumped me this morning, effectively leaving me homeless, given that the flat was his, and the landlord didn't *technically* know I was living there. Or that I existed, for that matter.

I'm not even sure *Ben* knew I existed some of the time, to be honest.

Well, no need to worry about that now, I suppose.

I close my eyes against the wave of exhaustion that suddenly assails me, and, when I open them again, the bus is being heaved backwards out of the ditch, then shunted forward until it's almost level with the sports car. As we pass it, Jack Buchanan glances around, and I get a quick glimpse of even features and full lips: a pretty-boy face, roughened up by a hint of stubble and dark, ruffled hair that looks like he's been running his hands through it in frustration. Which he probably has, given the circumstances.

He looks a bit like James Dean might have done, if James Dean had lived in modern times, and held off on the hair gel a little. This is actually quite inconvenient for me, really, because James Dean is my secret imaginary boyfriend, who I

8

love unreservedly, and this Jack Buchanan is... well, a Grade A asshole, it would seem.

What a waste.

As the bus moves past the car, our eyes briefly meet through the dirty window. He scowls, as if the very sight of me has offended him, and I instantly scowl back, treating him to my fiercest grimace; the one Ben says makes me resemble a pit bull on steroids.

There. That'll show him.

I sit back, refusing to drop my gaze until he finally drops his, turning away with a look of disgust on his face.

I win.

Well, if you consider pissing off a random stranger in the remote Highlands to be "winning", that is.

It's a small victory, to be sure.

A minuscule one, in fact.

It is, however, all I've got for now, so I'm counting it.

And, if the look on his face is anything to go by, Jack Buchanan is counting it, too.

Chapter 2

**Possible Reasons for the Sudden and Mysterious
Disappearance of My Ex-Boyfriend, Ben:
A List**

1. Another woman. *Unlikely, considering that he still sometimes tucks his shirts into his underpants despite my best efforts to get him to stop, but I don't suppose I can rule anything out at this stage.*
2. Witness protection program. *Possible. Unlikely, but possible.*
3. Secret double life. *See above.*
4. Suddenly called away to care for an ailing aunt. *Except, as far as I know, his aunt is alive, well, and in training for the London marathon. So probably not.*
5. Found out his sister's honor has been compromised by a dastardly officer, and now Ben must avenge her. *Think that's the plot of Pride & Prejudice.*
6. Uncovered a terrorist plot and now has 24 hours to save the world. *It's possible I watch too much TV as well as reading too many romance novels.*
7. Just decided he'd finally "had enough of my shit", like he always used to say he would one day.

I wrote my list on the train from London to Edinburgh, and I present it to my parents as soon as I get home, in a bid to stave off any questions they might have about the whole situation.

Unfortunately for me, though, it just creates even *more* questions.

"I dinnae understand," Mum says, looking worried. This isn't exactly unusual: Mum always looks worried. It's her natural state. Ruby Taylor is a Grade A Worrier. If worrying was an Olympic sport, she'd be a household name, for sure.

My mum worries about everything from whether she's left the iron on by mistake, to what would happen if someone (By which she means Dad) stacks the cutlery the wrong way up in the dishwasher, then someone (Dad, again), trips and falls onto the pointed ends of the forks and knives.

Mostly, though, she worries about me. Which I suppose is fair enough, really, considering how much I've given her to worry about over the years.

"I dinnae understand," she says again, the line deepening between his eyes. "Ben always seemed like such a nice, steady, lad. But now ye're saying ye think he was mixed up with the Mafia the whole time, Emerald?"

"Well, I didn't say that *exactly*," I say, squirming in my seat. "I just... I mean, there has to be some kind of explanation, right? And he didn't leave a note or anything to tell me what it might be, so—"

"So yer imagination has gone to work, as usual?" says Dad, shrewdly. "And what's this about losin' yer job? How did that happen? The Mafia again, I suppose?"

Oh yeah: *that*. What with all the drama of Ben's sudden departure this morning, I'd almost forgotten I'd *also* been laid off from my job just a couple of hours earlier.

But yes, that also happened to me today; meaning I've essentially just lost my boyfriend, my home, *and* my livelihood almost simultaneously. Which would be almost unbelievable if it wasn't... well, *me*, basically.

It's all just very *me*. And that's *without* even mentioning the way my bank card decided to stop working earlier today, leaving me with just enough money for the train to Fort William, and nothing more. I haven't even told Mum and Dad about that yet.

"No, the job thing really *was* an accident," I say earnestly, leaning forward in my chair. "You know what the publishing industry's like; no one's job's safe. They just couldn't afford to keep me on, they said. It could've happened to anyone, given the current economic climate."

Mum and Dad have no idea what the publishing industry's like, of course, and, to be totally honest, *I'm* only vaguely aware of "the current economic climate". It *is* true that people are being laid off right now, though, so I'm sure my sudden unemployment was nothing personal. I'm much less certain the same could be said of Ben, though; and the main reason I'm pushing this "Mafia" theory so hard is simply because him being involved with the Mafia would be much easier to understand than him just... *leaving me.*

Why would he just leave me?

And why don't I care more about it?

"But surely there was some kind of *sign*?" Mum persists. "What was the last thing he said to ye, lass?"

I think carefully back to this morning — was it *really* only this morning? — when I came home from work less than an hour after I'd left, to find Ben frantically packing a suitcase.

He was in such a rush he didn't even bother with those stupid little packing cubes he always loved so much. That's how I knew something was up. Well, that and the fact that he waited until he thought I'd be at work before trying to do a runner, obviously.

That was a major clue, too.

He didn't tell me where he was going, or why. All he said was that he was sorry, and that I'd "understand one day". Oh, and there *was* one other thing:

"He told me to remember to switch off the lights when I left," I tell Mum and Dad as the memory returns to me. "He was always fussing about the electricity bill."

"That's wise of him," Dad starts to say, before Mum silences him with a look.

"And was that it?" she asks, confused. "He didnae say anything else?"

I shake my head miserably. That was really how it happened; how the most serious relationship of my life came to an end. Those were the final words of the man I'd lived with for the past five years and had been tentatively considering getting a cat with, up until Ben decided he would probably be allergic to it.

Remember to switch the lights off. Don't run up a huge electricity bill.

Profound stuff, for sure. With a relationship as mundane as ours was, no wonder I'm struggling to feel anything but relief at its demise. Relief, and, okay, *confusion.* It would be safe to say confusion is probably my over-riding emotion right now. Because it would never even have occurred to me that Ben might just up and leave like that, without warning. It's the most un-Ben thing he's ever done. This was a man who had

13

Days of the Week underpants, for God's sake. Spontaneity was never really his thing. If it had been, I guess I might be feeling a little more upset at his sudden departure. As it is, though, I don't think it's really sunk in yet. None of it has. In fact, sitting here at the kitchen table, with a glass of Dad's homemade wine and a plate of suspiciously green looking chicken in front of me, I'm starting to wonder if I've over-reacted by rushing back here.

There has to be a reasonable explanation for all of this, surely? Like... aliens, for instance. There's one I didn't put on my list!

"Maybe he's been abducted by aliens?" I suggest, taking a tentative sip of my wine.

"Maybe he's dead?" Mum counters, upping the ante considerably.

"Yes, hopefully," I agree. "That would at least be a decent explanation for all of this."

"That's the spirit, lass," says Dad, slapping me cheerfully on the back. "Here, have one of these!"

He offers me a plate of the cakes I've been eyeing hopefully ever since I arrived, and I take one gratefully.

That's way too much sugar, Emerald. You'll get fat.

That's Ben again. I kind of wish he'd shut up, to be honest. This is *my* crisis, after all, not his. And if I want to eat my feelings about it, I damn well will. Then I'll hide the evidence at the bottom of the recycling bin, and he'll never know.

Not that it's any of his business.

Not any more.

"And how long do you think you'll be staying?" Mum asks, trying to sound casual. "It's just, we didn't think you'd want to come back after The Thing."

"Oh, just a few nights," I say, nonchalantly ignoring the last comment. "Just until I figure out what my next move is going to be."

Dad nods obediently. I think Jude is pretty convinced, too. But Mum knows me too well to be taken in by my act.

"Is that right, love?" she asks, looking at me doubtfully. "And what's that going to be, do you think? Will you go back to London? To publishing?"

I pretend to consider this carefully.

"Yes, probably," I say confidently.

Nope, absolutely not, says my brain, surprising me with its sudden ability to seamlessly contradict the words that have just come out of my mouth. *You're never going back there and you know it. You hate it there. And you hated your relationship with Ben, too. That's why you're not more upset about it. That's why you're sitting here eating cake and talking about alien abductions, instead of crying into your pillow, or whatever it is that people who've just been dumped would normally do.*

The brain might be speaking out of turn here, but it is telling the truth. It's a truth I've never spoken aloud; or even admitted to myself, really. But it's a truth all the same, and as soon as I acknowledge its existence — albeit silently — I know I'm never going to escape it.

London had always been my dream. Even as a teenager, I'd pictured myself sitting at a picturesque little pavement cafe, tapping away on my laptop, wearing a cute pink beret and soaking up the atmosphere and creativity of the city as I worked on that novel I'd always been meaning to write. I... think that might have been Paris I was thinking of, actually, now I think of it?

Because London was nothing like that for me. Actually, it

was just busy, and dirty, and too loud to hear yourself think, let alone write. The flat I shared with Ben was smaller than even the tiniest fisherman's cottage back home, and my job as a book editor wasn't nearly as glamorous as I'd imagined, either. I thought I'd just have to read mystery novels all day, and go out to fancy parties in the evenings. Instead, I ended up editing academic journals for a man called Darren, who always smelt of onions. Oh, and I didn't even *own* a pink beret. Which was unfortunate, really.

(Note to self: buy pink beret. Just, you know, *in case*.)

In the end, leaving wasn't as hard as I'd thought it would be. It's just the "coming home" part that hurts.

"Well, if you need something to tide you over," Mum says, clearly not fooled by my show of confidence, "You could always call Francesca. Her cleaning firm is doing really well now, you know; she's got an office on the High Street and everything, and she's always looking for cleaners. I'm sure she'd help you out."

"I don't *need* helping out," I say, stung.

This is a straight-up lie, obviously. I have never needed "helping out" more than I do right at this moment; and my best friend, Frankie, would be more than willing to do it, I know. That's just what she's like. Even if she *hadn't* somehow managed to set up a successful cleaning business in my absence, I'm pretty sure she'd have done it now, just so she could offer me a job in it.

But I don't want to work for Frankie; a truth that has nothing at all to do with Frankie herself, and everything to do with me.

Taking a job with Frankie would mean committing to staying in the Highlands, at least for now. It would mean admitting to myself that I'm never going back to London — and probably never going back to publishing, either.

It would mean admitting I'd failed. Again. And, okay, I think it's fair to say I know that already, but knowing it and admitting it are two different things. I might know it, but if I don't *admit* it, it can't be true, can it?

On second thoughts, don't answer that.

"I can't get a job here, anyway," I point out, taking another sip of Dad's wine. It tastes like vinegar mixed with feet, but I swallow it down anyway. "No one wants me here. Not after The Thing."

"Ach now, that was a long time ago," says Mum soothingly. "I'm sure everyone's forgotten about it by now."

"They haven't," Dad pipes up. "Old Jimmy mentioned it in the pub last week, in fact. It seems Bella McGowan is setting up a committee to try to finally get the village hall fixed, after our Emerald ... well. Did ye know we haven't had a Gala Day ever since ye left, Emerald? Because of The Th—"

"Is this chicken green, or am I imagining it?" I interrupt him, desperate to change the subject.

"Aye," Mum confirms, without a hint of embarrassment. "The recipe said to use mint, but I didn't have any, so I just used some green food coloring, so I did. It's the same thing. Have some more, Emerald; ye look like the cat's elbow, so ye do. Did they not have any decent food in that London?"

Dad and I look doubtfully at the chicken, and I make a mental note to go grocery shopping tomorrow, so I don't waste away from Mum's cooking. Then I remember I don't have any money to pay for it, and the panic starts to rise.

"Well, I'm exhausted," I say, pushing back my chair so suddenly that Jude Paw jumps up and starts barking at me in surprise. "I think I'll go to bed. Night, then!"

I am pretty tired, it's true. This day has been approximately two weeks long already, and almost as traumatic as The Thing itself. Tired as I am, though, I'm really just going to bed so I can lie on it and stare at the ceiling, doing my best not to think about the fact that I'm back in my childhood bedroom again, at the grand old age of twenty-eight.

Other things I don't want to think about include:

1. Ben.
2. Why Ben left.
3. Me losing my job.
4. What the hell I'm going to do now.

I'll make a list of the things I don't want to think about, I decide. Because it's honestly getting hard to keep track of them all. For now, though, it's time to go to bed.

* * *

My parents' house has been fully renovated at least twice since I moved out, thanks to Mum's post-retirement passion for interior design.

My old room, however, remains frozen in time; a shrine to my teenage self, complete with a large collection of stuffed animals on the single bed, and dog-eared posters of Flying Haggis, the Highland's very own answer to One Direction, on the walls.

Determinedly ignoring the painful pang of nostalgia that this step back in time evokes, I cross quickly to the window and pull back the curtain to look out.

The views were always my favorite thing about this house, which sits on top of a hill, high above the Bay itself. My narrow bedroom is in what used to be the attic, and it has a window on each side: one looking down over the town, and out to the sea beyond, while the other faces inland, over Heather Glen to Loch Keld, and the hills beyond it.

The loch is basically our back garden, then. From here, it feels almost as if you could throw a stone from my bedroom and hit it. You can't — don't ask me how I know — but, all the same, the water is close enough that it's always felt a bit like having our own private loch.

Although it's still only April, the days here are long, and the sun is only just starting to set, lending a golden hue to the landscape and a sparkle to the sea. Even though I don't want to be here, I still feel strangely comforted by the hulking presence of the hills.

It's beautiful.

And, well, also a bit sad, really.

I used to spend hours up here, flitting aimlessly between the two windows and plotting my eventual escape. But now here I am, right back where I started, and as I press my forehead against the window and watch my breath mist up the glass, I would give anything in the world to be somewhere else; or some*one* else, even.

But I'm not.

I'm Emerald Taylor, and I'm finally home.

And I have a *really* bad feeling about it.

Chapter 3

The next morning, three Very Bad Things happen in quick succession.

The first thing is my phone call to the bank, which confirms that my faulty bank card yesterday was not, in fact, an accident, like I'd assumed. There's no technical glitch, no hacking of the account, and I have absolutely *not* slipped into an alternate reality, no matter how hard I try to convince the man on the end of the phone that this must surely be the case.

I just have no money.

Actually, I have *less* than no money, because it seems that *someone* has spent all of my overdraft, as well as maxing out my credit card. And I have a pretty good idea who it was, too.

The second thing is my call to Ben's landlord back in London, who confirms that Ben ended the lease yesterday morning, forfeiting the deposit he'd paid when he moved in and everything. So I can't go back now, even if I wanted to. Ben really has gone. There's no "reasonable explanation" for what happened yesterday; not even a totally implausible one involving Mafia overlords or alien abduction. Or, if there is, then I have to accept that I'm probably never going to know what it is.

Shit.

(Oh, and the third thing is Jude Paw pooping in my shoe

again. Which, to be honest, seems like much less of a big deal that it would have done, had its discovery not been preceded by the first two Very Bad Things. I'm adding him to my list of Mortal Enemies, anyway. As Mum would say, he's worth the watching, that one.)

As I hang up the phone on the landlord, I realize something weird is happening in my chest. It's probably my heart breaking. Yes, that must be it. This must be what heartbreak feels like: a bit like how I've always imagined a heart attack might feel, only slightly more painful. If this was a movie, this would be the moment someone would ask if I needed a glass of water. I've always wondered why people do that, actually? What is it about water that's supposed to be good for shock? Why not gin, say? Or vodka? Or anything other than stupid old water? And why am I thinking about this, anyway? Why am I not thinking about Ben, given that he's apparently just broken my heart?

Concentrate, Emerald. If you're going to get your heart broken, the very least you could do is pay attention to it.

I poke gently at the edges of this new emotion, wondering what else is hidden underneath it. And what I discover is quite surprising, under the circumstances.

Because it isn't heartbreak.

It's relief.

I'm relieved that Ben ended things. I'm not happy about the way he did it, obviously, and I'm downright furious — not to mention *terrified* — about the fact that he's apparently taken all of my money with him. What he's done has changed my life — much more than losing my job ever could.

Then again, maybe my life needed changing? And, okay, this is obviously not the way I'd choose to do it. Not even close.

The more I think about it, though, the more I start to realize that while I desperately want my money back, I don't want Ben or my job. Because I wasn't happy with either.

And maybe not all "accidents" turn out to be for the worst.

* * *

"It was Ben," I tell Mum and Dad over breakfast. "The account was in both of our names, and he... he just cleared it. Then he bought a flight to L.A. on my credit card. He's flying first class, apparently."

I do my best to deliver this news as matter-of-factly as possible, but I can't quite keep the tremor of outrage out of my voice when I tell them my ex-boyfriend's in sunny California with my life's savings (Well, such as they were, anyway. Look, London's an expensive place to live, okay?) while I'm stuck here in the Highlands, with nothing.

I hope his first class plane seat came with a screaming child to kick him repeatedly in the back. I hope the turbulence made him spill his glass of complimentary champagne all over his crotch. I hope... I hope the wind blows really hard and messes up his hair, and that he can't find the particular brand of tea bag he claims is the only thing he can drink.

That's how much I hate him.

"He's a first class mutt," says Mum fiercely. For a second, I'm not sure whether she's talking about Ben or Jude Paw, who's staring at me accusingly from across the room, as if he thinks I might just have spent the money myself.

"But honestly, Emerald, what were you thinking?" Mum

starts vigorously wiping down the kitchen worktops as she fires questions at me. "Why didn't ye have your own bank account, for goodness sake? And why was he using your credit card? Have we taught ye nothing? I always said ye should have gone out with McTavish when ye had the chance. He'd never have pulled a stunt like this."

I stare at her blankly, quickly running through the words of wisdom she and Dad have imparted to me over the years. There's the thing about eating lots of blueberries to prevent UTIs, and the much-quoted advice about gargling with salt water to fend off a sore throat. There's a dizzying number of random facts about fish from Dad. There's been nothing about bank accounts or credit cards, though, as far as I can recall, and I feel momentarily brighter as I digest this fact.

This is *their* fault, not mine! My parents never told me *not* to open a joint bank account with my boyfriend, so how was *I* to know it was going to end up like this? Ben was an accountant, as well as being "a nice, steady lad," to quote Mum herself. I'd thought my money was safer with him than it was with me; which is why I'd agreed to make him an additional cardholder on my credit card.

But no. As it turns out, my money *wasn't* safe. And Ben wasn't a "nice lad" at all, was he? No, it seems Ben — nice, steady Ben, with his sensible haircut and his matching socks and pants — had a secret identity as a world class ass. For a split second, I wish I'd known this about him; it might have made him a little more interesting. Finding out now, however, has been the same kind of shock I got when I was twelve years old and the McTavish's horse bit me on the bum.

"I never liked the lad," says Dad, who's fussing with the lid of tropical fish tank that takes up almost an entire wall. You'd

23

think that after a lifetime as a fisherman, Dad would have had enough of fish when he retired, but apparently not. "He didn't like whisky. You cannae trust a man who doesn't like whisky."

I resist pointing out that I don't like whisky either and simply nod solemnly in agreement. I would much rather not think about Ben right now. He's not answering his phone — it seems to be disconnected — and, anyway, I really need to concentrate on what I'm going to do next, and how I'm going to get out of this mess he's left for me. Because, the fact is, I can live without Ben, but I can't live without money. And my heart might not exactly be broken, but it does feel like it's well on the way to exploding from the sheer panic that's coursing through my body right now.

"Have ye called the police?" Mum says, as if this brainwave won't have already occurred to me. "I'm sure young Dougie will be happy to advise ye. He has a half-day on a Wednesday, though, mind."

Young Dougie is Heather Bay's one and only police officer. He's fifty-eight years old, and I don't need to speak to him to know he won't be able to help me, because Brian-at-the-Bank told me as much when I spoke to him this morning.

"No, the police won't be able to do anything," he said cheerfully, sounding as if he was thoroughly enjoying the details of my financial crisis. "If the account was in both your names and this Ben was a cardholder on the credit card, well, I'm afraid he has every right to take the money. It's not theft. It's just a bit shit, really. So, do you really think he could have mafia connections, then?"

I'm pretty sure "a bit shit" isn't a phrase Brian's taken from the bank's handbook, accurate though it may be. I'm starting to think Brian-from-the-bank isn't taking this whole thing quite as seriously as I am.

"So, what *can* I do, then?" I ask, tearfully. The panic has taken firm control by this point. It's blocking out all rational thought. It's also making my legs feel a bit funny, as if they're not keen on holding me up any longer.

"Oh, there's nothing you can do," Brian assures me brightly. "You will call back and let us know what happens, won't you? I want to know what Ben's getting up to in L.A."

"You and me both," I say before I hang up. I would *love* to know what Ben's getting up to on the other side of the world, and I'd be even more interested in why he thought it would be okay to use my money to do it.

I'll go and see Dougie at the police station first thing tomorrow morning, I decide, checking my watch and realizing it's too late to get there before noon. I know Brian said there'd be nothing the police can do, but I have to at least try, don't I?

First, though, there's something far more important I have to do.

I need to call Frankie.

It looks like I'm going to be needing that job Mum suggested I ask her for after all.

* * *

In the decade I've been away from the Highlands, my best friend Frankie has somehow turned into a businesswoman — which is all the more strange given that, if our school had been the type to have American-style yearbooks, Frankie would've been voted Most Likely to Get Arrested.

25

Now, though, she's a pillar of the community and fully-fledged career woman, with her own thriving cleaning business, and I am absolutely in awe of her.

"Do you prefer 'girl boss' or just 'QUEEN'?" I joke, watching with a mixture of surprise and amusement as she switches effortlessly from one task to the next, pacing importantly around the little office she rents on Heather Bay's High Street, while answering her constantly ringing phone with a sing-song, "Highland Maids, Francesca speaking!" in an accent that doesn't sound entirely like hers.

"I prefer it when you shut up and lend me a hand," she fires back sharply, once the call is over, "Instead of just sitting there watching me work like a big southern softie."

"Sure, sure. That's why I'm here. *Highland Maids*, though?" I ask doubtfully, taking the logo-embossed sweatshirt she's handing me, which I can already tell is going to be at least two sizes too large. "Wouldn't a French maid's outfit or something be more appropriate with that name?"

"Then I'd have to call it *French Maids*, not *Highland Maids*," Frankie counters, unimpressed. "Och, I know the word 'maid' probably offends your feminist sensibilities, Emerald," she adds, going back to flicking through the diary. "But the tourists lap it all up. You know what they're like. They come here thinking they're going to bump into a real-life Laird, and they like the idea of having their very own Highland Maid to look after them while they're here."

I nod, taking a quick swig of the exceptionally bitter coffee she handed me when I arrived. It's true that tourists flock to this part of the Highlands, thinking some brawny Highlander in a kilt is going to come along and sweep them off their feet. Given that so much of Frankie's business comes from

Londoners with second homes, or from the holiday cottages down by the beach, I guess it makes sense to play up to it all a bit, even though anyone visiting Heather Bay is going to be disappointed to find it completely lacking in Lairds — or even a rugged band of peasants, to be totally honest.

"Do you think they're disappointed in it?" I ask Frankie thoughtfully, swinging my feet as I perch on the worktop opposite her. "When they find out they're not in an episode of *Outlander*, I mean? Because I'm still not over that myself, really. I could be doing with seeing Jamie Fraser emerging from the mist from time to time."

I glance wistfully out of the window as I speak, trying to pretend that the harr drifting in from the coast is romantic and mysterious, rather than just cold and wet. Ever the pragmatist, though, Frankie is there to bring me back down to earth with a practiced eye-roll, as she snaps her work diary closed, and turns to face me.

"We might not have Jamie Fraser," she points outs, "But we do have our very own Laird again, now that Jack Buchanan's moved up from Edinburgh. That should keep them going for a while."

"Speaking of Jack Buchanan," I say, remembering, "Did I tell you I saw him yesterday?"

"You saw Jack Buchanan? The *actual* Jack Buchanan?"

Frankie likes to pretend she's above the local gossip, but I can tell she's interested by the way she rakes her hand through her riotous blonde curls, grooming them as if she's expecting the man in question to walk through the door at any second.

"Yes, the *actual* Jack Buchanan," I reply, amused. "According to everyone on the bus, anyway."

"I don't know anyone who's met him," Frankie says, wonderingly. "I was starting to wonder if he was a real person, or just something the locals made up to bring the tourists in, like the Loch Ness Monster."

To be fair, that *is* the kind of thing we do here. This is a country that has the unicorn as its national animal; you can't say we don't understand branding.

"No, he's real enough," I confirm. "He's a real asshole, actually. Ran the bus off the road in his sports car, then gave me a dirty look as we passed him."

"A dirty look?" Frankie waggles her eyebrows suggestively. "Lucky you."

"Not *that* type of dirty look," I reply, shuddering at the thought. "An *actual* dirty look. An I-hate-you-and-I-want-you-to-die kind of look. Like he absolutely despised me."

"Och, you think everyone despises you, Emerald," Frankie replies dismissively. "It's just because of The Thing. Did you know he's living on the estate now?"

"Is he?"

This little nugget of information interests me in spite of myself. The Buchanans are one of the wealthiest landowners in the Highlands, but I've never known any of them to actually *live* here. Well, why *would* they, really?

The Buchanan Estate occupies the same side of the loch as Mum and Dad's cottage, and the old mansion house at the center of it has been boarded up for as long as I can remember. It's been boarded up for as long as *Mum and Dad* can remember, in fact, which is really saying something. The house itself was looking rather the worse for wear when I last saw it, and it's *huge.* I know, because... well, because Frankie and I used to sneak into the grounds at night when we were teenagers, to drink illicit cans of the strongest, cheapest cider we could find, and tell ghost stories about the despotic old Laird who we liked to imagine once lived there.

But now it seems there's a dashing *young* Laird in residence; although, if what I've seen of Jack Buchanan so far is anything to go by, I definitely can't rule out the possibility of him being just as despotic as the old man of our teenage imaginings.

I'm not here to talk about the mysterious Jack Buchanan, though, fascinating though the subject may be. I'm here because I've had no other choice than to ask Frankie for a job. A job which, just as I predicted, she was more than happy to give me.

"You do know how to clean, Emerald, don't you?" she asks now, looking at me suspiciously.

I sigh. "Yes, of course I know how to clean," I tell her. "Ben ran a tight ship, you know."

He did. He always said it exactly like that, too. "I run a tight ship," he'd say, fussily polishing the wine glasses the dishwasher hadn't done quite a good enough job of cleaning. It was like *being tidy* was his substitute for having a personality.

"I don't know what you saw in him," Frankie says, rolling her eyes.

"I don't know what I saw in him," I say, almost simultaneously.

Frankie grins, looking suddenly like the carefree 17-year-old who used to steal her brother's booze and go exploring the old estate with me, just because she knew I needed a good scare to remind myself I was still alive.

"Och, it'll all work out, Emerald," she says comfortingly. "You'll be fine, you'll see. And it'll be fun working together. Just like old times, no?"

I smile back at her, feeling just a tiny bit better. Cleaning houses together might not be remotely like the "old times" she means, when Frankie was the town tearaway and I was her faithful sidekick, but I'm not sure I'd even want it to be. Those old times weren't exactly good times — or not for me, anyway — but it's true that we did have fun together, and if there's a bright spot to me being back in the Highlands, then Frankie would be it. And while working as a cleaner isn't exactly my dream job, at least there's very little chance of me getting laid off from it, like I did from my "real" job.

How much trouble can a cleaner get into, after all?

Chapter 4

"**O**uch!"

Frankie and I are striding together down Heather Bay High Street; or Frankie's striding, rather. I'm stumbling along behind her, dragging a vacuum cleaner called Bessie (So Frankie tells me, anyway), and desperately hoping no one recognizes me.

And that's how I find myself walking straight into Jack Buchanan.

Or how *he* finds himself walking into *me*, even. Because, let's face it, he can't have been looking where he was going either, can he? That seems to be something of a habit of his, now I come to think about it. Is this man seriously just barreling around the Highlands, knocking buses off the road and women off their feet? Because it certainly looks like it, and the apology I was about to utter for getting in his way dies on my tongue as soon as I look up and see who I just hit.

Oh.

Him.

Again.

"Ouch!" I say again, bending down to rub at my ankle, which

scraped against Bessie's plastic exterior during the collision. It's not the worst injury in the world, but all the same, I'm a damsel in distress here; is he *really* not even going to ask if I'm okay?

Apparently not.

Jack Buchanan (Who, from what I've gathered, is always referred to by his full name by the residents of Heather Bay, as befits the local Laird) is walking down the street in the opposite direction to me and Frankie, and with serious looking men in suits on each side of him, taking up the entire pavement. His companions look like they might be lawyers or something. He looks like a movie star, with his sunglasses still over his eyes and his hair flopping over his forehead, and he is literally parting the crowds as he walks, with everyone he meets jumping unquestioningly out of his way.

Everyone except me, that is.

I *didn't* jump out of his way. No, me being me, I saw him coming, and I decided to play "chicken" with him; deliberately standing my ground and waiting to see which of us would step aside first.

It was me, obviously.

Well, it clearly wasn't going to be the great Jack Buchanan, was it? As it turns out, I'm playing this game on my own, anyway. The great Laird doesn't even notice me standing there in his path; doesn't even bother to shoot me one of those dirty looks of his as I attempt to move out of the way at the last second, his shoulder clipping mine as we pass. No, he just sweeps on by as if I don't exist, not even noticing that the brief moment of contact has almost sent me flying.

I hate him.

No, really: I hate him.

Seriously, though, who *does* that? Who just walks into people and doesn't even apologize? Or *notice*? And, okay, I get that it wasn't *totally* his fault, so maybe he doesn't feel like he has anything to apologize for. Me, though, I apologize for everything; whether I'm responsible for it or not. I even apologized to the dishwasher last week, when I tried to open it in the middle of its cycle by mistake. But Jack Buchanan can't spare a second of his oh-so-important time to make sure the woman he barged past is okay?

Nice.

Not.

"Oh my God, was that *him*?" Frankie asks as Jack Buchanan disappears around the corner, totally oblivious to the burning hatred I'm now harboring for him. "Was that Jack Buchanan?"

It's not like Frankie to be star-struck, but, in the short time I've been here, I've already noticed that Jack Buchanan seems to have some kind of mysterious hold over the people of this town, my best friend included.

"Yup," I confirm, still rubbing my ankle. "What a dick, right? That's the second time I've been involved in an accident he's caused."

*An accident **you** caused, Emerald. You could have just gotten out of his way, you know.*

"Stop it, Ben," I say sternly as Frankie turns away. "You left *me*, remember? So you don't get to be the voice in my head any more. You're fired. So there."

This short speech makes me feel momentarily better, but then Frankie looks over her shoulder at me, her forehead wrinkling in concern.

"Are you okay, Emerald?" she asks, her voice softer than usual. "I thought you were talking to yourself for a second

33

there. I worry about you, you know."

I arrange my features into a carefully neutral expression. Frankie and I don't really do this. We're close enough to be sisters, but ours is not one of those touchy-feely relationships where you sit braiding each other's hair and sharing confidences long into the night — and not just because Frankie's hair refuses to be contained in anything as pedestrian as a braid. I'm used to Mum worrying about me, but for Frankie to be doing it means my current situation must be *really* serious. Much more so than I'd thought, even. That's really not a comforting thought.

It's not a thought I have to entertain for long, however, because by the time I've picked myself up and limped a few more steps along the High Street, we're almost level with the old town hall, and suddenly I can't breathe.

The building in front of me is a crumbling, derelict eyesore, slap in the middle of the picture-postcard street, and it appears to be sucking all the oxygen out of the atmosphere. The rest of the street is a rainbow of pastel colors, which *Culture Focus* magazine recently described as "made for Instagram". The town hall, however, is in black and white, and passers-by are crossing the street rather than walking directly past it.

I stop in my tracks, not wanting to look at it, but not quite able to look away, either.

My fault. It's all my fault.

In the years that have passed since I last saw it, I'd managed to convince myself it wasn't as bad as I thought. That it was probably only a *little* bit burnt, rather than completely and utterly destroyed, like Manderley in *Rebecca* after Mrs. Danvers lost the plot.

"Last night I dreamt I went to the Heather Bay Village Hall

again," I mutter under my breath, as I continue to stand there and stare at it. To be fair, it's not like it's been razed to the ground. It is still standing. It still has a roof. Well, *part* of a roof. The rest of the roof is made up of a sad piece of plastic sheeting that flaps miserably in the wind, sounding a bit like a slow, sarcastic handclap.

Ladies and gentlemen, let's have a warm Heather Bay welcome for Emerald Taylor, Destroyer of Town Halls and Ruiner of Relationships.

The street is empty now that Jack Buchanan and his cronies have disappeared, but I can't shake the feeling I'm being watched. Which is always a possibility in Heather Bay, to be fair.

Mum told me the town hadn't been able to afford to fix the place up after The Thing. There had been various attempts at fundraising, I knew, but none of them had been enough to return the building to its former... I want to say "glory" here, but the hall was fairly nondescript really, even before it almost burned down, so let's not get carried away.

All the same, it may not have been the nicest looking building on Heather Bay High Street, but it was as least *usable,* until I came along and accidentally burned it down. It's in the state it's in now because of me.

I'm in the state I'm in now because of me.

And I may not be able to do much about the burned-out town hall, but I *can* do something about the rest of the messes I've managed to make of my life. Or I can *try.*

"Emerald! Come on!" Frankie snaps her fingers in front of my face, startling me out of my reverie.

"You were miles away there," she says, twirling her car keys impatiently around her fingers. "You can't do stuff like that while you're on the job, you know. We get paid by the hour. Are you sure you're okay, Emerald? I'm *really* starting to worry about you now."

"You don't have to worry about me," I tell her firmly, straightening my shoulders and taking a firm hold of Bessie's plastic handle. "I'm fine. I'll be fine. Like a new woman, in fact. The old Emerald is gone, Frankie. This is Emerald 2.0 you're looking at: a totally different person."

The more I think about it, the more this idea appeals to me.

Maybe instead of thinking of my return to Heather Bay as a bad thing that's brought me right back to square one, I could try to reframe it; to see it as an opportunity. I'm not going backwards, I'm starting over. I'm not a complete screw-up, I'm... I'm a work in process. Emerald 2.0, as I just told Frankie. And, okay, this idea literally just occurred to me, right this second. It's probably going to need a bit of refining.

But it's a start.

And it's happening just as Frankie's about to drive me to my first job as a Highland Maid, which seems as good a time as any to reinvent myself.

Emerald 2.0, here I come...

Chapter 5

The ever-present rain is drumming persistently against the windscreen as Frankie pulls into the driveway of number 6, Selkirk Lane, and lets Bessie and I out of the *Highland Maids* branded van before speeding off to her next job.

"Well, Bessie," I say out loud, making a mental note to stop speaking to my vacuum cleaner. "This is nice, isn't it?"

It is, too.

Selkirk Lane is a row of modern townhouses set on the banks of Loch Keld. These houses didn't even exist when I left for London, and their sudden appearance on the loch-side is testament to how popular this village has become. I can tell even from the outside that number 6 is going to be the sort of house that leaves me feeling weak with envy, and, as I slot the key Frankie's given me into the neatly painted front door, I'm grateful that she decided to start me off small, with an easy job that should only take a couple of hours at most; or so she says, anyway.

"The owner isn't there," she'd told me on the drive here. "She hasn't even moved in, actually; she'd only just got everything unpacked when she got called back to London early. Some kind of emergency, apparently. The removal company made a bit of a mess, though, so she just wants a quick clean so it's ready for her to move into when she gets back. You can do that, Emerald, can't you?"

I nodded, relieved to know that the owner of the house wouldn't be breathing down my neck while I cleaned. Because that would be all kinds of awkward, really, wouldn't it? Not that letting myself into someone else's home when they're *not* there is any *less* awkward, mind you; as I find out when I open the door to number 6, and hesitate for a second before stepping inside.

"Highland Maids!" I call out, just like Frankie instructed, cringing slightly at the name. "Anyone home?"

But there's no answer, so I quickly turn and haul Bessie inside, before closing the door behind me with a bang.

I was right; this house is enough to make a girl weep with jealousy. Not because it's particularly big, or grand, or anything like that — in fact, it's actually fairly compact by 'rich folks' standards — but because the person who owns it is clearly a woman after my own heart.

The shelves in the living room are filled with books.

The shelves in the bedroom are filled with shoes.

The shelves in the fridge are filled with wine.

"Mystery woman, I salute you," I say, plugging in Bessie and getting to work. "Because you obviously have your priorities straight, whoever you are."

Belongings aside, however, there aren't many clues to the owner's personality; no framed photos or postcards lying around — not even a collection of "quirky" fridge magnets with the names of the places she's visited to give her away. It makes sense, I suppose. Frankie said she hadn't moved in yet, so she probably hasn't had much of a chance to make it feel homely yet, even though it looks like most of her stuff is already here.

I bravely try to contain my curiosity about the homeowner and keep the comparisons between us to a minimum as I work my way around the house, mopping floors and wiping down surfaces. It's no use, though; my imagination has already started to run riot, and by the time I haul Bessie upstairs to make a start on the bedrooms, I've dreamed up an entire life and personality for her.

She's an artist, I decide. A wildly-successful one, who's bought this house, here in the wilds of Scotland, so she can paint in peace and quiet. She never makes mistakes or has "accidents". She has never, for instance, had to walk to her friends' house in her pajamas because she got locked out of her own flat while she was taking the bins out. She has never slapped nail polish remover on her face, thinking it was eye-makeup remover. Or spent twenty minutes pretending to know someone she doesn't actually recognize, rather than just asking their name. She doesn't lie awake at night cringing over something stupid she said as a teenager which she can never, ever get over, and she *certainly* didn't try to shave her own eyebrows off when she was eleven, in a bid to make them less "eyebrowy".

(They did grow back, by the way. Badly, of course. But *still*.)

Oh, and she has never burned down any village halls, or lost any jobs. And she never will, either.

The woman who owns this house, I think, warming to my theme, is a *badass*. But in a good way, obviously. She's funny, and quick, and smart. She can make you laugh, but will also be there for you when you need a good cry. She's successful, yes, but she's still close to her family. Oh, and she has a drop-dead gorgeous boyfriend, who loves her more than anything in the world, and who would on no account walk out on her one day, taking all her money with him.

She also has really great hair. But that goes without saying.

She's me, in other words; but the *other* me — the me I could have been if my life hadn't gone so catastrophically wrong back when I was just about to turn eighteen. If she was real, I'd probably hate her. As it is, though, she exists only in my mind, because while *someone* obviously owns this house, it's highly unlikely to be a glossier, sassier version of Emerald Taylor, is it?

Still, it's fun to imagine what the person who lives here might be like, and I smile to myself, picking up a tube of lipstick from the dressing table I'm in the process of cleaning, and absent-mindedly swiping it across my lips.

Shit!

I stare at my reflection in the mirror, my lips now a rather fetching shade of cherry red, my expression as surprised as if I hadn't just painted them myself.

Why did I do that?

I look frantically around for a tissue, and, not seeing one, just manage to stop myself reaching up to wipe off the lipstick with the corner of my Highland Maids sweatshirt. That wouldn't do. I don't want to go back to Frankie with lipstick smeared all over my uniform, so instead I look at myself sternly in the mirror.

"This is not good, Emerald," I tell myself sharply. "You're being paid to clean, not to play with someone else's makeup. Now, put it back and get on with your job."

Heaving a heavy sigh, I snap the gold lid back on to the tube of lipstick, and place it back on the dressing table, in the approximate spot I found it. I just got a bit carried away, that's all.

Too busy daydreaming, as usual, comments Ben in my head. *That's why you never actually achieve anything. And now you're probably going to end up losing yet another job, aren't you?*

I grit my teeth as I give the dressing table one last wipe. Ben's wrong. No harm has been done, and I'll make sure it never happens again, that's for sure. Because that would be exactly the kind of thing the old Emerald would do, and I am no longer her, am I? Emerald the 1st would 100% have found a way to mess this job up somehow; whether it be by trying on a client's lipstick, spilling bleach all over the carpet, or simply falling headfirst down the stairs, and breaking her stupid neck.

Emerald 2.0, however, will do none of these things.

Because Emerald 2.0 is a different person. A *better* person. One who just puts her head down, gets on with her job, and absolutely does *not* look inside that wardrobe on the other side of the room, with its door temptingly ajar.

Emerald 2.0 does not have "accidents".

And I'm determined to keep it that way.

* * *

Fifteen minutes later, I'm standing in front of the mirror in the master bedroom, wearing a slinky white dress with a pair of high, strappy sandals I found under the chair beside the bed.

Whoops.

I didn't mean to do it, I swear. It was... whispers it... an *accident.*

No, really, it *was*.

The things is, she'd left the clothes all heaped on a chair in the corner of the room, and when I picked them up to tidy them away, I couldn't help but notice we were the same size; clothes *and* shoes. Even then, I *still* wasn't going to actually do it, but the fabric of the dress was so invitingly silky, and the label inside was one I'd never even seen up close, let alone tried on. How could I resist?

(Rhetorical question. Please don't answer.)

I was only going to try on the dress; I promise. Just quickly, to see if it felt as gorgeous as it looked. But then the shoes were so obviously made to go with it, and when I finished fastening the slender straps, it felt almost like I was slipping into someone else's *life*, rather than just her clothes. I even *looked* different — which I guess isn't surprising, really, given that I would never normally dress like this. Not ever.

I've always been more of a jeans-and-sweater kind of girl. Or leggings-and-sweater. If I'm feeling *really* fancy, I might swap out the sweater for the ubiquitous "nice top", but I have never in my life worn anything like this; it wouldn't even occur to me.

I never wear white, for instance. I mean, I'm the kind of pale that's more of a blue-ish gray than white, but combine that with my red hair, and I can very easily look like one of the un-dead if I wear the wrong color.

White is the wrong color for me; or so I've always been told — which is why I normally stick to black, like a *proper* vampire. This dress isn't just white, though; it's also *tight*. It's tight n' white and strapless, and it shows way more of my cleavage than has ever been seen in public before. In Heather Bay terms, this dress is positively scandalous. And yet, when I look at myself in the mirror, I see someone else looking back at me. Someone taller (thanks, heels), sexier (thanks, lipstick), and altogether *better* than me. Someone with the confidence to wear a little white dress and bright red lipstick, and not give a damn when people try to tell her that redheads shouldn't wear white.

Someone like the owner of this house, as I've invented her in my head.

I quite like it, actually.

Let's face it; I've been wishing I could be someone else my entire life, so it's good to finally *look* the part. So much so that I discover I don't really fancy changing back again. Or not right now, at least.

Telling myself it'll just be a few minutes, and that I'll put everything back where I found it as soon as I'm done here, I switch Bessie back on and resume my hoovering, while pretending to be Freddie Mercury in the 'I Want to Break Free' video. Oh, don't pretend you've never done it.

Music! As soon as the thought comes to me, I wonder why it didn't occur to me before. Music is one of the few things that I can rely on to help pick me up when I'm down, and it would be the perfect way to make this job a little less boring, wouldn't it? In the movie of my life, this will be the montage scene — and every good movie needs a montage scene, right?

I dash back downstairs to grab my phone from my bag, being very careful not to fall down the stairs in the process, and use Bluetooth to connect it to the speakers I saw in the living room, before selecting a playlist and hitting "play". There! A bit of Taylor Swift will be just the thing to get this job done.

I've just reached the first chorus of *Shake It Off* — and I *am* shaking it off, believe me — when the sound of the doorbell chiming downstairs rudely interrupts my cleaning. Okay, my *dancing*. And maybe just a *little* bit of singing, too. Look, I love Taylor Swift, what can I tell you?

I pause, panting slightly from my exertions, wondering what I'm supposed to do.

Do I answer it?

Is that what a maid's supposed to do in this situation?

I mean, I know that's what a maid would be supposed to do in *Victorian* times, obviously, but, despite the slightly dubious name Frankie's chosen for her firm, we're just cleaners, really, not actual *servants*, and I'm not sure whether answering the door would be over-stepping the mark here. Then again, if I *don't* answer, and it turns out to be something important, will I get in trouble? Will Frankie?

Wait: it probably *is* Frankie, isn't it? I bet she's come to check up on me, or... or to bring me more cleaning supplies or something.

As the doorbell rings a second time, echoing through the house, I swipe my hand quickly across my mouth to get rid of the telltale red lipstick, then quickly untangle myself from Bessie's cable before heading downstairs, taking a quick swig from the can of Diet Coke I brought with me as I go.

I'm just about to open the door when the bell rings again, the sound louder now that I'm standing right next to it.

That's when I remember I'm wearing someone else's clothes as well as her lipstick. And, for all I know, the "someone" they belong to could be standing on the other side of that door.

Shit.

There's no time to worry about that now, though, because I can see the person's shadowy figure shifting impatiently behind the glass, which means they can see me too. There's no option but to open the door, so, as the figure behind it raises a hand and impatiently presses down on the bell yet again, I grab the handle, and, not giving myself time to think about what I'll say if it *is* the owner of the house standing there, I pull the door open.

There on the doorstep is none other than Jack Buchanan.

Yes, the *actual* Jack Buchanan.

Again.

"You!" I splutter before I can stop myself, almost choking on my drink in shock. "What are *you* doing here?"

For a millisecond, I wonder if he's here to apologize for almost knocking me over, then I realize the idea of him somehow knowing where to find me, then turning up at my cleaning job, is even less plausible than the idea of a man like this lowering himself to apologize.

Behind him, I notice the red sports car from yesterday sitting crouched on the driveway, as if lying in wait for its next victim.

And that's when I spill my can of Coke all over my dress.

Her dress, rather. The homeowner's dress.

Her now *soaked* dress.

Shitshitshit.

Jack Buchanan looks at me, confused, a small line appearing between his eyes.

"Er, hi," he says, finally, holding out his hand. "I'm Jack. And you must be Scarlett?"

Chapter 6

"**S**carlett?"

I stare at him in horror, trying not to think about the cold liquid seeping through my — her — dress, and onto my bra. (Which is my own, thankfully, just in case you were wondering.)

Why is he calling me 'Scarlett'?

"Er, yes. You *are* Scarlett, aren't you?"

I can't quite work out whether his tone is irritated or just plain puzzled. What I *do* know is that his eyes are a shade of blue that would have Taylor Swift reaching for a pen to write down some lyrics about them, STAT, and I wouldn't blame her one little bit. Can I get a guitar over here? Because I have a sudden urge to write me some country music, all of a sudden.

"Um, I think you have the wrong... color," I blurt stupidly, still trying to make sense of his question. "Did you mean to say Emerald?"

And how did you know my name — or something approximating *my name — anyway?*

Jack Buchanan sighs heavily, then gives a small, forced smile, in a transparently half-hearted attempt to make up for it. Ah, okay, he *is* irritated, then. Glad we cleared that one up.

"Scarlett Scott?" He tries again, this time speaking deliberately slowly, the way you would to a toddler. Or simpleton. "Finn McNeil's cousin? He somehow convinced me that it would be a good idea for us to go out to dinner? My assistant Elaine called to arrange to set up a date last week?"

OK, now he's just saying names as well as colors. I open my mouth to tell him that, but then two thoughts strike me simultaneously:

1. It looks like the woman I've been imaging has a name. She's called Scarlett Scott. Which makes everything I've just been doing in her house feel a whole lot worse, somehow.
2. Did he just say "date"?

I close my mouth sharply again, my mind whirring. I obviously have to tell him he's got it wrong; that I'm not this Scarlett Scott he's looking for, I'm just the cleaner. But I'm wearing her clothes. And her lipstick. And listening to music on her speakers, in her house, which I've made myself right at home in. This man may not have a clue who I am, but he's presumably going to know that cleaners don't normally wear tight white dresses and strappy sandals while they work. And, if he figures out that they're not actually mine...

Shit. Shit, shit, shit.

I can feel the panic rising in my chest as I gaze stupidly at his infuriatingly handsome face. Up close, Jack Buchanan is almost disturbingly attractive. His hair is rumpled, his jaw has the faintest trace of stubble, and his lips are full and slightly sulky. He really would make a great James Dean. All he needs is a quick change of clothes and a cigarette dangling from his

47

mouth and he'd be golden He already has the mean and moody look down pat — and from what I've seen of him so far, I'm going to hazard a guess that it's not an act.

Right now, Jack Buchanan has the demeanor of a man who is trying desperately not to look at his watch, and I know I have to say something soon, or he's going to turn and walk away, back to tell Finn, and Elaine, and God knows who else, all about the idiot woman they set him up with, and who answered the door soaking wet and refusing to say a word. A woman they will have a really good chance of working out could not possibly have been Finn's cousin, Scarlett.

If it was just me who'd get in trouble over this, I'd 'fess up at this point, no question. But it's not just me, is it? No, in fact, it won't be me who'll take the fall for this *at all* — even though it's 100% my own stupid fault. It'll be Frankie. Or Frankie's business, more accurately. Because no one wants a maid — a Highland one or otherwise — who's going to wear their clothes and make themselves right at home. So it doesn't take a genius to work out that Highland Maids could go out of business in roughly the time it took for me to dance to one Taylor Swift song in someone else's clothes.

You had one job, Emerald. Literally one job. And you well and truly blew it.

Which means there's only one thing for it.

"Hi!" I say through gritted teeth, offering Jack Buchanan my soaking wet hand. "Yes, I'm Scarlett! It's so nice to meet you!"

* * *

As accidents go, this is a pretty major one, even for me, and the fact that I'm doing this for Frankie's sake rather than my own doesn't do much to ease the nagging sense of guilt that accompanies me back into the house.

My plan — which I hastily concocted on the walk from the door to the living room — was to bring him inside, offer him a drink, then come up with some excuse why "Scarlett" couldn't go on a date with him after all. That seems like the easiest thing to do, under the circumstances. Other than just telling the truth, obviously, like I should have done in the first place. Or, you know, *not trying on someone else's clothes* to start with. That would've been the *actual* easiest thing to do, wouldn't it? For me, though, the easiest option has somehow always been the *hardest* option. Which is why briefly pretending to be someone else is the choice I appear to have taken.

And it *will* be brief. I'll just let him in, make my excuses, and then, once he's gone, I'll finish the job I'm being paid to do, and then go straight home. No harm, no foul. One hell of a lesson learned.

But it's just... it's Jack Buchanan. The man everyone in town seems to be obsessed with, right here in front of me. He looked so endearingly confused when I ushered him into the downstairs toilet instead of the living room, and he's wearing this beautifully cut suit...

I've always been a sucker for a man in a suit.

Ben never wore suits. Just "sensible" jumpers, and a selection of "smart casual" ensembles that always managed to look like his mum had picked them out for him. Maybe she did, actually.

This man, though, was born to wear a suit. He's exactly the right combination of lean and muscular to fill it out to

49

perfection, and his open-necked shirt is just begging to be opened a little more.

Er, not by *me*, obviously. Clothes have gotten me into enough trouble as it is today already; a fact I'm reminded of when I offer him a drink, and he simply looks at his watch (Wait: is that a Rolex?), then stares pointedly at the stained dress, which is starting to soak through to my bra.

"The reservation is for 7 o'clock," he says pointedly, running a hand through his dark brown hair and leaving it even more ruffled than it was to start with. "And I'm guessing you're probably going to want to deal with that first?"

His eyes drop to my chest, then quickly flick away again, an unreadable expression on his face.

"Oh! Yes, of course! It was just, the door, you know, it startled me. The Coke." I point unnecessarily to my chest, pantomiming the act of spilling my drink, and abruptly deciding to never go out in public ever again. Or, at least, not until I've learned how to speak like a normal human, anyway.

He nods silently, and I take the opportunity to turn and head for the stairs which lead directly out of the living room, tripping over Bessie's cable as I go.

Smooth, Emerald; really smooth.

Back in Scarlett's bedroom, I glance into the mirror and let out an involuntary shriek of horror when I see the red lipstick smeared across my cheek.

"Is everything all right up there?"

Jack Buchanan sounds like he could not conceivably give less of a shit whether everything's all right up here or not. In fact, he sounds almost hopeful. Like he might somehow be about to wriggle out of this "date" we're supposed to be having.

You and me both, buddy. You and me both.

"Everything's fine!" I yell back cheerfully. "I just... I just stubbed my toe. Ouch!"

Silence.

I rush to the bathroom to clean my face and scrub frantically at the Coke stain, which is, in my first stroke of luck of the day, not quite as bad as I'd feared. Most of the drink seems to have landed on my right breast — keepin' it classy as always over here — and I think it's going to come out. Or I hope so, anyway.

Please, God, make it come out. I know stains on dresses probably aren't your biggest priority right now, what with all the wars and famines and stuff, but if you could just do me a solid here, I promise I'll—

"Are you *sure* you're all right up there?"

The disembodied voice from downstairs just sounds straight-up irritated now, and I'm irrationally annoyed by him trying to hurry me along. Does he not realize I'm trying to make a deal with God here?

There's no time for that now, though, so abandoning the bathroom mirror, I pluck my discarded Highland Maids sweatshirt off the floor, where I left it, before realizing I absolutely cannot go back downstairs wearing this. I might as well just go down with a sign on my forehead saying, "Hey, I'm actually just the cleaner!"

The Coke stain has faded a bit, thanks to my efforts in the bathroom, but there's still a giant wet patch where I scrubbed it, so I do the only thing that seems possible and hastily rifle through Scarlett's closet once again, this time pulling out a crisp white shirt, which I throw on over the dress. The shirt covers the stain *and* some of my scandalous cleavage. My outfit is still totally inappropriate for anywhere in Heather

Bay, though, and it's only the sheer guilt of what I've done so far that stops me going back to the wardrobe and finding something more suitable.

I've already ruined one dress; I can't possibly risk destroying another one. And trust me: I *would*.

This is bad. No, seriously, this is really, really bad. Frankie is trusting me to clean this house, and instead, I'm basically robbing it. I've done some stupid things in my life, but this is right up there with the time I mistook the pizza delivery guy for a guest at a party my friend was having and tried to drag him into the house with me. So I speak with some authority on this matter.

I will put these clothes right back where I found them as soon as he's gone, I tell myself, as I hurriedly pull the shirt a little tighter around my body and start back down the stairs that lead to the living room, half-expecting it to be empty when I get there.

But it's not empty.

No, Jack Buchanan is still sitting there where I left him, a small frown of concentration on his face as he types something quickly into his phone. He's even managing to type moodily. I wonder briefly if he sleeps moodily too, and an image pops into my head of him lying in bed, his arms crossed sullenly over his chest and his lips pouting, even in sleep.

It's probably not the best idea for me to thinking about what Jack Buchanan looks like in bed, though, is it? I clear my throat guiltily, and he looks up and sees me watching him.

"Ready?" he asks in the voice of a man who's about to be dragged unwillingly to the gallows.

Why is this guy so unfriendly? Is he being made to go on this so-called "date" at gunpoint or something? Or he just really

52

disappointed in the person he's been set up with?

It shouldn't really matter to me, of course. It's not like I'm actually going to *date* the guy. But this is the third time our paths have crossed now since I've been back in Heather Bay, and the third time his reaction has been less welcoming than Jude Paw's was when he realized I was home again.

Every instinct I have tells me to continue with The Plan: to go downstairs, make some polite excuse, then show Jack Buchanan out of this house, and out of my life.

But I've never been one to trust my instincts — and now I *really* want to know just what it is that apparently made this man hate me on sight. Which is why, instead, of showing him the door, I simply flip my hair over my shoulder, and give him what I hope is my most winning smile.

"Yup," I say brightly, as I descend the staircase, like Rose in Titanic. "Ready when you are!"

Chapter 7

"**I**'m in a car with Jack Buchanan! I'll see you at work tomorrow," I type frantically — and surreptitiously — into my phone, so what comes out is more like, "I Mina bar with a cancan." But Frankie will know what I mean, I'm sure.

I shouldn't be telling her this at all, of course, given that it's inevitably going to lead to awkward questions about where I met him and how on earth I ended up here. But, well, I guess I'll worry about that later; just like I'll be worrying about how to tell the man beside me that I'm not actually who he thinks I am, how I'm going to fix the dress I ruined, and, oh yeah, how I'm going to get my sorry excuse for a life back on track.

I'll make a list of things to worry about. It'll be easier that way.

As I slide the phone back into my bag, I steal a quick glance at the driver's seat. I'm crammed uncomfortably into one of the bucket seats in the front of the convertible, my knees somewhere near my chin. Our not-so-friendly local billionaire, however, looks perfectly at ease as he expertly steers the little car down the winding roads that snake through the hills towards town. I can smell his cologne. It literally smells like money.

"You're going too fast," I say, before I can stop myself.

"You're going to run someone off the road at this rate."

I clamp my mouth shut, resisting the urge to clap both of my hands over it to stop myself from saying anything else. I was thinking of the bus, of course, but if *Jack* starts thinking of the bus, he might remember seeing me *on* the bus — and I really don't want that.

Fortunately for me, though, it seems the intensity of our bus window eye-lock that day existed only in my head. I made no impression on Jack Buchanan at all, and although I know I should be feeling grateful for that, I can't help but feel a bit dejected by how utterly forgettable I apparently am in my natural state.

I bet he'd have remembered Scarlett.

Especially if she was dressed like this.

"Thanks for the tip," he says shortly. "I'll certainly bear that in mind."

Huh. So it's like that, then.

He drives in silence, concentrating on the road, and not bothering with small talk. I'm grateful for that too, actually. I mean, okay, I guess it *is* a little rude that he's barely spoken a complete sentence to me since he knocked on my — Scarlett's — door, but still, no conversation means no opportunities to either make a fool of myself, *or* reveal my true identity, so it's probably for the best.

"So, do you come here often?" I blurt out suddenly, as if to prove myself wrong on the "no chance of making a fool of myself" front.

"Where? This road?"

The faint line between his eyes deepens as he frowns in my direction.

"No, of course not! I meant... wherever we're going. Where

are we going, by the way?"

"I made a reservation at Sartori," he says, naming the best restaurant in Heather Bay. "I hope that's okay with you?"

I nod my assent, determined not to say anything else if I can possibly help it.

"And to answer your question, no, I don't go there often," he says, his eyes still on the road. "Hardly ever, in fact. I don't go to many places around here. I value my privacy too much."

You're telling me, I think, but — for once — don't say. Not that I blame him, mind you. If I were a billionaire, I probably wouldn't be hanging out in a small, rain-soaked Scottish town, either, whether I owned it or not. I'd be on a beach in the Bahamas. Or shopping on Rodeo Drive.

I would be anywhere but here, in other words. Here, however, is where fate has brought me, and as Jack pulls up directly outside the restaurant, I find myself opening my big mouth yet again.

"Oh, you can't park here," I say importantly. "Not on the High Street. These spaces are only for the owners of the businesses."

"I am the owner of this business," he replies, as if it's obvious. "Didn't Finn tell you?"

"Finn?" I look at him blankly, before dimly remembering that Finn is the name of the person who set us up on this "date". He's Scarlett's cousin, apparently, and his name is going onto my list of Mortal Enemies as soon as I get home.

"Oh, yes, right," I say casually, swinging my legs out of the low-slung car and doing my best to stand up gracefully, even though Scarlett's shoes have a much higher heel than I'm used to. "It's just, you said—"

"I said I didn't come here often," Jack says smoothly,

holding the door open for me. "Not that I didn't have any connection to it. Anyway, I don't, really. It's purely a business investment; I don't take anything else to do with it at all."

I follow him obediently inside, tugging my dress down self-consciously as I walk. Imagine owning a restaurant and hardly ever visiting it. Imagine having "business investments" you barely even know about. Imagine running your hands through that boyishly rumpled hair, then sliding them under his... no. Let's *not* imagine that, on second thoughts. This might be a "date", but it's not *my* date. It's Scarlett Scott's date. And I'm going to have to do my very best not to totally screw it up for her.

The thought of Scarlett makes my stomach lurch with nerves. I was so busy thinking about Jack Buchanan and his hair that I'd almost forgotten I was supposed to be Scarlett. And now, as I follow Jack to a table in the corner of the room, I realize that pretending to be Scarlett is going to be a problem, given that I'm doing it right in the heart of my hometown. And while Jack might not come here often, pretty much everyone else I know *does*; and might be here right now, for all I know.

I can do this, I tell myself sternly, taking the seat Jack's politely holding out for me. *I can be Scarlett Scott for an hour; or however long it takes me to get out of this. I can be smart, and sassy, just like I imagined she'd be. I can be confident. I can be anything other than my usual self. Because I* **have** *to be.*

Oddly enough, the thought calms me down a little. It's not me, Emerald Taylor, who's currently sitting opposite Heather Bay's recently returned Laird. It's Scarlett Scott; renowned artist, white dress-wearer, owner of truly magnificent hair. *He* thinks that's who I am, after all; and if Scarlett Scott is the woman he thinks he's having dinner with tonight, then

Scarlett Scott is who I'll be.

Let's just hope there's no one I know here to recognize me.

"Mr. Buchanan!"

Jack's expensively clad derrière has barely made contact with his seat, when Tony, the maître d' is upon us, thrusting two menus roughly the size of the Bible into our hands, then standing back to beam enthusiastically in Jack's direction, while completely ignoring me. So far, so good.

"Wonderful to see you, Mr. Buchanan," Tony says, his hands clasped in delight. "Always a pleasure. You'll see we kept the best table for you, as always! I'll be right back with some of The 39 you had sent over."

"Excellent," says Jack, looking vaguely pleased for the first time since we arrived. "I can't wait to try it. I know Scarlett here's going to love it."

He looks at me expectantly, and my stomach flips over in apprehension. I have absolutely no idea what a "thirty-nine" is, but Scarlett presumably does, so I'm going to have to go with the flow here.

"Ooh, lovely," I say, rubbing my hands together, and desperately hoping that a "thirty-nine" doesn't turn out to be some kind of weird sex act, which is what it sounds like to me. "I love a good sixty-nine! *Thirty*-nine, I mean. *Thirty*. Nine."

Ouch.

Did I *really* say that? And did I *have* to rub my hands together at the same time? Can a person actually die of shame, do you think? Because I suspect I'm about to test that theory out.

"I'm sorry?"

Jack frowns. He does that a lot, I've noticed. He's going to need Botox by the time he's much older if he's not careful with that.

58

I look down at my menu, pretending I didn't hear him, but he just keeps on staring at me with those Taylor-Swift-song eyes of his, so I'm forced to look back up and answer him.

"Um, yes, I do," I say assertively, wishing Tony would hurry up with the drinks so I have something to do with my mouth other than speaking with it. Because, let's face it, speaking hasn't really been working out too well for me so far, has it? "I... I just really love a thirty-nine. Like you said I would."

Jack's blue eyes widen in surprise.

"But you can't possibly know that until you've tried it," he says tersely. "And you can't possibly have tried it, because—"

"Emerald? Is that you?"

I spin gratefully around in my chair, so relieved at the interruption to this tortuous conversation that I could hug the person responsible for bringing it to an end.

Then I realize it's Frankie's mum, Joan; who's banging enthusiastically on the restaurant window and waving in my direction.

Oh no. Please God, no. Don't let her come in here and blow my cover.

"Emerald! I thought it was you! Your mum told me you were back," she exclaims, ignoring Tony's protests as she comes bustling into the restaurant, briskly shaking the rain off her umbrella as she approaches.

"Um, hi Mrs. Allison." I squirm uncomfortably in my seat, wondering if I could get away with telling Jack that "Emerald" is just some weird local greeting that everyone uses around here. No? Didn't think so.

"How are you, Emerald?" she's saying now, her face filled with concern. "I know Francesca said you were going to be—"

"Great!" I interrupt her. "I'm really, really great! But, oh wow, is that the time already? Mr. Allison will be wondering where you are!"

"Och, he'll be fine, Emerald," she replies, sounding like someone's dared her to say my name as often as possible. "You know Jim; as long as he's got his pint and his football, he's happy as Larry!"

The way this conversation is going, I'm amazed she didn't say "Happy as Emerald." I feel like she must have wanted to.

"Well, I'm sure he must be missing you," I say, leaning back in my seat, and trying desperately to act like it's the most normal thing in the world for me to be sitting in a restaurant, having a romantic dinner-à deux with the Laird who just so happens to own the place.

"I suppose so, Emerald," Frankie's mum says, tucking her bag under her arm as she finally gets the hint. "Well, I best be away. You mind and tell your mam I was asking after her, Emerald."

"I will, Mrs Allison," I say, knowing that I absolutely will not, or I'll have to explain how I bumped into her. "Bye now!"

And with a cheery wave, and one last "Bye, Emerald!" she's gone.

As silence descends on the table, I pick my menu back up and pretend to be studying it intently. Maybe he didn't notice her calling me "Emerald" I think, desperately. She only said it, what, six times? Seven, maybe? In the space of about two minutes?

"Emerald? I thought your name was Scarlett?"

Jack's expression is inscrutable, but that line between his eyes has deepened. My cover is about to be blown.

"Emerald's my middle name," I say quickly, the lie tripping off my tongue with an ease that surprises even me. "But it's what most people call me."

"Your... your name is Scarlett Emerald?" he asks, the hint of a smile playing around his lips. "Really?"

I flush as red as the name I just laid claim to. When you put it like that, it does sound pretty stupid, really, doesn't it?

"Yup," I say nonchalantly, picking up my menu again. "My parents, er... they like colors. You should see their house. It's like a children's TV show in there."

I cross my fingers tightly, hoping Mum will forgive this lie. The cottage is actually furnished in tasteful shades of cream and white, which Mum describes as "all the rage on that Instagram," and Dad describes as "a nonsense", considering they live on a muddy hill in the Scottish countryside.

For a fraction of a second, Jack *almost* laughs. I see it flirting around the edges of his beautiful lips, but then it's gone, replaced by the carefully neutral expression that seems to be the norm for him. This is probably not a good time to tell him Mum's name is Ruby — even though that *is* actually true.

"I think I'm going to call you Emerald too," he says at last, his gaze holding mine just a nanosecond longer than is comfortable. "It suits you much better than Scarlett does. It goes with your eyes."

"I like your eyes too," I tell him, awkwardly returning a compliment he didn't actually give me. "They..." I want to tell him they remind me of the deep blue of the sea off Heather Bay when there's a storm approaching, but that feels like too much, even to me, so I settle for, "They're... very *blue*," instead. I'm starting to see why my career as a writer never took off. And why I don't have a boyfriend anymore.

He looks at me for a second, the corner of his mouth twitching before once again settling into its customary puzzled frown.

"So, Finn said you were from London," he says. "But your accent sounds Scottish to me? Or am I getting that wrong?"

"Finn? Oh, right, yes. Finn. My cousin Finn."

Screw this Finn, though, seriously. His name is definitely going on my list. Right at the very top.

"Um, I've been in London for a while now," I say at last, deciding to stick as close to the truth as I can manage. "I moved there for university and just stayed on. But I was born in Scotland. Not far from here, actually."

"Right," he says, his face clearing. "So you're moving back home, then? That must be nice?"

There are a lot of words I'd use to describe my return to Heather Bay, but "nice" is not one of them.

"Oh yes," I reply brightly. "Lovely. And what about you? Are you from around here?"

I know he isn't, but I'm not sure whether or not Scarlett does, so I decide to err on the side of caution with my questioning. In any case, I'm sure it'll do the mighty Laird good to think I don't actually have the slightest idea who he is. Or how rich and important he might be.

His accent is what Frankie and I refer to as "Posh Scots". So there's a Highland burr in there somewhere, but you have to listen pretty hard to find it. The tourists would be deeply disappointed in him. He hasn't used the word "Sassenach" once, or even told me not to "fash" myself. He might be almost indecently attractive, but he's definitely no Jamie Fraser, that's for sure.

"Edinburgh," he says in a tone of voice that warns me not to ask any more questions. "Although my family is from the Highlands originally, so in a way, I suppose I've come back home, too. So I guess that's one thing we have in common."

He says this as if he's just figured out the final clue in the pub quiz. It's like he expects a medal for having managed to find something in common with the awkward woman he's been forced out on a blind date with.

My hackles rise.

Jack Buchanan and I might both have recently returned to Heather Bay, but that's the only thing we have in common.

"And do you like it?" I ask, fiddling with my cutlery. "Heather Bay, I mean?"

"Like it?" Jack looks up from his menu, his blue eyes surprised. "I love it," he says, as if stating the obvious. "I love the solitude of it. The wild beauty. I didn't grow up here, but it somehow feels like home to me."

See? I told you we had nothing in common.

"Now, shall we order?"

This time, his tone is that of a man who has completed all the small talk he's willing to engage in. He's checked it off his To Do list, like a task that has to be completed. I am a task that has to be completed. Or Scarlett is. Which makes my presence here all the more incomprehensible, really.

"So, why did you agree to this, then?" I can't resist asking him once Tony's taken our orders. "This dinner, I mean?"

This *date*, I mean. I wasn't going to ask him, but I just have to know. Why *would* a filthy rich businessman, with the type of movie star good looks Jack Buchanan has, need to be set up on a blind date, after all? And why me, for that matter? Scarlett, rather.

Why Scarlett?

Jack leans back in his seat and runs a hand through his hair.

"It was Finn's idea," he says, shrugging slightly. "You know

63

what Finn's like when he gets an idea in his head."

I nod, rolling my eyes slightly. "That Finn," I say knowingly. "What's he like, eh?"

(What is he like, though? Because I have absolutely no idea — which is unfortunate given that he's supposed to be my... cousin, was it? Uncle? God, this is horrific. Note to self: find out what Finn is like. Whoever he is.)

"Um, and how do you know Finn again?" I dare to ask, hoping desperately that he's not about to somehow produce the guy from the back of the restaurant. "I don't think he said?"

"Oh, we were at university together in Edinburgh," Jack replies, sounding bored. "We started chatting because I knew he was from Heather Bay, too, and I wanted to know what it was like. I hadn't seen him for years, though. His message was a bit out of the blue, actually. I only really agreed to it because—"

I lean forward eagerly, but before I can find out what he's about to say, Tony's back with two glasses, plus a bottle of what looks suspiciously like whisky.

Please don't let it be whisky.

It's whisky.

Of *course* it is.

"The 39," Tony says, presenting it to Jack as if he's handing him an Oscar. "Enjoy."

He disappears again, leaving Jack to pour us each a generous helping of the amber liquid.

"I've been looking forward to this," he says, holding his glass up to catch the light, and looking at it in a way I wish someone would look at me. Him, ideally. "I hope you have, too. *Slàinte.*"

I glance up, wondering what he meant by that last bit. Not the "slàinte", obviously; I know that's Scots Gaelic for "cheers". But why would I — Scarlett — have been looking forward to drinking whisky? Why would *anyone*?

There's nothing for it, though. Jack's waiting for my response, so I smile grimly as I pick up my glass and touch it to his.

Maybe this whisky will be nice *whisky? Maybe this will be the moment I finally figure out just what it is people see in the horrible stuff?*

Or *maybe* it will just burn the back of my throat, like it always does, leaving me goggle-eyed and gasping for breath in the middle of the restaurant?

(Clue: it's the second one. It's *always* the second one.)

Jack stares at me, looking shocked and not particularly pleased.

"Are you okay?" he asks, eventually. "Maybe you should take a drink?"

It's only as I raise the glass to my lips a second time that I realize he meant water, not whisky. He's even reaching for the jug Tony left when he brought us our menus. It's too late for that, though, because by this point I've gone all in with another gulp of whisky; an even bigger one this time.

And that's when I start choking.

Really choking, I mean: as in, the whisky is completely filling my airway, to the point I can't breathe.

Jumping instinctively to my feet, my eyes bulging in panic as tiny black dots start to blur my vision, I do the only thing I can think of, which is to lean forward and cough, pressing my hands to my stomach in a kind of Heimlich maneuver.

Thankfully, it does the trick. With a sound a bit like a toilet

65

flushing, the trapped liquid comes right back up the same way it went down. "She's gonna blow!" I think stupidly to myself, feeling as if I'm having some weird out-of-body experience as I watch a fountain of golden liquid exit my body like it's being exorcised, spattering in all directions as it lands...

...all over Jack Buchanan.

Chapter 8

Well, that *was a complete and utter disaster.*

I wake up the next morning with Ben's voice listing all the things I did wrong yesterday, starting with the lipstick and ending with that moment in the restaurant where I... nope, it's no use: I can't even think about it without doing a whole-body cringe so intense it's basically a workout.

If you'd just told the truth from the start, you wouldn't be in this position.

"Right back atchya, Ben," I mutter, fumbling for my phone. "Maybe if you'd just told me the truth right from the start, none of this would've happened. Didn't stop to think about *that*, did you?"

To silence Ben's voice, I open up a note and make a list:

Emerald's Master List of Things To Worry About:

1. Impersonating another woman. Totally illegal, or just *slightly* illegal, depending on how far I take it?
2. Possibility of getting found out for the above: jail, or just being completely shunned by everyone I know forever more?

3. Borrowing someone else's clothes without permission.
4. Spilling Diet Coke over one (very expensive) item.
5. Being spotted by Frankie's mum.
6. Making an absolute tit of myself in front of Jack Buchanan and everyone else in the busiest restaurant in Heather Bay.
7. Completely covering his suit — his really, really expensive looking suit — in regurgitated whisky.
8. How to pay off my credit card before the bailiffs come for me?
9. What am I going to do with the rest of my life?
10. What if there's a zombie apocalypse?
11. I think I might have fallen for Jack Buchanan, local billionaire, and all-round-man of mystery. Who presumably hates me even more after my little display last night.

With the exception of number 10, which I've worried about for as long as I can remember, all of these worries are fairly pressing, so, once I'm done with my list, I re-open the Notes app on my phone, and start another.

TO DO: URGENT

1. Finish cleaning Scarlett's house.
2. Go to work, and face Frankie.
3. Come up with a convincing reason for me being out with Jack Buchanan last night. One that doesn't involve impersonating one of Frankie's clients. I just bumped into him in the street and he invited me to dinner? It wasn't him, just some other incredibly rich, implausibly handsome man? WHAT?

4. Find out how to get whisky out of suits
5. Google the cost of a Saville Row suit.
6. Find a new job.
7. Move to Paris.
8. Stop thinking about Jack.
9. No, seriously, Emerald, just STOP.
10. I mean it.

I put the phone down with a sigh and heave myself up from the couch, which is where I slept last night.

Oh, yeah: I'm back at Scarlett's. I should probably have added that to my list of things to worry about, shouldn't I? Or maybe I should just start a new one called Things to Feel Guilty About instead? A list of Lists I Need to Make? Sounds like a plan.

I stayed at Scarlett's, though, not because I *wanted* to, but purely because that's where Jack dropped me off after our disastrous "date" last night, and it was too late to call my dad and ask him to come and get me, like a teenager who's been at her mate's house.

Still, at least I know I'll never see Jack Buchanan ever again. Which doesn't help me figure out how I'm going to go about replacing the suit I ruined, obviously, but which *does* mean I won't have to keep up the ridiculous charade of being Scarlett Scott. Which, I wasn't exactly doing a stand-up job of, was I?

Needless to say, our "date" came to an abrupt end after I'd comprehensively covered Jack in the contents of my whisky glass, via my mouth. He didn't speak at all on the way home, and I didn't dare to. The tense set of his shoulders and jawline had told me all I needed to know about his state of mind, and I'd been glad to finally stumble out of the car in Scarlett's driveway, which, of course, was where he'd brought me back to.

"Please send me the bill for the dry cleaning, or—" I squeaked, my voice trailing off as he finally looked round at me, his expression as impassive as ever.

"It's fine," he said shortly. "Please don't mention it."

Then he'd reached over and slammed the door closed behind me, before roaring off into the night.

Fantastic.

I'd let myself into the house, and quickly changed back into my own clothes, carefully hanging Scarlett's things back in her wardrobe, before falling asleep on the couch. I'm just congratulating myself on the rare moment of good sense that had made me choose the couch rather than the bed — which would really have been taking the piss, quite frankly — when the sound of the doorbell makes my head throb in protest.

Shit.

I crouch behind the sofa, my mind whirling. It can't be Scarlett, I tell myself, my heart thudding in my chest; she'd just let herself in. But it *could* be Frankie, coming to check up on the cleaning I was supposed to do yesterday afternoon, or Scarlett's annoying cousin, Finn, who, from what little I know of him, seems overly invested in everyone else's lives, or —

"Emerald, are you in there?"

It's Jack Buchanan.

I mean, of *course*, it is.

Well, nothing else has been going right for me since I arrived back in Heather Bay, so why should this be any different?

"Emerald, I know you're in there. I can see you through the door," he shouts, his voice impatient.

Busted.

There's nothing for it, so I drag my unwilling self to the door, and open it just wide enough to peer out.

"Hi."

Jack is wearing a different — but still immaculate — suit from the one he had on last night and is clean-shaven and gorgeous despite the earliness of the hour. I scowl, hating him for being so perfect. I guess that's his toxic trait. Well, that and his personality, obviously.

"Hi," I croak in my morning voice. "If you're here about the suit, I'm really, really sorry. Just tell me how much it cost and I'll transfer the money as soon as I have it. It might take me a few—"

"I'm not here about the suit. I don't care about the suit."

I stare at him, surprised.

"You must do," I whisper, hoping my voice sounds husky, rather than croaky. "What was it: Gucci?"

"Prada, actually." He looks annoyed. "But it's fine. I have tons of suits."

"I suppose you do, being a billionaire and all."

I can't believe I just said that, but he just smiles slightly — or frowns slightly *less*, rather.

"I'm not a billionaire," he says. "Well, maybe on paper—"

I can't tell if he's joking or not, so I simply file this piece of information away and shrug. It's safer if I just don't speak around this man, I decide. Or anyone else, for that matter.

"I wanted to make sure you were okay," he says, when I don't answer him. "You seemed quite upset when we left the restaurant."

"Well, yeah." I open the door slightly wider. "Wouldn't you be? I felt so stupid."

Jack Buchanan has probably never felt stupid in his life,

though, I realize, as he looks me up and down, taking in my rumpled clothes and uncombed hair. He's the kind of person who goes through life getting everything right, and never knowing what it feels like to be out of place or embarrassed. He wears Prada suits, and is a billionaire-but-only-on-paper. He's the exact opposite of me, in every way possible, and I just want him to leave me alone now, so I can go and be awkward on my own, the way I always have been.

"Perhaps," he says, his expression thoughtful. "I haven't really thought about it. Anyway, I can see I've caught you at a bad time —" He glances pointedly at my outfit again "— so I won't stay. I just wanted to give you this."

He hands me a stiff white envelope — the bill for his dry cleaning, I assume — then turns and walks back to his car, which is a different one from last night's, I notice. How many cars does he have, anyway?

As soon as he's gone, I race to the bathroom and look at myself in the mirror. My hair is like a haystack, my mascara is pooled under my eyes, and the remains of Scarlett's lipstick is smeared across one cheek. I have never looked sexier. There is, however, one saving grace, and that's the small, but significant, fact that, when I put my own clothes on last night, I hadn't noticed that I had my *Highland Maids* sweatshirt on inside out, the logo hidden from view.

At least that's one less thing to worry about. Now I just have all the other things on my list to get through.

* * *

72

Frankie doesn't have me scheduled to start work until noon today, so as soon as I get home from Scarlett's — courtesy of a lift from Dad, who refuses to let me sit in the front with him as Jude Paw has already called shotgun, apparently — I open up my laptop, flop onto the single bed, and spend the next hour reading everything I can find about Jack Buchanan, ignoring the WhatsApp messages that keep pinging in from Frankie.

"What's a cancan?" she'd written, at some point last night. "Are you drunk?" And, then, earlier this morning, "Remember, you're supposed to be starting work at 12:00, so if you're hungover, just drink loads of coffee or something before you come in."

Nothing about her mum spotting me and Jack at Santori, thankfully, so she must not have heard from her yet; one more small mercy. The coffee Dad delivers to my room a few minutes later is another, so I sit there sipping it, and make another list:

Things I Know About Jack Buchanan:

1. He's 35. (Source: Wikipedia.)
2. He was telling the truth when he said he wasn't a billionaire. According to CelebrityNetWorth.com he's still a few million shy of that particular status. So, basically a pauper then. Just an ordinary guy, who just so happens to have a helicopter pad on his lawn.
3. He has a helicopter pad on his lawn. (Source: Mum's friend Shona, who was in the kitchen when I got back this morning, and who knows everything about.... well, *everything*, really.)
4. Although some of his fortune was inherited, he made a large chunk of it himself, by launching a tech startup

73

which seems to develop apps of some kinds, although I kind of skimmed over that part. He made the rest, meanwhile, by investing in other businesses, primarily ones involved in trying to reverse climate change. (Source: Tatler's Most Eligible Bachelors in Britain List, 2019) So he's a Laird with a conscience, basically. Which is going to make it a whole lot harder for me to hate him.

5. In addition to his estate in Heather Bay, he's also believed to own apartments in London and New York, plus a house in the South of France, which I'm going to pretend is a château, and which his parents live in most of the time. (Source: Same Tatler article.)

6. He has a younger sister called Rose, who has a penchant for pop stars and was once rumored to be dating Prince Harry, apparently. (Source: Daily Mail sidebar of shame.) I'll stalk her later.

7. He has a deep dislike of awkward Scottish redheads with a habit of either spilling or spitting their drinks. (Source: Emerald Taylor, Last Night.)

8. Er, that's pretty much it, really.

That *is* it, too. No mention of a girlfriend. Not even rumors of a fling or blurry photos of him falling out of a nightclub with a reality TV star. Other than the bare facts I've just listed above, Jack Buchanan is a true man of mystery. That was how Tatler described him, in fact: "Jack Buchanan: Tech giant, Scottish Landowner, and Man of Mystery." Their writer manages to make his elusiveness sound enigmatic and sexy, but, as far as I'm concerned, it's just deeply suspicious. What kind of person doesn't have Instagram? Or even an ancient Facebook profile? How am I supposed to stalk him without social media?

Then again, I shouldn't be stalking him at all, should I? Numbers 8 through 10 on my To Do list all involve not thinking about him, and I'm already a filthy impostor: I can't add "stalker" to my list of crimes — that would be a bit much, even for me.

I will stop thinking about Jack Buchanan, I tell myself firmly as I stuff my feet into my shoes, ready for work. *Right now. This very instant.*

Because, let's face it: he definitely won't be thinking about me, will he?

* * *

It's only as I'm hauling Bessie outside to wait for Frankie to pick us up that I remember the envelope Jack gave me during our awkward doorstep interaction this morning.

Damn.

It's going to be the bill for his dry cleaning; it has to be. I know he said he didn't care about the suit, but what else would he have felt the need to present to me in writing? Unless it's a restraining order. A legal document banning me from ever coming within 10 meters of Mr. Buchanan; or —

An invitation.

To a party.

Well, a ball, to be exact. A masquerade ball. On Midsummer Night. At his mansion.

I stand outside the house, staring down at the piece of thick, cream-colored card in my hands. Jack Buchanan has invited me to a ball at his house — the one with the helicopter pad and the sauna, and the indoor swimming pool, and... okay, I made that up about the swimming pool, but it seems like the kind of thing he'd have, doesn't it?

The rain starts to fall as I stand there on Mum and Dad's driveway, my heart racing as I imagine myself arriving, Cinderella-like, in a beautiful evening gown (Where will I get a beautiful evening gown?), my eyes hidden behind a jeweled mask (And a jeweled mask?), and my luscious red curls (Extensions, maybe?) swishing behind me. "Who is this beautiful, yet mysterious stranger?" I hear voices whisper, as I sweep past them, towards Jack, who turns as I approach, and holds out his hand.

"Scarlett," he smiles down at me, taking my hand in his. "My beautiful Scarlett—"

And then, all of a sudden, I come back down to earth with a bump. Because, the fact is, he hasn't invited *me* to his ball at all, has he? No, he's invited *her*: Scarlett Scott. It says so right here in black — well, gold — and white. "Mr. Jack Buchanan requests the company of Ms. Scarlett Scott at a masquerade ball..."

I don't bother reading any more, because it doesn't matter. It's for Scarlett, not me. Scarlett, with her perfect house and her perfect clothes, and what I imagine to be her perfect skin and hair. Scarlett, with her whole perfect life that could've been mine, if I'd just somehow managed to stop messing things up all the time.

But men don't invite women like me to their parties. They don't invite us anywhere, really. And Jack Buchanan hasn't invited me *this* time, either: he's invited Scarlett — and Scarlett will be the one who gets to go.

"Well, I didn't want to go to your stupid masked ball anyway,

Jack Duchanan," I tell my reflection in the front window of the house. "I wouldn't have come even if you *had* asked me."

If only I actually believed it.

Chapter 9

"Oh my God, Emerald, I can't believe it! Jack Buchanan! THE Jack Buchanan!"

Frankie's just pulled up outside the house, and she doesn't even bother to get out of the van before she starts shrieking at me from the driver's seat.

Shit.

I take my time loading Bessie and the rest of her cleaning cohort into the back of the van, trying to avoid looking Frankie in the eye as my mind whirs.

She knows about me and Jack. Her mum must have told her. And I have absolutely no reasonable explanation I can give her for it.

"Look, Frankie," I say, finally mustering the courage to turn round and face her, "I know it looks bad, but—"

"Oh, it's not bad; it's amazing!" Frankie says, almost dancing out of the van to help me slam the doors shut. "I mean, I couldn't believe it when I got the phone-call! I thought she must be joking at first!"

"I know," I reply mournfully. "I should have told you, it just it all happened so fast, and —"

"Told me?" She looks puzzled, but not angry. Which is welcome, if just a *little* bit confusing. "Why would *you* have told me? D'you know Elaine, then?"

"Elaine?"

The name rings a bell, somehow, but I can't place it, until—

"Aye, Elaine, Jack Buchanan's assistant?"

Bingo.

Shit. How does *she* know? Did Jack say something that made her realize I wasn't Scarlett? But what? And *how*?

"Frankie, I can explain," I start to say, but Frankie isn't even pretending to listen as she gets back into the van and turns the key in the ignition.

"Like I say, I couldn't believe it when she told me who she was," she rattles on as I join her. "And then when she said she wanted to book Highland Maids for the next few weeks, well! It was a good job I was already sitting down, let's put it that way!"

"Wait, what? The next few weeks? Frankie, what are you talking about?"

"Emerald!" She looks round at me, exasperated, as she pulls out of the driveway. "Have you not been listening to a word I've been saying? Elaine? Jack Buchanan's secretary? She called me this morning?"

"Yes, I got that bit," I say impatiently, "But what's this about a booking?"

Frankie rolls her eyes, but I can tell she's bursting to tell me by the way her cheeks have turned tomato red, the way they always do when she's excited.

"So, Jack Buchanan is hosting this masquerade ball," she begins.

"Yes, on Midsummer Night, I know."

"It's going to be huge. Massive. Everyone who's anyone will be there, apparently. *Everyone.*"

I'm guessing she got this last hit from Shona or someone, rather than from Elaine; it doesn't sound like something a professional assistant would say, somehow, but it *is* very Shona. Telephone, telegram, tell Shona McLaren.

"So, they need the house cleaned for it, obviously," Frankie continues, "But, the thing is, it's much too big for the house-keeper to manage on her own. In fact, between you and me and Elaine, it sounds like she's not been doing much at all, really —just dusting the rooms that get used the most, which is hardly any, on account of him hardly ever being there."

Of course, Jack Buchanan *would* have a full-time house-keeper. Of *course* he would. Well, it's not like he'd have been cleaning that gigantic house on his own, would he? A sudden image of Jack Buchanan with a frilly apron tied over the top of his immaculate suit and a feather duster in his hand makes me smile suddenly, but a quick look from Frankie brings me back to reality.

"Anyway, it seems the housekeeper called in sick as soon as she heard about this party she'd have to cater for," she says, "And they're going to need to use the whole house for it, because there'll be people staying over for a few days before and after. I think he wants to treat them to the whole 'Highland Laird' experience, you know? House party complete with hunting, shooting, fishing, and all that jazz?"

"So, a bit like when Mr. Rochester had the house party in Jane Eyre?" I interrupt eagerly, interested in spite of myself. And, okay, I must admit, I'm a bit disappointed to learn that Jack is apparently the huntin'-shootin'-fishin' type — it doesn't seem like his kind of thing somehow — but that's a problem for Future Emerald to deal with. I'll make a new list as soon as I get home.

"Uhh, yeah, I guess." Frankie gives me an odd look, then returns her eyes to the road.

"Anyway, that's where we come in," she tells me. "They're going to need us a few days a week in the run-up to the party, and again for a few days after, to clear up. Can you believe it, Emerald?"

She looks up, her eyes shining. "This is such a great opportunity. It'll be hard to manage it because we're busy enough as it is, but I couldn't turn it down. It could be the making of Highland Maids. Imagine when word gets out that we're the cleaning firm used by Jack Buchanan! Everyone will want to book us! Anyway —"

She's snapped back to businesswoman mode again. "I'm going to need all hands on deck for this. I'm so glad you're here, Emerald, it's going to be such a huge help. I don't know what I'd have done without you."

I return her smile as best I can, even though my stomach has started to churn uncomfortably with nerves.

What was that I was just telling myself about how I was going to forget all about Jack Buchanan? How, exactly, am I supposed to do that when he keeps throwing himself right into my path, I wonder?

* * *

Problems for Future Emerald to Worry About:

1. How to get out of cleaning Jack Buchanan's house with Frankie? Call in sick? Fake own death? Develop mysteri-

ous allergy to millionaires? What?

2. How to make sure he doesn't recognize me if I can't get out of it?
3. Where to buy a ballgown in the Highlands?
4. How to afford a ballgown?
5. What if my future boyfriend really *does* enjoy killing animals for sport?

After a few seconds' thought, I draw a line through number 5, too. The fact is, if Jack actually *is* into blood sports, then so much the better. Not for the animal kingdom, obviously — sucks to be them in this scenario — but for me, Emerald Taylor, who will have a hard time fancying someone who may or may not have killed Bambi's mum. Maybe while wearing a fetching pair of tweed trousers and a deerstalker.

Yes, that'll do it. That'll stop me liking him, for sure.

And if I don't like him, then I won't want to see him again — and I definitely won't consider going to his masquerade ball. Nuh-uh, not me.

At least, that's what I'm telling myself.

For now, however, I have a problem for current Emerald to think about. A really quite pressing one, in fact, because we're still in the van, on our way to my next job, and Frankie's just told me whose house I'll be cleaning next.

"It's Lexie," she says, not looking at me in a way that feels deliberate. "Lexie Steele. You remember her from high school, right?"

Oh, yes. Yes, I do. I remember Lexie, all right.

Lexie Steele: the most popular girl in high school. The girl everyone else wanted to be. The girl *I* wanted to be. And, you know, I'm not saying Lexie was a *bitch*, exactly. It's just—

"But Lexie's a straight-up bitch," I tell Frankie, before I can stop myself. "Please tell me you're joking? Please tell me it's just Voldermort's house you're taking me to clean? Or Dracula's, maybe? Anything other than Lexie Steele's."

"Och, she's not that bad, Emerald," Frankie says carefully. Frankie always did see the best in everyone. Even me. "She's changed since high school. You're still just upset because she wouldn't let you into her clique."

"No, I'm not," I say, even though this is absolutely true. "I didn't even *want* to be in her clique. I don't know what you mean."

"Emerald, you tried to dye your hair blonde," Frankie points out. "It went bright orange, remember?"

I nod reluctantly. Red hair does *not* take well to bleach, let me tell you. But Lexie Steele had the most beautiful honey-blonde waves, to compliment her blue eyes, and so *I* wanted honey-blonde waves, too. Lexie even had a hint of a suntan, and, to this day, I have no idea how she did that, living in the Highlands. My own skin is so pale it burns if I stand under an electric light for too long. Lexie, on the other hand, could have played the cheerleader in an American made-for-TV movie. She was all blonde and glowing, and I, with my red hair and freckles, and my way of falling over my own feet without warning, absolutely worshiped her.

From afar, though, because, like I said, Lexie was a bitch. Not in some big, dramatic kind of way, though; this isn't *Carrie*, after all. But in that subtle, incredibly painful way some people have of letting you know you're not welcome, without saying a word.

I was not welcome in Lexie's world as a teenager, and I most definitely will not be welcome in it now. I know that as surely as I know that Jack Buchanan will never call me again, and that Jude Paw is probably just biding his time until he can poop in my other shoe. Because I don't fit in. Not in London, not here in the Highlands, and definitely not in the house we've just parked outside of.

Lexie's house is pink; which figures, really. As a child, Lexie was one of those pink-obsessed girls whose mother liked to dress her like a real-life Barbie, and, as an adult, she's obviously kept the color theme going.

Her house is one of the pastel-painted stone cottages that line the Heather Bay seafront, although Lexie's sits a little apart from the rest, almost as if it's embarrassed to be seen with them. It's out on a little promontory, with a garden stretching down to the sea, and I'm pretty sure I can even see some roses in the garden. Pink ones, naturally.

"She might not be at home," Frankie says doubtfully, as she helps me haul Bessie out of the van. "She's often at work at this time of day."

"Or she might be dead?" I suggest, in an attempt at optimism which proves to be as unfounded as it usually is for me, when I reluctantly push the polished front door of the cottage open to reveal Lexie Steele, in the flesh.

And what a lot of flesh it is, too.

Lexie is lying on a yoga mat (I don't need to tell you what color it is, do I?) in front of the bay window of her sunny living room, wearing a pair of tight cream leggings which compliment her golden glow (From a bottle, surely?) and show off her taught midriff. Her matching bra is stretched to capacity, and I have just a few seconds to think about how long it would take me to spill something on that pale fabric when she sits up and locks eyes with me.

84

Maybe she won't recognize me? It's been over a decade, after all.

"Emerald?" says Lexie, her green eyes narrowing as she takes in my Highland Maids uniform. "Emerald Taylor? Is that really you?"

Chapter 10

You know those women who never seem to have a hair out of place, even in a hurricane? Lexie Steele is one of those women. (Not that I've seen her in a hurricane, mind you; I just feel a bit like I'm in the eye of one right now. Hurricane Lexie, now approaching the east coast of Scotland, with considerable risk to life and limb. Better batten down the hatches, folks...)

Lexie doesn't seem to be wearing makeup, but there isn't a visible pore on her skin. As she stands up and makes her way towards me, her blonde hair falls obediently into place, like a shiny golden curtain dropping at the end of a show. She's the kind of woman who can make Primark look like Prada, whereas I can only work that trick the other way around. She is the walking personification of the word *glossy*.

I, by contrast, always look *unfinished*, somehow. I am the walking personification of the word *disheveled*. No matter how much time I spend on my hair and makeup, by the time I leave the house, I look like I haven't bothered. My hair tangles in the slightest breeze. My lipstick always ends up on my teeth. I feel myself getting grubbier just standing next to Lexie, in the pristine cream workout gear that would be ruined in two minutes flat on me.

"Emerald?" she says again, taking a step closer. "*Is* it you?"

For a second, I think about denying it. I told Jack Buchanan I was Scarlett Scott and got away with it, after all. Maybe I could tell Lexie the same thing? As Scarlett, I could be different. I could move fearlessly through the world, without worrying that everyone who met me was thinking about The Thing. Being Scarlett could be the thing that saves me.

Or I could just tell the truth and be boring old Emerald.

"Um, yeah," I say, sounding even stupider than I feel. "It's me. Hi." Then I give a weird little wave, which makes me want to cut off my own hand.

"Oh wow, I thought it was you! How are you?"

To my utter shock, Lexie throws her arms around me, enveloping me in a thick cloud of *Le Vie Est Belle* as she hugs me as if she actually *likes* me.

Okay, this is weird. Why is Lexie Steele being nice to me?

It's a fair question. If it wasn't for The Thing, I'm pretty sure Lexie wouldn't even remember me. And yet, here she is, acting like we're besties. What's even weirder, however, is that she keeps on doing it the whole time I'm plugging in Bessie and unpacking the dazzling array of cleaning products Frankie has provided for me, all in their own little carrying case.

Lexie keeps on talking as I work, following me around the house (Which, I'm gratified to note, isn't quite as nice on the inside as it is on the outside. It has a bit of a "little-old-lady" feel to actually, which makes me wonder if she inherited it from her granny or something), still chattering away about herself. Within twenty minutes or so, I'm in possession of the full set of facts pertaining to Lexie Steele and her life since I last saw her, including:

1. Her move to Edinburgh, for university.
2. Her return to the Highlands, to take over the running of the family business, which is something to do with whisky, as far as I can tell. *Everything* in Heather Bay has something to do with whisky, though, so I kind of tune out at this bit.
3. Her string of disastrous relationships, and her absolute horror of being single at almost 30. ("I know you're probably used to it, Emerald," Lexie says sweetly, "But it's just not how I imagined my life, you know?")
4. Her crush on Jack Buchanan. Which, wait: what was that?

"Wait. You know Jack Buchanan?" I say, standing up from my position on hands and knees under the kitchen table so quickly I almost knock myself out. "How come?"

This is the longest sentence I've uttered to Lexie Steele since I walked into her house. It's probably the most I've said to her in my entire *life*, actually, and I'm horrified to realize I'm blushing as I say it, as if I think she's going to instantly know why I'm asking. Or maybe she won't even notice?

"Oh my God, Emerald, are you blushing?" Lexie squeals excitedly. "Don't tell me you like him, too? Because I have first dibs, you know." She waggles a manicured finger at me as she pulls a virtuous looking bottle of water out of the fridge.

"I don't actually *know* him as such," she admits at last, leaning against the kitchen worktop and taking a swig of her drink. "But he's in the same industry as ours, so I've seen him around a bit, at events and stuff. God, he's hot. Don't you think he's hot?"

I nod mutely as she turns and gazes out of the window, which looks down to the sea. The waves are a moody looking dark gray today, but there's still a small group of tourists determinedly pitching their beach tent and laughing as the wind almost whips it out of their hands. Lexie and I stand there watching them for a few minutes while I gather the courage to ask my next question.

"You said Jack Buchanan's in the same industry as you," I say finally, trying my best to sound casual as I start unloading the dishwasher. "But I thought you said you were in the whisky business? Or did I pick that up wrong?"

Lexie rolls her eyes slightly and makes no move to help me with the dishes, which I suppose is fair enough — she's not paying Frankie so she can do her cleaning herself, after all — but still feels weird to me. I can't imagine just standing there watching someone else do my dirty work: literally. Then again, I can't imagine what it must feel like to be Lexie at all.

"No, silly," she says, downing the rest of her water and leaving the empty bottle on the counter for me to clear up. "My family has a distillery, remember? And so does Jack Buchanan. Or, at least, he will do; he's setting it up now. It's called The 39, after the year his grandfather founded his original distillery. He'd made a few caskets of this special blend of his, apparently — the grandfather, that is — and he was planning to make it a whole *thing*—" Lexie gestures expansively. "But then he got conscripted and *died*, and that was that."

She says this without any emotion whatsoever, but my heart is thudding so rapidly I can hardly speak. *The 39?* Wasn't that what Jack called the drink he tried to give me last night? The one I spat all over him? Did I *really* just spit out Jack Buchanan's grandfather's legacy, as if it was a dodgy batch of Irn Bru?

Yes. Yes, I did. No wonder he hated me.

"So, Jack's trying to set this distillery up to, what, honor his grandfather, then?" I say carefully, hoping desperately that Lexie's going to say no, of course not: that he's doing it to, I don't know, rob orphans of their inheritance, or some other nefarious reason that will make him sound a little less noble.

"Yes, I think so," Lexie replies brightly. That's what I've heard, anyway. Oh, it's so good to see you again, Emerald," she bursts out suddenly. "I probably shouldn't say this, but I used to be really jealous of you back in high school. Can you believe it?"

Her eyes flick quickly up and down my body, as if to confirm the sheer absurdity of her ever having envied someone like me.

"You did?" This piece of information is so surprising that it banishes all thoughts of Jack Buchanan, and my ruthless dismissal of his grandfather's legacy, out of my mind. Lexie Steele was jealous? Of *me*?

"Why, though?" I blurt out, frozen in the act of pulling a casserole dish out of the dishwasher. "You didn't even talk to me back then?"

You didn't even know I was alive, I want to say, but don't. That would be needy even for me.

"Didn't I?" Lexie looks away, her voice vague. "I don't remember that. I just remember when you were voted in as Gala Queen that time, and how much I wished it had been me instead. Although that didn't work out too well for you in the end, did it?"

With a sickening crash, the casserole dish slips out of my hands and shatters on the tiled floor, its fragments rolling off in all directions, as if they're as eager to escape the awkwardness of this scene as I am. I take advantage of the next few chaotic minutes, as Lexie finally deigns to come and help me, to firmly squash down the memories that are trying their best to surface as a result of Lexie's words.

The Gala Day; the event of the year in Heather Bay, when everyone dresses up and parades through the streets, complete with brass bands, decorated trucks, and over-excited school children.

The year Lexie's talking about is the year I was voted Queen of the village: an honor granted to one final-year student each year. An honor that somehow fell that year to the least likely person in Heather Bay: me.

I will not think of these things. Because thinking of these things means thinking about The Thing, *and I absolutely cannot think about The Thing. I just can't.*

Of course, it makes sense that Lexie would have been jealous of me being Queen that year. She was the natural choice for it, after all; the one everyone had assumed would be picked for the role. She was so certain she'd get it, in fact, that I'd heard her mum had already bought her a dress for it; some frothy pink concoction, no doubt, that Lexie would somehow have managed to make look like it was straight off the Paris runways.

But then the votes had been counted, and somehow it was *my* name that was pulled from the hat — well, the Tupperware bowl. I can still remember the silence that followed the announcement, then the whispers, then the stares. Even Frankie had been surprised. Lexie's mum had demanded a recount, but the recount had been done, and the result was right enough: it was me. I was to be Heather Bay's Gala Queen. Which meant I was the one who rode in the carriage to the town hall that day; and I was the one responsible for the accident that burned it down.

"I wish it had been you, too," I tell Lexie rucfully, as we sit back on our heels, scanning the floor for any last remaining shards of the now departed casserole dish. "I really do."

Lexie flashes me a smile, and for just a second I wonder if we could possibly be friends, now that we're older and she has absolutely no reason to envy me any more. Not that she ever did, as far as I'm concerned. Then the front door opens with a bang, and suddenly Lexie's mother is standing there in front of us, looking almost exactly as I remember her, with dyed blonde hair and a sharp, brittle look about her. She's wearing a pair of jeans almost as tight as Lexie's leggings, and her face looks oddly stretched, somehow, as if someone's taken the skin and tucked it into her hairline. She's like Lexie, only older. And, well, *scarier*.

"For goodness sake, Alexandra," she tells Lexie, completely ignoring me as her eyes sweep the room. "Get up off that floor. The maid can finish up whatever it is you're trying to do down there. It's what we're paying her for."

It's no more than I'd thought myself, just a few minutes earlier, but the woman's haughty attitude instantly gets my back up, as does the way she's refusing to so much as acknowledge my presence, even though I can tell by the way her eyes widened when she saw me that she knows exactly who I am. "*The maid?*" Does she think we're in a Regency romance here?

I make a mental note to speak to Frankie again about the name of her business, and how it's encouraging the clients to treat us like... well, like *maids*, basically... as I shuffle apologetically off the floor, desperately trying not to draw attention to myself — an attempt which fails spectacularly as I somehow manage to trip over Lexie's outstretched foot and find myself right back on the floor again

"Sorry," Lexie mouths apologetically as she holds out her hand to help pull me back up. I'm not sure whether she's apologizing for her mother's supercilious attitude, or for inadvertently sending me flying, but, either way, I'm grateful for the small act of kindness. I think I'm going to cry, actually.

Oh, please not now, Emerald. Please don't make yourself look even more stupid than you already have. I'm begging you.

Swallowing back the tears with difficulty, I mutter my excuses and head back to the living room to gather up Bessie and co. The entire time I'm packing up my stuff, I can hear raised voices from the kitchen as Lexie and her mum argue back and forth. The stone walls of the cottage are too thick for me to be able to make out what they're actually saying, but as I push open the heavy front door at last, and make my way down the path, hauling Bessie behind me, I can still hear them going at it. Or Lexie's mum is, anyway. Whatever she's saying, it sounds like she's really berating her daughter, and Lexie's just taking it, almost as if she's used to it.

Poor Lexie. She may have perfect hair — and perfect skin, and teeth, and, oh, *everything*, really — but, right now, I don't envy her one bit. I think we might even be friends, actually. Just think of it; me and Lexie Steele — just two Cool Girls, together at last. This could be the one thing that makes coming home almost bearable!

It's only as I reach the rose-covered gate at the end of the path that it hits me; Lexie told me everything I could possibly want to know about her life — but she didn't ask a single thing about mine.

Chapter 11

I was expecting Frankie to be waiting to pick me up, but when I get to the designated spot, just a little further along the street from Lexie's house, it's McTavish I find there instead.

In his tractor, naturally.

His bright yellow tractor, which is taking up the entire breadth of the narrow road it's currently parked on, with a string of irritated motorists queuing impatiently behind it.

What a way to end the day.

"Hiya, Emerald," McTavish says cheerfully, jumping down from the driver's seat and taking Bessie from me. "I hope you dinnae mind. I thought it would be nice to catch up now ye're back, but when I went to yer mam's she said ye'd went off to see Frankie, and when I went to see Frankie, she said ye were here. So here I am."

I pause, looking up at the tractor in horror. Being paraded through the streets of Heather Bay on it is pretty much the last thing I want right now — or *ever*, really for that matter — but it doesn't seem like I have much choice in the matter; several of the cars McTavish is blocking have started honking aggressively at him, and there's no way I'll make it home with Bessie on foot, so I allow McTavish to sling the vacuum cleaner up into the cabin, before hauling myself up behind him.

I don't know if you've ever ridden on a tractor, but, well, let's just say they're not exactly passenger vehicles. I'm practically perched on top of McTavish as we start to inch our way forward at a grindingly slow pace, and I'm not sure it's even legal for me to be up here, now I think of it. I guess it's a good job Dougie, the village policeman, has the afternoon off.

McTavish, however, is completely unperturbed to be traveling painfully slowly through our home town, with a wild-haired woman and a vacuum cleaner on his lap. Much like Lexie, he looks exactly as he did the last time I saw him; and the time before that, actually, which was when we were both still in our teens, and I was leaving Heather Bay for what I hoped would be the last time. He's wearing a pair of chunky work boots with worn blue jeans, an ancient navy fleece, and he has a *Flying Haggis* cap crammed over his straw blonde hair. He looks like he's just time-traveled back from our youth to save me from myself.

Well, other than the missing teeth, obviously.

I *really* want to ask him about the missing teeth.

I absolutely *cannot* ask him about the missing teeth.

"What happened to your teeth?" I blurt out, as we set off down the road which snakes along the seafront "Sorry," I add instantly. "I don't know why I said that. Just ignore me, please."

Fortunately for me, not much phases McTavish — not even me — so he just laughs good-naturedly.

"Och, it's fine," he says, looking me right in the eye in that way he has. Most people don't really look at you when they're talking; they'll glance around, and only make very occasional eye contact. McTavish, on the other hand, always seems to be

95

looking right into your soul, and he's doing that now. I shiver uncomfortably, wondering if he can somehow tell that I've been impersonating Scarlett Scott for the benefit of the local Laird. Because I feel a bit like I have the word "IMPOSTOR" stamped on my forehead in invisible ink, and if anyone could read it, it would be McTavish.

"Got knocked out, didn't they?" he says now, as if he's reminding me of something obvious. I don't like to pry any further, so I simply nod as if I know exactly what he's talking about, instead.

McTavish, however, isn't the world's greatest conversationalist; when he said he wanted to "catch up" he apparently meant "sit quietly together on a tractor", so once we've exchanged the requisite "How've you been?" and "What have you been up to?" we travel the rest of the home in companionable silence.

"Thanks, McTavish," I say as I finally jump down from the tractor in front of my parents' house. (I can see Mum peering excitedly out of the window, not even trying to hide behind the curtain. She'll be thrilled to see me arriving home with "a nice lad" like McTavish, I'm sure). "It's good to see a friendly face around here. Although Lexie was pretty friendly, too, actually, to be fair. We had a really nice conversation."

"Aye? Did ye? Well, I've always said, if patter was water she'd drown, would that one."

If I hadn't been looking at him when he said it, I'd have totally missed the expression that passes fleetingly over his face as he says it, and, as it is, I can't even begin to decode it anyway; or the weird comment about water, for that matter.

Before I can devote too much thought to McTavish and his facial expressions, however, I have a much more pressing issue to think about, because just as I'm about to take Bessie and go into the house to face Mum and her questions, my phone beeps with a message alert, and I look down to see a name I really didn't expect to ever cross my screen:

Jack Buchanan.

Is messaging me.

On my phone, which... wait: how did he get my number?

I glance around nervously, almost as if I'm expecting to see him hiding in the bushes or something, spying on me... then I cringe as I suddenly remember how I'd insisted on giving him my number after our "date", so he could let me know how much I owed him for the dry-cleaning. I think I might have even grabbed his phone and typed it in myself, actually, so I can only hope I typed in my name as Emerald — or Scarlett, even — rather than as Princess Consuela Banana-Hammock, which is what I sometimes do when I'm drunk. Okay, it's what I *always* do when I'm drunk.

I probably didn't do it this time, though, I tell myself confidently as I wave goodbye to McTavish before opening up the message.

> *Princess Consuela (?).*
> *Apologies for yesterday. I'd like to make it up to you.*
> *I'll pick you up tonight at 8pm.*
> *Jack.*

Shit.

I sit down on the front doorstep, still staring at the phone as my brain scrambles to unpick the many oddities of Jack's message; like the way he phrased it as an order, rather than a suggestion; how it doesn't seem to have even crossed his mind that I might not be free — or even want to see him. Oh, and the way he signed his name on a text message, like Mum does. (Mum even signs off like that on voicemails, though. She'll say whatever it is she has to tell you, then pause for a second and go, "Love, Mum," as if she's writing a letter.) It's cute on mum, but slightly less cute on a man who supposedly made his fortune designing apps, and who should presumably know how phones work by now.

That, however, is the very least of my worries, because not only does Jack Buchanan not seem to know how modern technology works, he doesn't seem to know how *women* work, either. I mean, you don't just *summon* someone to a date with you, do you? Or assume they'll say yes?

But Jack obviously does — and now I'm in a whole mess of trouble, because as much as I want to be annoyed by his officious manner, if I'm honest, what I'm really feeling is excitement.

He wants to see me again.

Me, Emerald. Well, Scarlett.

He must have liked me — her — just a *little* bit, then. Just enough to want to see me — her — again the very next day. Which, given that he's hands-down the most attractive man I've met in — well, *ever*, really — is the ego boost I badly need right now.

Not that I'm going to actually *meet* him, of course.

I mean, of *course* not.

Even if I *wanted* to — which I most emphatically *do not* — it would be absolute madness, on a scale that not even I am normally capable of. Because, the fact is, he thinks I'm Scarlett Scott. And there's absolutely no way to explain that I'm not without:

a) Making myself sound certifiable

and

b) Potentially getting Frankie's cleaning business sued. Or whatever it is that happens when a cleaner decides to wear her employer's clothes.

(What *does* happen, though, I wonder? Because my frantic internet searches have turned up surprisingly little on the subject.)

Then again, I've been feeling terrible about what happened with the whisky ever since Lexie's revelation about Jack's grandfather and how it was his dying wish or something that his grandson continued his legacy. Okay, I might have made it up about the dying wish. But it seems like the kind of thing the entirely fictional grandfather I've just made up in my own stupid head would say. And how horrible would it be to be honoring that wish and have some idiotic redhead practically throw up on you?

Horrible.

Terrible.

I should really apologize. Again. Properly this time, though. While I'm sober, I mean.

I could just meet him for a minute or two, I suppose? Just to explain? (Explain *what*, though? The fact that I can't stand whisky, or the fact that I'm not the person he thinks I am? Because I somehow don't think either of those things will go down any better with Jack Buchanan than his grandfather's whisky went down with me.)

Then I remember Frankie, and how excited she was when she told me she'd won the contract to clean Jack's house. Now that she's actually going to be working for him, it's even more important that I stay out of his way and make sure he never,

ever finds out about my little accidental deception I might have done a lot of stupid things in my life, but I'd never forgive myself if I took my best friend down with me by ruining this deal for her. Never. Hoes before bros, as they say. (Wait: *do* they say that? Or did I just make that up, too?)

So I will not be going on this date. No way. Never. Not even if you paid me.

And besides: I have absolutely nothing to wear for a date with a billionaire-but-only-on-paper. Or even with your common-or-garden millionaire.

Case closed.

Chapter 12

I go on the date, obviously.

Oh come on, you've read this far; do I really sound like someone who'd make the right decision to you? Even in the face — the really quite impossibly handsome face — of someone like Jack Buchanan?

Of course not.

I blame Lexie. Lexie and her heart-rending story about Jack's ailing grandfather and his dying wish to start a whisky brand; a story that gets even more heart-rending every time I think about it — mostly because I'm pretty much making it up at this point. I mean, the grandfather wasn't actually "ailing" in Lexie's version, was he? He was probably quite fit, in fact, given that he was young and healthy enough to be sent off to war. Also, I really doubt that his dying words were about whisky, somehow; although he *was* Scottish, presumably, so you never know. Even taking all of that into account, however, this new vision of Jack Buchanan as devastatingly attractive family man has intrigued me. It's a bit like when Elizabeth finds out that Darcy was the one who paid for Wickham to marry her sister, and once I've had that thought, it's impossible to shake it off.

Which is how I come to find myself back at Scarlett Scott's

house, less than 24 hours after I swore I'd never go back there.

Whoops.

I'm not going inside this time, though. Nuh-uh. I mean, I might be known for my bad life choices, but I'm not quite *that* bad. At least, not yet, anyway,

So, here's the plan:

I'm going to tell Jack the truth.

I'm going to beg him not to get Frankie into trouble over it; it's not her fault I can't get through a single day without messing up somehow, after all.

I'm going to apologize — again — for my reaction to his whisky.

And then I'm going to politely excuse myself and never see him again.

(Or not unless he *really* wants to.)

(I wonder if he'll want to, though?)

That's the plan, anyway, and as I drop my bag onto Scarlett's doorstep and start to struggle out of my Highland Maids uniform, I'm feeling pretty pleased with myself about it, too. I'm *terrified*, obviously: that goes without saying. I might not know much about Jack Buchanan, but one of the few things I picked up on last night was that he is not a man to suffer fools gladly. And, let's face it: I've been a real fool, haven't I?

So, I'm worried about Jack's reaction to my big "I'm Not Scarlett" confession, but I'm going to do it anyway. Because that's what Scarlett *herself* would do; or so I've been telling myself, anyway. I'm well aware of the irony in channeling the imaginary Scarlett I've invented in order to gather the courage to tell Jack I'm *not her*, but, the fact is, the Scarlett Scott who exists in my mind is everything I've ever wanted to be and more. And I hate to admit it, even to myself, but there's a part of me that actually enjoyed pretending to be her the other night.

It wasn't *fun*, exactly — or, not unless you consider almost choking to death in front of an audience "fun", anyway. But it was liberating, in a way. To step into someone else's shoes; literally *and* figuratively. To step into someone else's *life*. Isn't that what I've always wanted? To be someone else? To not have to be *me* for just a little while?

"Do you ever wish you could, I don't know, just *take off your own head* for a while?" I asked Ben once. "Just to get a break from yourself?"

Ben just frowned and rolled his eyes in his favorite, "Don't be so stupid, Emerald," expression. Then again, Ben had nothing to escape from, I suppose. He knew exactly who he was and where he was going. He had a ten-year-plan, and a twenty-year-plan, and a pension-plan. He had a closet filled with tasteful shirts, and he'd spend every Sunday night ironing them, in preparation for the week ahead. He couldn't even have imagined wanting to be someone else. Why would he want to be someone else, after all, when he was so extremely good at being *himself*?

I did, though.

I always knew I wanted to *do* something with my life; to be *someone*. I just didn't know who that someone was; and now I do.

I want to be the fictional version of Scarlett Scott —the one I've created in my own head. I don't mean I want to keep on pretending to be her to Jack; quite the opposite in fact. But I want to be *like* her. To live fearlessly, the way I imagine she would. To do the *right* thing, even if it's also the hard thing. The *honest* thing. To do... a bunch of other appropriately noble-sounding things that I can't bring myself to think about right now, because I forgot to unbutton the polo shirt Frankie makes us wear under our sweatshirts before I tried to pull it off my head, and now it's stuck somewhere around my ears, blocking my vision, and making my face turn slowly purple.

Thank goodness Scarlett's doorstep is hidden from the main road.

Oh yeah: Scarlett's doorstep. I'm waiting for Jack here, rather than on my own doorstep — well, my parents' doorstep — not because I want to continue the deception, but because the news I have to deliver isn't exactly the type you want to just send in a text, is it? No, I want to ease him into it gently, so I'm going to meet him here, in the place he thinks I live, and then tell him the truth in person.

As for why I'm getting undressed here, well, that's Frankie's fault, really. She sent me off to another cleaning job almost as soon as I got back from Lexie's, and I knew there wasn't going to be time for me to go back home and change before I meet Jack, so I hastily threw some clothes into a bag to change into later. And now here I am: arms trapped above my ears, head stuck in a polo shirt, old, graying bra on full display... so it figures that now would be the perfect moment for me to hear the purr of a car engine turning into Scarlett Scott's driveway, doesn't it?

Oh shit. Oh no. Oh please, God, no. Please don't let it be Jack, here already. And please let me get this bloody polo shirt off my head...

It's no use. The more I struggle, the more stuck in the shirt I become. I think it might be trying to suffocate me, actually. Leave it to me to be the first person in the world to be killed by her own clothes; what an obituary *that'll* be, for sure.

I'm straight up panicking now. Not because of the shirt situation — I really wish it wasn't the case, but this actually isn't the first time my clothes have turned against me in this manner — but because of the *him* situation.

The *Jack Buchanan* situation.

The *Oh My God, the sexiest man I've ever met is probably looking at my dingy gray bra right the hell now* situation.

As situations go, it's not the best one I've ever been in, I have to say. Like, this is not remotely how I'd have planned for Jack to see me naked for the first time. Or *any* time. It's almost definitely going to be the *last* time he ever sees me naked too, though, because there's no mistaking the sound of that car engine. Only a very expensive little sports car makes that particular purring sound as it comes to a stop, and only Heather Bay's resident billionaire-on-paper owns one of those.

I actually *want* to die now.

It's okay, shirt; take me. Do your worst. Just, for the love of God, make it quick, so I don't have to face him.

The shirt, however, doesn't listen, and, a few seconds later, I hear the crunch of feet on gravel before a pair of hands reach out and wrench the offending garment from my head.

"Oww!" An involuntary squeak of pain escapes my lips as the tight collar of the shirt almost takes both my ears off with it.

I really must speak to Frankie about these uniforms.

My eyes are closed, and, for a moment, I consider just *keeping* them that way. Just turning and walking blindly away, and pretending this didn't actually happen.

"Um, Scarlett? Emerald, I mean? Are you okay?"

I reluctantly open my eyes, and there he is: white shirt, dark blue jeans, dark hair flopping over one beautiful blue eye. And there I am: graying bra, un-toned abs, saggy black joggers that I've spent the entire day scrubbing other people's floors in.

Another excellent first impression from me, then.

"Hi!" I squeak nervously, pretending to be surprised to see Jack standing there. "Wow, if I'd known you were going to see my underwear, I'd have worn something nicer!"

And then I drop dead, right there on the driveway.

Okay, no, I don't. I just *wish* I could drop dead, because *seriously*, Emerald? *Seriously*?

There is no trace of a smile on Jack Buchanan's full lips this time. Probably because there's absolutely nothing funny about turning up for a date and finding the woman you're supposed to be meeting standing half-naked on the doorstep, is there?

On second thoughts, don't answer that.

"Do you need to go and change?" Jack asks, his expression deadpan. "Or is that what you were just doing?"

"Oh! No! Just... just give me a second," I say, putting my hand quickly into the pocket of my joggers and heaving a sigh of relief when I realize Scarlett's key is still in there. Frankie was so excited by the news of her new cleaning commission that she forgot to ask for it back, so I still have it.

And that's how I end up shame-facedly letting myself into Scarlett Scott's house for the third time.

Accidentally, of course.

* * *

I'm twenty minutes into my second date with Jack Buchanan, and so far it's playing out almost exactly like the first. Let's

- Me pretending to be someone else: check.
- Me having some kind of clothing-related accident: check.
- Jack driving us both in stony silence to some unknown destination, while giving every indication that he'd rather be anywhere else at all: check, check.

I can only hope he was too distracted by my near-nudity to notice Bessie sitting by the front door when he arrived.

There is one big difference between this date and the last one, however; I'm wearing my own clothes this time. Which is progress, right?

In less positive news, however, when I rushed guiltily up to Scarlett's bedroom to change, I upended the bag of clothes I'd brought with me out onto the bed, only to find the following:

- One slinky black negligee that I bought for what I *thought* was going to be a dirty weekend with Ben, but which turned out to be just me sitting in the hotel room on my own, drinking the mini-bar dry and watching *Eastenders* while Ben played golf with "the boys".
- A pair of bikini bottoms, at least two sizes too small.
- My trusty denim jacket, which I've had since I was a teenager.
- A single black sock, owner unknown.

In the toss-up between the black negligee and my grubby old joggers, the nightie wins, so I pulled it on as quickly as I could without getting stuck in it — I *really* didn't want Jack to have to help me out of this one — then threw the denim jacket over the top. The Emerald who packed this bag apparently didn't see any need for shoes (Unless the sock was supposed to fulfill that particular role?), so I stuffed my feet back into the trainers I was wearing when I arrived, hoping the combination of silky "dress" plus jacket and trainers looks casually cool, instead of making me look like a bag of laundry that got up and walked. Which, to be blunt, is how I suspect I look.

With that done, I quickly stuffed the bag containing my Highland Maids uniform and the rest of my clothes under Scarlett's bed, then thundered my way back downstairs, carefully avoiding the mirror I had to pass in the hallway.

And now here I am, sitting beside a silent Jack Buchanan, who doesn't speak a single word to me until we finally pull up outside what appears to be a giant warehouse on the banks of the loch. There's a huge sign with the number '39' on one side, so I guess this must be the distillery Lexie told me about; a fact that's confirmed by Jack as he holds the car door open and waits for me to clamber out.

"I'll show you around the distillery later, if you like," he says, gesturing for me to follow him down a path that leads around the back of the building. "I thought we'd eat first, if that's alright with you?"

I nod silently, not trusting myself to speak just yet. I'm just wondering where on earth he's planning to eat in a whisky distillery, when a sudden flash of color catches my eye, and I glace round just in time to see a bright yellow tractor pulling out of the gate we've just driven through.

McTavish?

What would McTavish be doing here?

That's going to have to be another question for another day, however, because by now we're rounding the corner of the huge building, to find ourselves standing by the side of the loch, which glistens softly in the dying light of the sun. To our left, a set of wooden stairs leads up the side of the distillery, to what looks like a glass box sticking out the side of it.

"This will be the restaurant, eventually," Jack explains, as he leads the way up the stairs. "I'm assuming Finn told you about my plans to open the building to the public? So, we'll have distillery tours, a gift shop, a restaurant... you know the kind of thing."

I don't, of course, but it seems Scarlett does, so I just nod again and say nothing, while Jack pushes open the door to the glass box which he called a restaurant.

"Oh, wow!"

The words burst out of me as I step through the door and into what feels like a window directly onto the loch. The floor-to-ceiling glass that makes up each side offers panoramic views from one shore to the other, while the polished floor is almost exactly the same shade as the water itself, making me feel as if I'm part of the stunning scenery that's spread out before me.

"You like it?"

I glance around at Jack, who's smiling that rare smile of his; a smile that feels a bit like the sun coming out after a rainstorm, and makes him look almost boyish. It must really be something to be the reason for that smile. But, of course, it's not directed at me, but at the loch itself — which I suppose is fair enough, given that *it's* not the one wearing a pair of old trainers and a nightie.

"I *love* it," I say, truthfully. "I've never seen anything like it. I feel like I'm floating just above the water. It's amazing. Really."

"It is, isn't it?" He's grinning broadly now; this project of his obviously means far more to him than even I could have imagined, and his enthusiasm is so infectious it's impossible not to smile back at him.

"Shall we?"

The vast space above the water seemed empty when we walked in, but as I look in the direction Jack's pointing in, I see a table set for two at the far end of the room, nestled in a corner where two glass walls meet. There's a champagne bucket next to it, and I feel a rush of relief that I'm apparently not going to be subjected to the dreaded whisky again. Then, with the same sinking feeling I get at the very top of a rollercoaster — or every time I check my bank balance — I remember the reason I came here; not to have a romantic, lochside date with the man in front of me, but to apologize to him for my behavior on the last one. And to come clean about who I really am.

"Jack, there's something I need to tell you..." I say, deciding it's probably best to just get it over with, before I lose my nerve. Before I can spit out my confession, though, a loud bang makes me jump as a set of double-doors on the other side of the room burst open and a waiter appears, carrying two plates.

"Welcome to The 39," Jack says, his eyes twinkling with pleasure. "You're our very first guest."

Chapter 13

I t's just over an hour later, and I still haven't told Jack I'm not actually the woman he thinks I am.

It's not that I don't *want* to tell him, you understand. Well, I mean, it kind of *is* that I don't want to tell him. Let's face it, no one actually *wants* to be all, "Oh, by the way, did I mention I've been pretending to be someone else this whole time?" on a second date, do they? That's much more of a third date scenario, if you ask me. Or a *never* kind of scenario. Never works for me too.

I *am* going to mention it, though, I swear. The guilt will eat me alive if I don't. I'm just not going to mention it *right this second*, because the fact is, something unexpected happened when Jack Buchanan smiled at me. I started enjoying myself.

I can't help it, though; he's just so *interesting*. And, okay, sexy. Jack Buchanan is so distractingly sexy, in fact, that, for the first few minutes of our date, while the waiter serves a smoked salmon starter and Jack expertly pours the champagne, I pretty much sit there gawping at him, looking a bit like the salmon probably did before it made it onto our plates.

There's just something about the easy way he opens the champagne bottle, as if he's been doing it his entire life. His strong, elegant hands on the neck of the bottle. His full, slightly pouty lips on the glass. He shouldn't be allowed to be this attractive, I think, as I take a sip of my own drink, feeling the bubbles go straight to my head. He shouldn't be allowed to just walk around making people feel the way I'm feeling right now. It's such an unfair advantage, being born beautiful.

I'm suddenly uncomfortably aware of the fact that I'm wearing a nightdress under my old, beat-up denim jacket, and I tuck my feet carefully under the table to avoid drawing attention to my unsophisticated trainers. I'm a fish out of water here; which is *also* a bit like the salmon I'm currently eating, actually. I suspect the fact that I have more in common with my dinner than with my date probably doesn't bode all that well, does it?

Then Jack starts talking about his grandfather and the distillery, and I allow myself to relax and just *listen* to him — which isn't particularly difficult, as it happens, because when Jack Buchanan talks about something he's passionate about, his enthusiasm is utterly infectious. I actually find myself wishing I didn't hate whisky so much, because he's making it sound so amazing.

The story Lexie told me turns out to be pretty accurate; as she'd said, Jack's grandfather, who'd lived in Heather Bay his entire life — in the old estate house which Jack now owns, no less — had dreamed of starting his own whisky brand since he was a young man. He'd started working on his first malt in 1939, just before the war started. And that, as Lexie said, was that.

"I never met him, of course," Jack says wistfully as our main courses are placed in front of us; a very posh version of haggis, neeps and tatties, that instantly makes my mouth water. "And neither did my dad, actually; he was born a few months after my grandfather went to war. I've no idea how my grandmother coped. It must have been such a rough time for her."

I pause in the act of shoveling a forkful of haggis into my mouth.

"That's so sad," I say, meaning it. If I'm not careful, I could very easily start to cry at the thought of Jack's unknown grandmother giving birth to her first child, only to find that her husband wouldn't ever meet him. Her grandchild, however, is determined to fulfill his legacy, and I bite down hard on my fork to stop myself from embarrassing myself by starting to weep over someone else's family. This is really not the time to be indulging my super-sentimental side, and I'd ideally like to get through at least *one* date with Jack Buchanan before letting him find out about my tendency to cry over everything. That *also* seems like a third date kind of thing to me.

"He'd love this place, though," Jack says, looking around. "He always wanted to give something back to the village, and I really want to make that a reality. I'm planning to launch it at the masquerade ball next month. I didn't want to make a big fuss, but my PR manager convinced me it would be a good idea, so there's going to be a whole thing, with some kind of tedious hiking party and, oh, I don't know, a whole bunch of stuff they've been organizing. I haven't been paying much attention, to be honest."

"You don't like the fuss?"

This seems very on-brand for him, to be honest. I can imagine him sulking in a corner somewhere, like Mr. Darcy, while everyone else has a wild time at his party.

"Nope." Jack grins ruefully. "I hate it. I hate all the schmoozing, you know? The fake conversations, pretending to be someone you're not just to get people to buy into what you're selling them. I'd much rather just hide in my office and get on with the work. Or be out on the distillery floor, surrounded by the smell of hops, and the copper stills. That's what home feels like to me. Not stuck in a room making small talk with people who're only interested in my money, or what I can do for them. None of that's real. None of it actually matters."

I swallow nervously. This is *really* not feeling like a good time for my big "I'm Not Scarlett" announcement. And it's not exactly news that Jack Buchanan doesn't like people who pretend to be someone they're not — who *would*, after all? — but what *I'm* doing is next level fakery. Off-the-charts. He's going to hate me when he finds out. And, all of a sudden, him *not* finding out is the most important thing in the world to me.

"And you?" he asks suddenly, fixing me with those blue eyes of his. "What does home mean to you, Emerald?"

I hesitate, wondering how on earth I'm supposed to answer this. Because I'm not like him. I don't have a grand passion in life, or a legacy to try to fulfill. I don't even have a dead grandfather, whose last wish I must honor. Seriously, though, what does a girl have to do to get herself a dead relative or two around here?

Over Jack's shoulder, the sun is slowly sinking in the sky. From here, I can see Westward Tor, the hill that sits on the banks of the loch, its jagged cliff face covered in the purple heather that gave the village below its name. Most people find the Tor ominous and unwelcoming; and with good reason, too — barely a winter goes by here without some hapless climber having to be airlifted off the summit. For me, though, it's always been a place of refuge — somewhere to escape to when I just can't be inside my own head any more. Like on the day I burned down the village hall, for instance, and ran all the way to the Tor, to sit on its blustery summit, and cry into the wind.

Suddenly, I know how to answer Jack's question.

"See that hill?" I say, pointing behind him.

He twists round in his seat to stare at it.

"That mountain, you mean?"

I chuckle to myself. You can tell he's a city boy.

"It's just a hill," I tell him. "A big one, sure, but not quite big enough to be a mountain."

Jack nods, in the manner of someone who's making notes in his head, in case he's going to be questioned later.

"I can see I have a lot to learn about this place," he says ruefully. "I was hoping it would just sort of come to me, I suppose, once I moved here. Like it was in my blood or something."

"I'm sure it is," I say softly. "But it takes a bit of getting used to, too. Even for those of us who grew up here."

I bite my tongue, realizing I'm on the verge of saying too much here, but he's watching me with a curiously intense expression, which makes me want to go on; to open up to him.

I must not do that. That way trouble lies.

"It's okay for you, though," he says, still holding my gaze. "You're a local, even if you've been away for a while. I'm an incomer. An outsider."

"Not really," I assure him, touched by this moment of vulnerability. "I mean, okay, you didn't grow up here, true. But your family did. That means something. In any case, it's not like we're living in the 17th century or something, where it's all clan warfare and... and *witches* and stuff. And you know we don't actually stone people anymore, right?"

Jack grins, his cheeks dimpling delightfully, and I feel a

sharp pang of guilt for lying to him.

Because most of that was a lie. Not the bit about the witches and the stoning, obviously; that was true enough. But it's still easy to feel like an outsider in a place like Heather Bay. Trust one who knows.

"I'm disappointed," Jack says archly, twirling the stem of his champagne glass in his long, elegant fingers. "I was hoping to find the Highlands rife with witches. I thought they might be rather fun."

He raises one eyebrow, and my heart-rate rises with it.

"Oh, don't worry, there are still plenty of witches," I assure him, thinking of Lexie and her mum. "But enough about me," I add quickly, earning another flash of those dimples. "I want to know more about you."

"No, wait," he interrupts, his expression suddenly serious. "You didn't finish telling me about the mount... the *hill*. What were you going to say about it?"

Oh.

I look at him, surprised. I can't believe he actually remembered what I was talking about and came back to it. I can't believe he was actually *interested*. Ben never was.

"Oh, um, you asked me what home meant to me?" I reply, stumbling over my words slightly. "Well, it's that hill. The Tor."

Jack nods, waiting for me to go on.

"Back when I lived here," I say carefully, trying to remember what I told him about my past on our ill-fated first date, "I used to climb the Tor whenever I felt sad. And sometimes when I felt happy, too, actually. Anytime I needed space to think, basically. To just be *me*, without the pressure of everyone else's expectations of me. It's ... well, it's a good place to just sit and be alone with your thoughts, you know?"

I'm blushing by the time I get to the end of this short speech, but, to my surprise, Jack's still nodding, as if he knows exactly what I'm talking about and doesn't find me remotely stupid for saying it.

"I get that," he says, his expression wistful as he turns to look again at the hill, now just a silhouette against the sky. "Sometimes you just want to get out of your own head, don't you? Switch off all the noise."

I blink rapidly to stem the tears that are suddenly pricking at the back of my eyes. Jack can't possibly know how closely his words echo what I've just been thinking. But he said it like he meant it, and, now he's not just some sexy, rich guy who drives too fast and looks down on everyone. He's a real, flesh and blood person; and one I'd really quite like to get to know.

"So," I say thoughtfully, taking another sip of my champagne. "You don't like parties, or schmoozing; what do you like?"

"What do you want to know?"

Hmm. What *do* I want to know?

There are a lot of things I'd *love* to ask Jack Buchanan right now. Like what, exactly he's doing here with me, whether he has any recent ex-girlfriends he might be thinking about getting back together with, and exactly *how* annoyed he'd be if he found out I was lying to him. Instead, though, I decide to play it safe with the very first question that pops into my head.

"In the movie of your life, who would play you?"

In my defense, it's a perfectly reasonable question; the kind you might be asked at a job interview, say, or as part of one of those awful ice-breaker exercises they make you do as a "team building" activity. I've always thought you can tell a lot about

117

a person by who they want to play them in a movie, though, and, to his credit, Jack actually takes the question seriously, his brow creasing as he thinks about it.

"Jett Carter," he says at last, naming the hottest actor on the planet. "Not as good-looking as me, of course, but he's the only actor good enough to capture my mercurial nature."

His eyes twinkle as he says it, and there's suddenly not enough air in the room. Either that or there's actually something wrong with my breathing.

"Go on then. What about you?"

"Oh, I've never really thought about it," I say casually, even though it would definitely be a red-haired Vivien Leigh. "You're wrong about Jett, though. You'd definitely be played by James Dean. Before he died, obviously."

There's a short pause as I register the sheer stupidity of my final comment, and then, to my relieved amazement, Jack bursts out laughing. *Properly* laughing, I mean. And not in the, "Oh my God, Emerald, why are you such an idiot?" way Ben used to laugh at me, but as if he actually thinks I'm *funny*.

This is new.

"I'm glad you clarified that for me," he says, grinning as he refills our glasses. "As for you, though, Miss *I've-Never-Really-Thought-About-It*, I'm going to say you'd be played by Nicole Kidman. Before she got all the plastic surgery."

I smile, delighted. When I asked Ben this question, he said I'd be played by the girl who was Little Orphan Annie. Lexie Steele once said I could be Ginny Weasley's uglier sister. But Jack Buchanan just compared me to one of the most beautiful actresses in the world, and if I didn't know better, I'd almost be tempted to think he was flirting with me.

Is he flirting with me?

Please, God, let him be flirting with me

The sun has almost hit the water now, and we sit there for a few moments in companionable silence, watching as it sinks under the waves, leaving the sky streaked with red and gold. It's the golden hour — the "gloaming" as we call it in Scotland — and I've always thought it was the most beautiful time of day here; a magical, almost mystical time when you could almost believe you've slipped into a fairytale.

It's almost perfect.

Almost.

The only thing that would make it truly perfect would be if this was actually *real.* If Jack and I were *really* on a date. If he knew exactly who I was, and didn't care.

I should tell him. I *have* to tell him. It's the right thing to do; the 'Scarlett Scott' thing to do. And I've had just enough champagne now to give me the courage to do it. Picking up my phone, I snap a quick photo of the sunset that's filling the entire window first, just so I have something I can look back on to remind myself of this moment, before everything went tits up. Then I take a deep breath, and an equally deep glug of my champagne, and turn back to the table...

... to see Jack staring intently at his phone, a frown line creasing his beautiful brow.

Oh.

Okay.

Maybe this isn't going as well as I'd thought it was? I'd really thought we were starting to form the beginnings of a connection, what with him opening up about his distillery and me... well, banging on about witches, and mountains, and did I *really* say something about stoning people? Seriously, Emerald?

119

As I open my mouth to speak, though, I see that Jack isn't just looking at his phone; he's now standing up from the table, still looking at the device in his hand, as if I'm not even there.

"I'm really sorry about this, Scarlett," he says, not even bothering to look at me. "But I'm going to have to go. Please, feel free to stay as long as you like. Enjoy the rest of the champagne. My driver will take you home whenever you're ready."

And then he's gone; striding out of the restaurant without looking back, while I just sit there looking at his retreating back and wondering what the hell just happened.

What the hell *did* just happen, though? Because I honestly have no idea. I flick quickly back through my memory, searching for whatever it is I must have done to send him rushing off so quickly, but, for once, there's nothing. Aside from that awkward incident with me basically flashing him on Scarlett's driveway — which, okay, wasn't my finest moment, to be sure — I've behaved impeccably this evening. I haven't choked on my drink, or spat whisky over anyone. I haven't fallen over, or broken anything. I haven't even asked a single awkward question, or tried to break an uncomfortable silence with a joke that falls flat. It's been very unlike me, in fact. The real Scarlett surely couldn't have done better.

And yet, Jack has gone, leaving me sitting here alone, without explanation. And, okay, I know two dates don't exactly count as a relationship — especially when both of them are cut as exceptionally short as these ones. But, even so, I can't help feeling a bit like I've been dumped. Again.

Chapter 14

For the next three days, I throw myself into my new job. It's the start of the summer season, so the holiday chalets that make up the bulk of Highland Maids' work at this time of year are all booked: a blessing for Frankie and her business, but something of a blessing for me too, because at least the work helps distract me from my increasingly long lists of Things I Don't Want to Think About Right Now and Mortal Enemies.

Emerald's List of Mortal Enemies:
Ex-Boyfriend Ben
Jack Buchanan
Finn Whateverhisfaceis
Brian-from-the-bank
Jude Paw

There's something therapeutic about cleaning, I think, as I plug in my earbuds and get to work every morning. It's just me and Taylor Swift, smoothing sheets, emptying bins, and bringing order to chaos. Well, if I can't manage that in my own life, at least I can do it at work, right?

So I clean and I tidy, I make beds and I sweep floors, and I don't think about Jack Buchanan at all. Or not much, anyway. Not more than a few times an hour, which is hardly anything, really.

I haven't heard from him since he walked out on our date at the distillery. Not a single word. Not so much as a text message saying he'd just found out his pet parrot had died, or that the long-lost twin he didn't know he had had turned up at his house, demanding his share of the inheritance.

Nothing at all.

I'll be honest: I'm kind of pissed about it. Even if it had been a normal date, it would have been shockingly bad manners for someone to just leave like that. But this had been no ordinary date, had it? No, this had been the date on which I was going to come clean — to admit that I wasn't Scarlett Scott, and to redeem myself for the terrible way I'd behaved by wearing her clothes and stealing her identity. It was going to be hard, but honorable, and I'm really quite annoyed that Jack Buchanan has robbed me of the opportunity to vindicate myself like that.

I mean, how dare he, right?

(Oh, and it was also the date on which I really started to fall for him. Well, he certainly managed to nip that in the bud, didn't he?)

If I'd just been able to tell the truth, I'd be a whole different person by now. 'Fessing up to Jack — owning my mistakes instead of simply running away from them, like I normally do — would've turned me into Emerald 2.0. Instead, though, I'm still just Emerald the 1st: back in Heather Bay, sleeping in her childhood bedroom, head stuck in the toilet.

"Cup of tea, Emerald? The kettle's just boiled."

I sit up, bumping my head on the cistern in the process. I wasn't joking about having my head stuck in the toilet, by the way; I've been cleaning it for the past twenty minutes, while its owner, Bella McGowan, offers me an increasingly tempting selection of hand-baked treats from the kitchen. She started off with just a biscuit — which I declined, on account of the whole "toilet" situation — but has been upping the ante ever since, with scones, cakes and shortbread.

Bella is one of those elderly ladies who isn't happy until they've over-fed you to the point of bursting, and if I don't finish this job soon, she'll probably be well on her way to cooking me a three-course meal, and Frankie will sack me for eating on the job or something.

Then again, a cup of tea does sound good, and the bathroom is positively sparkling, so...

"That'd be lovely, Bella," I call back, peeling off my rubber gloves. "Be with you in a second."

Bella's house is a 1950s bungalow, of a type tourists are always surprised to find actually exist in the Highlands. They think it's all ruined castles and charming stone cottages, but this house was probably considered the height of luxury when Bella and her late husband, Frank, bought it as newlyweds, and its barely changed since, as far as I can tell.

Neither has Bella, for that matter. She's been a Heather Bay fixture for as long as I can remember, and she already seemed ancient when I was a little girl (Mind you, so did my own parents, who can't be *that* much younger than her...), so I'm assuming she must be about 117 by now, even though she looks pretty much the same as always, with her clever brown eyes, her spiky gray hair and her purple Doc Martens.

Oh, and the One Direction badge she has pinned to her fluffy magenta cardigan.

That's certainly different.

("Och, I love wee Harry," Bella said fondly when I commented on it. "He cheers me right up, so he does.")

Despite knowing more about me than most people do, Bella is one of the few people in Heather Bay who hasn't mentioned The Thing yet, which is why I figure it's probably safe enough to have a quick cup of tea with her before heading off to my next job.

Then I spot the box.

It's sitting on a small coffee table in the middle of the room, and, at first I think it's just a regular wooden box, containing, I don't know, jigsaw puzzles? TV guides? More cakes? Then Bella notices me glancing at it curiously and decides to casually give me a heart attack.

"Oh, I thought you might like to see that, Emerald," she says, passing me a steaming mug of tea, in a mug with Harry Styles' beaming face on the front. "It's some little mementos of the last Heather Bay Gala Day. I dug it out of the garage when Frankie told me she was sending you to do the cleaning, so you could see it."

I'm so shocked I almost choke on my tea. It's crazy how some people can just say the words "Heather Bay Gala Day" without having a panic attack. I, meanwhile, can't even *think* them without feeling sick to my stomach, and, all of a sudden, the plate of scones Bella's put in front of me doesn't look nearly as tempting.

"Och, for goodness sake, Emerald, you're not still fretting over that business, are you?" says Bella, shrewdly. "It wasn't your fault. You know that, don't you? Here, have a scone."

"But it *was* my fault," I say leaning forward and almost knocking my cup of tea over in the process. "It was *me*, Bella, *I* did it. And I don't think I'll ever get over it. Ever."

"Nonsense," says Bella crisply, fixing me with her best ex-headteacher glare. "Of course you'll get over it. It was an accident. Accidents happen, lass."

"Yeah, to *me*," I reply, giving in and taking one of the scones. "Accidents happen *to me*. And I can't seem to stop them, no matter how hard I try."

"Well, you won't with that attitude," says Bella, refusing to pander to my dramatics. "You're not helpless, Emerald. What happened at the Gala Day was an accident, but that doesn't mean your whole life has to be one. You're the one in control. You know that, though. You're a clever lassie."

I stare at her mutinously for a moment. I instinctively want to argue with her; to point out that I'm *not* a clever lassie and that I *don't* know how to take control of my life, but, the fact is, she has a point.

"Do you really think it was just an accident?" I ask, allowing myself to sink back into the sofa cushions. "I've always assumed it was my fault, and that no one would ever forgive me for it. I could hardly bring myself to walk past the village hall when I got back here. I can't believe I did that."

"I think you'll find that people have shorter memories than you think," Bella says kindly. This isn't strictly true, of course; in my experience, the good people of Heather Bay have almost total recall of everything that's ever happened in the village in the past 100 years or so; and, for the newcomers, there's always Shona McLaren to fill them in. I know Bella's trying to make me feel better, though, and I'm grateful to her, so I just smile weakly as I finish my scone.

"You know I was Chair of the Gala Committee, back in the day?" Bella asks as I wipe the crumbs from my chin. "Well, we decided to re-start it a few months ago. We've raised some funds which we're hoping might be enough to repair the roof of the hall, with maybe a bit left over. That young fellow — Jack Whatshisname, from the estate — he said he might chip in a bit for it. You'd be more than welcome to join the committee if you like? We could be doing with the help. Och, it would be good to have a Village Gala again, so it would."

"Um, I'm not sure I'd be much use to you," I reply, trying to stay cool despite the fact that my face instantly turned red at the mention of Jack's name. Well, part of his name, anyway. Between this and the talk of the Gala Day, I'm in actual hell right now. It's a good job the scones are tasty, because Frankie is absolutely not paying me enough for this.

"Jack Buchanan, you mean?" I ask cautiously once I've recovered myself. "How d'you know him, Bella?"

"Och, I don't," Bella replies, getting up and starting to clear the plates from the coffee table. She hasn't mentioned the box again, I'm grateful to note. I might get out of here without having a nervous breakdown after all. "I've heard of him, though. We all have. He's quite the celebrity around these parts. Quite dishy too, apparently. Although not as dishy as wee Harry, obviously."

She shoots me another one of those shrewd looks of hers, and I pretend to be studying the contents of my mug intently until she finally gives up.

"Anyway," she says, as I get up to help her, "He's starting a distillery by the loch, and we thought it could be a good opportunity for a bit of cross-promotion. Get him to sponsor the Gala Day in exchange for a banner on the town hall or something. It's all about 'branding' these days, isn't it?"

Bella might be old, but she's certainly not stupid, that's for sure.

"Do you think he'll do it?" I ask curiously, following her through to the kitchen with a pile of dirty dishes.

"I hope so. We've only had contact with his assistant so far, but from what I've heard, he seems to be quite community-minded. Keen to do his bit for the village and all that. Well, his family does own most of it, so maybe he sees it as his Lairdly duty."

I bite my lip as I put the dishes in the sink. I don't know Jack Buchanan at all, I realize. Every time I think I'm starting to get a handle on his personality, he does something to surprise me. It's hard to imagine the man who ran the Heather Bay bus off the road and literally ran out on our second date wanting to "do his bit for the village," for instance, but then I think about the warmth in his voice when he spoke about his grandfather, and the way his cheeks dimpled when he smiled at me, and suddenly I'm not so sure.

It's almost as if there are two different Jack Buchanan's, actually. I frown to myself as I mull this over. Could Jack have an evil twin, perhaps? It would certainly explain the two sides to his personality, that's for sure.

"You should consider joining us, Emerald," Bella is saying now, and I shrug non-committally as I start to wash up the dishes. I have absolutely no intention of joining a committee whose sole-purpose is to restart the Gala Day I inadvertently put a stop to over a decade ago. I don't want to even think about it if I can possibly help it. And I don't want to think about Jack Buchanan, either. I'm going to lock up all my thoughts of him, just like whatever it is Bella has in that box of hers in the living room. Then I'm going to throw away the key and never think of it again.

First, though, I'm just going to quickly see if Bella has any more of those scones...

Chapter 15

I'd kind of hoped Frankie might have forgotten her threat to make me part of the team that would be cleaning Jack Buchanan's house for his party, but I'm out of luck; the next morning she's banging on the door a full half hour before I was expecting her, waking up Mum, Dad and Jude — who immediately destroys one of Mum's favorite cushions in protest.

Frankie paces the kitchen while I get dressed, glugging down coffee like it's a life support system, and fretting aloud over the job ahead of us. Such are her stress levels, in fact, that by the time I make it downstairs, mum is borderline hysterical, and Jude has pooped in one of Dad's shoes.

It's going to be a very long day.

"Are you sure you should be taking Emerald, Frankie?" Mum asks, wringing her hands anxiously as she watches Frankie pace. One of Mum's more endearing traits is her ability to instantly take on other people's anxiety, almost as if it were her own. ("I'm one of those empaths," she says any time she's questioned about it. "I just can't help it.") She'll have to go for a lie down as soon as we leave, I can tell. "It's such an important job for you, love. I'm just worried that..."

She trails off as dad shoots her a warning look.

"Um, I'm right here, you know?" I point out, trying not to take offense. I mean, I *did* burn down the village hall, after all. It's not like her lack of faith in me is *totally* unjustified. She has nothing to worry about today, though, because there's absolutely no way I'm going to be so much as entering Jack Buchanan's house, let alone cleaning it. It's just too risky, what with the whole "impostor" situation and all. To say nothing of the "Huge, Inappropriate Crush on a Man Who Clearly Hates Me" situation.

I'm too late to fake my own death, unfortunately — I really wish Frankie had given me a bit more notice that today was going to be The Day, or I'd have been *on* it — but I *can* fake a pretty convincing stomachache. Which is why I'm currently doubled over, clutching my stomach and—

"Oh my God, what's that?"

I straighten up suddenly as I step in something wet and smelly, which immediately starts seeping through my sock. Across the room, Jude Paw stares at me, unblinking.

"What's what, Emerald? What's happened now?" Mum's anxiety has kicked up a notch as she turns in my direction, and I realize I can't possibly add to it by telling her I'm not feeling well, so, instead, I simply fetch a cloth and clean up Jude's mess, choosing to keep a dignified silence as I plot that furry little git's downfall.

"Come *on*, Emerald, we're going to be late!"

Before I know it, Frankie's hurrying me out of the house and into the van, Mum and Dad are waving us off like we're going to be receiving a Nobel prize rather than just cleaning some guy's house, and I have no idea how I'm going to get out of this now that my "stomachache" plan has been thwarted.

None.

My mind spins as we bump down the country lanes that connect Mum and Dad's house to the huge gates that mark the entrance to the Buchanan Estate.

"Last night I dreamt I went to Manderley again," I blurt out, as the *Highland Maids* van turns into the private road that leads to house itself and begins the mile long drive through the forest to the mansion.

Frankie, sitting tensely at the wheel, rolls her eyes briefly in my direction, but says nothing. She's more nervous than I've ever seen her before, but it's still nothing compared to the nerves I'm feeling myself. I know Frankie thinks the future of her business depends on this job, but I can only *dream* of having a problem like that. My problems, however, are not the, "Building a solid financial future" kind, unfortunately. No, mine are more the, "Being caught in the act of impersonating a complete stranger" variety, and, because of them, I'm so anxious I'm almost nostalgic for the days when my biggest issue was my ex-boyfriend stealing all my money.

Which is *another* problem I've yet to address, actually.

I... think I'm going to need another list. Or maybe just to re-read the original; it's not like I've managed to strike off any of the items on it, after all.

The narrow driveway that snakes down to the house has obviously been carefully tended since I last visited it — as a teenage tearaway, under cover of darkness — but there's still something very *Rebecca* about the place, and I shiver uncomfortably, hoping that's not a sign of what's to come. I've already burned down the town hall, after all; under the circumstances, I'm amazed Frankie's even letting me near this place.

The Buchanan Estate — I still can't bring myself to think of it as "Jack's house" — sits on the banks of Loch Keld, with its own pebble beach and boat dock, plus acres of surrounding land. As the road finally opens out into the circular driveway, I realize I'm holding my breath for the first glimpse of the house, which I've always found quite magical.

It's not a castle (Or, at least, I don't *think* it is. What does a very large house have to do to be considered a castle, I wonder?), but it does have a couple of satisfyingly fairytale-like turrets; one short fat one above the front entrance, and another taller, thinner one off to one side, which I assume is where Jack Buchanan will be keeping his mad wife.

"I thought you were pretending to be in *Rebecca*, not *Jane Eyre?*" says Frankie, when I make this observation aloud.

"I thought you were ignoring me?" I shoot back, both of settling into the gentle bickering we've always used to help steady our nerves. As it happens, though, Frankie's wrong: Buchanan House doesn't really look like Manderley *or* Thornfield Hall to me. It's entirely itself, as it has been for almost 200 years now, and it's almost impossible to imagine it as someone's actual *home.*

"Remember how you used to swear the place was haunted?" Frankie says, grinning over at me suddenly.

"I used to *wish* it was haunted," I correct her as we get out of the van. "So I could have a Nancy Drew–style adventure in it and solve the mystery of the haunted mansion."

"Scooby-Doo, more like, knowing you," snorts Frankie, lifting her hand to raise the giant brass ring on the front door of the house. Before she can knock, though, the door swings open, and we find ourselves facing a short, round woman with a kind face, and a pair of retro-style cat's eye glasses, which I immediately covet. If I was expecting Mrs. Danvers to greet us — and, let's be honest, I kind of *was* — I'd have been disappointed.

"Hello there," she says warmly, opening the door to let us in. "Highland Maids, is it? Come on in; I'm Elaine."

I freeze halfway across the threshold. I'd noticed Jack's car wasn't parked in the driveway when we arrived, and had assumed that meant he wasn't at home. I'd forgotten about Elaine, though. Elaine, the personal assistant. Elaine, who'd set up the "date" with Scarlett. Elaine, who knows Finn, who knows Scarlett. Scarlett, who doesn't currently know *any* of these people (Other than Finn, apparently), on account of the fact that it was me who ended up going on the date instead.

Whoops.

"Are you coming in?"

Elaine looks at me curiously (Unlike Frankie, who gives me a much less polite look behind Elaine's back), and I step quickly into the entrance hall of the house — which is appropriately vast, with two curved staircases which sweep up to the landing above — where I give myself a quick shake.

This Elaine might have set up Jack's date with "Scarlett", but it's unlikely that he told her much about it — maybe I'm wrong, but he just doesn't seem like the type to gossip with his staff around the water-cooler, somehow — and there's no way she could possibly know it was me who turned up instead. And if I'm right that he's not at home this morning, then I'm probably safe enough. For now.

Breathe, Emerald. Just breathe.

Despite my warning to myself, I continue to hold my breath as Elaine takes us into an office which sits to one side of the entrance, and chats to Frankie about the cleaning we'll be doing. Two other Highland Maids are already there waiting for us; a pair of (almost) identical twins, who Frankie introduces as Maya and Mirren, and they stare at me suspiciously the entire time Frankie and Elaine are speaking.

"Och, don't worry about them," Frankie tells me as we file out of the office at last, each clutching our respective hoovers, plus a little caddy of other cleaning tools. "They're just annoyed because they wanted their sister Mary to have this job, but I brought you, instead. Us besties have to stick together!"

I swallow hard as Maya — or is it Mirren? — turns and gives me what can only be described as a death glare. I'm touched that Frankie wanted me with her for this job; I know how important it is to her. I also know, however, that Maya and Mirren will probably never forgive me for usurping their beloved sister, so I'm relieved when Frankie suggests we split up and clean a wing of the house each, before moving on. At least that way I won't have to keep turning around to find the McChuckle sisters watching me like the scary twins in *The Shining*.

I really wish I hadn't thought about *The Shining* as I haul Bessie up what I can't help think of as The Grand Staircase, and allow Elaine to lead me down a long corridor which is a lot more *gothic* than I'd expected it to be, somehow.

The room Elaine shows me into, however, is innocuous enough, with a four-poster bed in the center, and a picture window looking out onto the loch. It's just a guest room, but it has its own en suite bathroom ("All the rooms do," Elaine tells me before she leaves. "Mr. Buchanan insisted on it.") and is so comfortable that I almost thank Elaine for letting me in, before remembering I'm a cleaner, not a guest.

Imagine being a guest in this house, though, I think, crossing to the window as soon as the door closes behind me, and gazing out at the loch. Imagine *living* here.

I can't allow myself to do that, though. Well, given that the *last* time I let my imagination run riot in someone else's home, I ended up pretending to be the owner, I reckon it's probably best if I just get on with the job in hand. You know, like a *normal* person?

So I put in my earbuds, select my favorite playlist, and get to work, stopping only to pull my sweatshirt off and tie it around my waist when I get too hot. I'm wearing an ancient black t-shirt underneath, instead of the regulation Highland Maids polo shirt, but as long as I put the sweatshirt back on before I see Frankie again, she'll be none the wiser.

I've been assigned all the bedrooms on this floor, and on this side of the staircase. Frankie's taking care of the other wing, and the Sisters of Death are on the next floor, probably sticking pins into a redheaded voodoo doll or something as they tackle the rooms up there. The work isn't exactly strenuous; the rooms on my wing of the house are all unoccupied guest rooms, which means none of them are in need of much cleaning. I make quick work of the first two, before pushing open the door to the very last room, which sits at the end of the hallway.

Then I stop short in surprise.

This room isn't empty.

Actually, this room clearly belongs to someone.

And I don't have to be Nancy Drew — or even Scooby Doo — to figure out who that someone is.

I'm standing in Jack Buchanan's bedroom.

Chapter 16

Don't snoop, Emerald. Whatever you do, don't snoop.

For a long moment, I stand there in the doorway of the room, wondering what the hell I'm supposed to do now. It feels wrong to go inside, somehow; awkwardly intrusive, in a way that cleaning the other rooms on this floor didn't.

Then again, none of the other rooms were Jack's, were they?

From the doorway, I can see almost the whole room, which occupies the entire corner of the house, with a bay window taking up a large section of one wall (With a window seat! I can't even tell you much I've always wanted a window seat!), and another, equally large window at the opposite end. The bed is another four-poster, dressed with crisp, hotel-quality linen, and I can't help notice that it doesn't look like it's been slept in.

Why doesn't Jack Buchanan's bed look slept in?

Where has he been sleeping, if not in his bed?

And why do I care, given that the last time I saw him, he was walking out on our "date" without looking back?

The room in front of me provides no answers to any of these questions. It doesn't really provide answers to *any* questions I might have about Jack, actually, because, aside from the pile of whisky- related magazines by the side of the bed, and the sunglasses sitting on top of them, there's very little — other than the sheer size of the space I'm standing in— to distinguish this room from any of the others I've cleaned this morning. It's meticulously tidy (I could have guessed Jack Buchanan would be a neat freak), but totally devoid of any kind of character, almost like a hotel room. It feels just as temporary, too, somehow; as if the person living here knows he won't be staying for long, and so didn't even bother to unpack, or make himself at home.

It *is* his home, though, and that's what's making me hesitate on the threshold. I know Jack instructed Elaine to hire a cleaning firm, so he presumably knew his room would be cleaned along with the rest of the house. He didn't know *I'd* be the one doing it, though, and the thought makes me feel so uncomfortable that when I hear the low murmur of voices approaching down the hall, I'm almost relieved at the interruption.

Then I look round to see who's speaking, and my legs almost give way.

Jack Buchanan is walking towards me down the hall, accompanied by another man, who I don't recognize, but, please God, don't let it be the mysterious Finn McNeil; I'm not sure my nerves could stand it.

"I left the paperwork in my room," I hear Jack say as the two men get closer. "It'll just take me a second to find it, then we can go over it together."

He's so intent on his conversation that he hasn't looked up, and nor has his companion, so I take the opportunity to quietly close the door I'm standing in front of, and open the one directly behind me instead, intending to step into whichever

137

room it is until Jack's safely out of site.

It's a good plan, I reckon. A sound one. It could totally have worked, too.

Except the "room" turns out to be a cupboard.

And the cupboard turns out to contain a tangled mess of brooms and mops, and God knows what else.

And the tangled mess is balanced so precariously inside the closet that, as soon as I open the door, it all comes tumbling out and lands right on top of my stupid head, with a noise that sounds a bit like how I'd imagine a landslide probably would, if you were standing right in front of it.

Gah.

I guess Jack's probably noticed me, then?

"Emerald?"

Yup. Busted.

"Emerald, is that you? What on earth are you doing here?"

I straighten up reluctantly, allowing the various brushes and mops that are covering me to clatter ostentatiously to the floor. I'm so sure I'm about to get yelled at — by Jack *and* by Frankie, once he tells her what I've done — that I'm almost too scared to look him in the eye. When I do, though, Jack's expression is confused rather than angry, and I feel a dim spark of hope somewhere in my frantically beating heart.

"Who, me?" I ask stupidly, as if he might possibly be addressing some *other* Emerald, rather than the one currently standing in front of him. It's definitely me, though, and my stomach twists into a knot of anxiety as I look at the mess around me, realizing there's really no way to explain what I was doing in Jack Buchanan's broom cupboard without sounding absolutely insane. Still, at least all of the cleaning supplies currently scattered across the floor are an excellent camouflage for Bessie and friends, who don't look remotely out of place amid the chaos. These are the kind of small victories you have to be grateful for when you're me.

"Sorry, I, er, I thought this was the bathroom," I mumble at last, seizing upon the first excuse that comes to mind, knowing even as I say it that it's just not going to cut it. For once, though, it seems my luck is in; Jack's companion is clearing his throat and looking pointedly at his watch in a bid to hurry him along, and, let's face it, anything that helps distract him from me right now has to be to my advantage.

"The bathroom? No, that's in the other wing," he says vaguely, before turning to the man beside me.

"Look, why don't you head back downstairs?" he suggests, apologetically. "I'll just grab the paperwork from my room, and I'll be right with you. Not you, Emerald," he adds sternly, as I prepare to slink off, thanking my stars that I'm at least not wearing the Highland Maids sweatshirt anymore. That would've been a bit of a dead giveaway, wouldn't it?

"You haven't told me what you're doing here?" Jack continues, oblivious to my need to be as far away from here as possible. "Here, as in my house, I mean; not here as in my... whatever's in that cupboard."

"It's cleaning supplies," I offer helpfully. "You should probably clear it out a bit, though. Before it hurts someone."

I trail off under Jack's gaze, which is most definitely not the gaze of a man who wants to talk about his broom cupboard, and more the look of a man who's rapidly running out of patience with the woman he just found stumbling out of it.

"I'm here to... to talk to you about the Heather Bay Gala Day," I say, as inspiration suddenly strikes. "Yes, that's it, the Gala Day! Bella McGowan sent me. You know Bella, of course?

Everyone knows Bella," Jack's brow creases in confusion, but I rush on before he can interrupt me. "She's the chair of the Gala committee, and they're looking for sponsors so they can get it up and running again, after it ... well, after it stopped for a while. She thought you might be interested. You know, as a way to get the distillery name out there? And she found out I know you... well, sort of... so she asked if I'd come over and talk to you about it."

I pause for breath, watching the line on Jack's brow to see if he's going to relax enough for it to disappear, then resisting the temptation to reach up and smooth it out with my fingers when it doesn't.

He's still confused. That much is obvious. He's not, however, *furious*, like I'd have expected him to be, and that gives me hope.

"The Gala Day," he says, frowning even more. "I think Elaine might have mentioned something about that. It's a kind of festival, isn't it? With a parade?"

"And a whole bunch of other stuff, too," I say eagerly, relived to be talking about anything other than what I'm doing in this house. Even the Heather Bay Gala Day — a.k.a. my own personal Waterloo — is a welcome change of topic right now, which is really saying something. "There's food trucks, for instance, and lots of different events; like Highland Dancing, and baking contests, and..." I wrack my brains, trying to think of something more interesting than the three things I've just named, but drawing a blank. "Oh, and there's normally a funfair, too," I add. "With a Ferris wheel and... stuff. It's a whole thing in the village, trust me. The event of the season."

Or at least it *was* until the year I got involved.

"Don't they crown one of the village girls Queen or something, too?" asks Jack, looking suddenly interested. "In fact, didn't one of them—?"

"I don't think so," I say shortly, interrupting him before he can go any further down this train of thought. "Anyway, like I said, lots of the local businesses sponsor various parts of the day, and Bella thought the distillery could be one of them. It would help the village, and it would help the distillery too, to be part of the local community. Good for your branding, you know."

I am being Scarlett right now; channeling her entirely imaginary personality in order to bolster my confidence and sound like I might actually know what I'm talking about. The strange thing is, though, the longer this conversation goes on, the more convinced I become that this actually *is* a good idea. Jack would get publicity for his business, Bella would get funds for her Gala Day. And as for me, meanwhile, I'd get the warm, fuzzy feeling of knowing that I'd in some way helped to rebuild the thing I'd inadvertently ruined.

Oh, and I'd also maybe stand a chance of getting out of this house without either Jack or Frankie finding out that I've been posing as Scarlett Scott from time to time.

Now that really *would* be a result.

I just have to convince Jack; and I suspect that's going to be easier said than done, because he's still just standing there saying nothing. He's not quite frowning, but he's definitely not smiling, and, all of a sudden, I've had enough of this. I've had enough of tiptoeing around him, never knowing what he's thinking, or how he feels. I've had enough of worrying that he's going to find out I'm not Scarlett, and that Frankie's business is going to suffer as a result of it. Most of all, though, I've had enough of wondering why he left me sitting there alone in his restaurant that night, without even the courtesy of an explanation.

I'm not going to ask him, though.

Oh, come on, I'm not *that* stupid. I know perfectly well that I'm going to be lucky to get out of this house without everyone in it finding out about my Scarlett-related deception without going out of my way to start an argument.

Instead, I'm going to do something even worse. I'm going to act a bit cold and aloof.

Because *that'll* show him.

"Anyway," I say stiffly, flicking my hair over my shoulder. "That's all I had to say. That's the reason I was here. Just that. I don't want to keep you from your very important business, though, so I'll be going now."

And, with that, I turn and march decisively off down the hallway.

I don't even trip up as I go.

Chapter 17

Okay, I could probably have done without the hair-flip. That was a *bit* much. And, instead of immediately leaving his house, with my dignity intact, I've just realized I'm going to have to hide in another cupboard or something until Jack leaves, so I can go back for Bessie. But, all of that aside, I'm quite impressed with what I've just done.

I walked away.

I didn't turn back.

I somehow managed to keep my mouth shut, and not get myself into trouble.

Any *more* trouble, I mean.

"Emerald, wait!"

The sound of Jack's voice stops me in my tracks, and I turn to see him striding down the hallway towards me. His shirt is open at the neck, his brow is furrowed, and he has a dark, brooding expression which I really shouldn't like, but which nevertheless makes me feel a bit like an Edwardian lady about to reach for her smelling salts.

Oh my God, this is it. He's going to sweep me into his arms and kiss me passionately, right here in the hallway. Then he'll tell me the reason he walked out was because he couldn't handle the strength of his feelings for me, and then he'll...

"You dropped this."

Jack stops in front of me and hands me a feather duster. It's neon orange and I have never seen it in my life before. My best guess is that it was one of the items inside the broom cupboard I opened by mistake, but why would Jack think it was mine? Unless he just wanted an excuse to keep talking to me? Which... no. That's insane.

Isn't it?

"Also, why are you being so weird?" he says, his brow creasing again, but with confusion rather than anger this time. "Have I done something to offend you? Because I'd really like to know, if I have."

I pause, looking up at him thoughtfully. I shouldn't answer this; or, at least, not honestly. No good will come of it. I know that. And yet...he actually sounds like he wants to know? Almost as if he... cares?

Well. This is *unexpected.*

"I... was a little offended by the way you walked out on me in that restaurant," I admit at last, staring at my shoes. "I mean, you're not into me; I get it. But you could've been a bit nicer about it, you know? It was... it was *ungentlemanly,*" I add, warming to my theme. "Caddish, even."

"Caddish?" Either I'm imagining it, or Jack's mouth is twitching upwards in what passes for an expression of amusement for him. Which kind of proves my point, really.

"Yes, caddish. Something only an absolute *cad* would do? A gentleman would *never* treat a lady in such a cavalier fashion, trust me."

Okay, I have no idea why I'm speaking like I'm in a Regency romance all of a sudden. This house, in all its Gothic splendor, has obviously gone to my head. Either that or Frankie's right, and I really do read way too many romance novels. Whatever the reason for my random segue into 'Jilted Heroine', however, a strange thing has happened as a result of it; Jack is smiling again.

Not *properly* smiling, you understand. I mean, Colgate isn't going to be calling him up to star in their next toothpaste commercial any time soon. (Although his teeth *are* beautiful, to be fair. On the rare occasions you actually get to *see* them.) But there's no mistaking it; his mouth is starting to turn up at the corners, and those dimples of his have appeared on his cheeks which... *Please God, no. Not the dimples. I can resist anything but that, I swear.*

"I'm so sorry," he says, making a visible effort to straighten his face. "I didn't mean... I just... well, I didn't *think*, is what I'm trying to say. And I should have. I'm sorry."

Because I'm a pushover, my natural inclination is to just accept this weird attempt at an apology. That's what I'd have done if it was Ben standing in front of me, rather than Jack; it just wouldn't have been worth the argument that would've ensued if I'd challenged him, so I'd have backed down, just to keep the peace.

But Ben left me.

And took all my money.

And ran off to L.A. with it.

So, when you really stop to think of it, *keeping the peace* didn't work out all that well for me with Ben, did it? Like, I'm probably never going to look back and say, "Gee, I sure am glad I didn't ever question that boyfriend of mine when he was acting a bit shady." And not just because I don't actually talk like that.

Instead, then, I decide to try something new.

What would Scarlett do, I wonder? How would my much-smarter alter ego handle this situation?

With sass, I expect. But calm sass. Scarlett would be polite, sure, but she'd still stand up for herself. And I will, too.

"I appreciate the apology," I say coolly. "But I'd have preferred it if you just didn't bother asking me to dinner if you couldn't stand to spend more than a few minutes with me. It would've saved us both a lot of trouble. So, you know, er, don't do it again."

This is quite a big speech for me, short though it is, and my heart is thudding with adrenalin by the time I get to the — admittedly rather awkward — end of it. I desperately want to leave now, but Jack takes a step forward, all traces of amusement now totally gone from his face.

"Is that what you thought?" he says softly, standing so close that I can smell his expensive cologne. "That I couldn't stand spending time with you? Emerald, you've got it all wrong. I got a message from my distillery manager while we were having dinner. There was a problem with one of the whisky stills — a pretty serious one. I thought I could handle it, but it got out of control, and we ended up having to call the fire brigade. It was... well, it was quite a night. And I should have called you after it to explain, but it's just been crazy, you know? We've had the insurance company to deal with, the police—"

He pauses to run an exasperated hand through his James Dean hair, and I notice the bandage wrapped around it.

Oh. Shit,

"The police? You mean Young Dougie has had to work on a Wednesday?"

I'm using humor to hide the fact that I'm confused as all hell right now. It's what I do. Frankie says it's my toxic quality.

She's probably right. Fortunately for me, though, Jack doesn't really *do* humor. Or maybe he just doesn't have a clue who Young Dougie is?

"No," he says, frowning again. "They sent someone up from Glasgow. I don't think his name was Dougie, though, it was Dylan something."

"So, I guess it must have been really serious, then, if they sent someone all that way? Is that how you hurt your hand?"

He holds his bandaged fingers in front of his face and stares at them as if seeing them for the first time.

"Oh… yeah," he says, lowering it again. "Don't worry, it looks worse than it is. I'll be fine."

I doubt that, somehow. For the first time since we started talking, I notice that Jack looks tired. I hadn't noticed it before, because he's the kind of man who wears "tired" well. But there are faint circles under his eyes, and if Mum were to get her hands on him, he'd have a plate of suspiciously green chicken sitting in front of him before he knew what had happened.

I, meanwhile, just feel like shit. He's been *literally* putting out fires at his distillery — doing his best to save his business, and getting injured in the process — and I, meanwhile, have been making his silence all about *me*. Why did he leave our date? Why hasn't he called me? Why doesn't he loooovee me? I'm like Taylor Swift in her *Red* era, and, no offense to Taylor, but I am not proud.

"Is everything alright now?" I ask tentatively, feeling like I've no right to even ask.

"Sort of." Jack rubs his un-injured hand across his eyes. "The distillery is back up and running normally, yes. But we still don't know how it happened, and the police think it's suspicious. They think the still might have been tampered with deliberately, and I just... I'm sorry, I don't want to burden you with all of this. I'm sure you've got much more important things to think about."

"Not really," I say truthfully, grateful that he doesn't know the only other thing I have to think about is the fact that I should really be cleaning his bedroom right now, and Frankie's going to be wild if she finds out I didn't do it. "And this sounds pretty important, really. I wish I'd known. Maybe I could have helped."

I couldn't have, obviously. Everything I know about whisky and the making of it would fit onto the back of a... there isn't an object small enough for me to be able to finish this comparison. But Jack's half-smile is back, and I have never been more relieved. At the same time, though, there's a niggling worry poking away at the back of mind. Something I don't really want to think about, but have to.

McTavish.

Didn't I think I saw McTavish that night at the distillery? Could he have...?

No. No, absolutely not. I know McTavish probably still holds a candle for me, but he wouldn't do something like this. Would he?

I shake my head briskly as if to rid it of this uncomfortable thought.

"That doesn't justify my... caddish... behavior to you, though," Jack is saying now, looking at me with an intensity that makes my stomach flip. "I really am sorry, Emerald. I just panicked and ran to the distillery. I should have at least explained myself."

"No, no, it's fine," I say, flustered. I can feel a blush rising in my cheeks, and I really need this conversation to end before it can take over my entire body. "Honestly. I shouldn't have said anything. It's not your fault. I was being stupid. I usually am."

"I don't think you're stupid," Jack says. "Clumsy, maybe." He gestures to the mess of cleaning equipment strewn around us. "But not stupid."

He's standing so close to me now that if I was anyone other than me, I really would think he was about to kiss me. Instead, he just keeps on standing there. There's absolutely nothing in his behavior to justify the way my heart has started to pound, but I find myself taking a deep breath anyway, to slow it down.

"Emerald, I'm... not much of a people person," Jack says at last, as if I wouldn't already have worked that out for myself. "I don't really like many people, to be honest. I work too much. I don't always think about how I might come across to other people. But I'm not the person you seem to think I am. I might not be perfect, but I'm not a... a *cad*."

"I'm not the person you think I am either," I admit ruefully, wondering what he'd say if he knew exactly how true that statement is. "I'm really not. You have no idea, seriously."

Jack looks at me curiously. We're so close now that I can see the stubble that's already starting to appear on his jaw. I am painfully aware of the feather duster I'm holding like it's a baton and I'm about to conduct an orchestra with it. Call me crazy, but this *doesn't* seem like a good time to come clean about my real identity for some reason.

"Well, what are we going to do about that?"

Jack's expression is still serious, but his right cheek is starting to dimple, and I already feel like I know that look. It's the look of a man who's starting to soften. A man who's completely forgotten to ask how the hell I got into his house, anyway. (Which is good news for me, because I have absolutely

149

no idea what I'd say to that one.) If I didn't know better, in fact, I'd say it was the look of a man who might actually *like* me, and if that isn't a good enough reason to keep quiet — for now, anyway — then I don't know what is.

"Do about what?"

I *think* I know what he's saying here, but, just to be sure, and avoid any further confusion between us, I'm going to make him spell it out for me.

"Well," he says, his dimple deepening as he starts to smile, "It seems that we need to get to know each other a bit better, wouldn't you say?"

I *would* say that, as it happens. I would very much say that. Instead, though, I simply nod mutely. It seems like the safest option.

"So maybe we can start again?" Jack suggests, offering me his hand. "Hi, I'm Jack Buchanan. And you are?"

Both dimples are in full effect now, and I can't help returning his smile as I shake his hand, hoping my own isn't quite as sweaty as it feels.

"Hi, I'm Emerald," I reply, grinning like a child at a birthday party. "Um, Scarlett Emerald. It's nice to meet you, Jack."

"And it's nice to meet you too, Scarlett Emerald."

He's still holding my hand. His is very soft. It feels so nice it almost makes me forget the blatant lie I just told him. It could easily make me forget *everything*; from the car crash that is my life, to the feather duster I'm still clutching in one hand.

"Emerald—"

He's standing very close now. So close that I'm suddenly very aware of his height, and how small I feel in comparison. Without dropping the eye contact that's become the most important thing in my universe, I slowly raise myself up onto my tiptoes, until our faces are level with each other,

Until our *mouths* are level with each other.

Until all of the air in the room evaporates and I have no choice but to drop my feather duster as Jack's hand finds its way to my waist, pulling me closer and closer, until—

"Buchanan? Are you coming back down, or do I have to come and look for you?"

It's the man I saw Jack with earlier, calling from halfway up the stairs. and he's just moved smoothly into the number one spot right at the top of my list of enemies.

"Sorry, John, I'll be right there."

Jack shrugs apologetically as he releases my hand.

"I'm so sorry," he says, sounding like he means it. "That's my PR manager, John. I'm being called away from you yet again. To be continued, though?" he suggests, his eyes still on mine. "I'll call you?"

"Sure."

I somehow manage to say it as if we've just been standing here having a totally normal conversation, and not even *remotely* about to kiss.

But we *were* about to kiss. I'm sure of it. And not even Annoying John, the PR Man, can take that precious little fact away from me.

I stoop down and pick up the feather duster, which bobs cheerfully in my hand as Jack darts back into his bedroom, then back out again with a sheaf of papers, which he carries off towards the staircase.

"Find Elaine before you leave," he says over his shoulder. "I'm guessing she let you in? If you give her some details of this Gala thing, I'll have a look at them as soon as I get a chance."

"Sure," I say again, knowing I absolutely will not be doing

this. "No problem."

Jack smiles again, then he's gone, leaving me standing there hugging my feather duster and feeling like Cinderella when she finds out she *will* be going to the ball after all.

And then, just like Cinderella, it all falls apart.

"Sorry about that," I hear Jack say to his companion as he meets him on the staircase. "Just a bit of business I had to deal with. It took longer than I expected."

There's a thick, ornate pillar between me and the stairs, and I'm standing just behind it. I can't see him, but I can hear him, and I edge forward slightly, unable to stop myself from listening in.

I'm "just a bit of business?" Is that really *what he's calling what almost happened between us?*

"No worries," I hear the other man say. "Was that the journalist you mentioned? Scarlett something? The one who's supposed to be writing a feature on the distillery."

"She's supposed to be," comes the response from Jack. "I'm not sure if she will yet. We didn't get off to the best of starts, really. I hope she still will, though. I'm working on it."

"I'll bet," the man says, with what can only be described as a chortle. "Got to keep 'em sweet, isn't that right, Buchanan? Anything for the press coverage."

Their voices are moving away now, as they continue on down the stairs, so I don't catch Jack's reply. I don't need to, though. I've heard more than enough to know my conversation with him wasn't quite what it seemed on the surface, and the fact that *I'm* not quite what I seem on the surface either does absolutely nothing to quell the hurt that's rising up inside me right now.

"The journalist."

Scarlett is a journalist.

Who's apparently writing a feature on Jack and his distillery.

This can't be right. Scarlett — my Scarlett — is an artist, not a *journalist*. A successful one, too. But of course, *my* Scarlett isn't actually real, is she? She's just a character I invented, so I could pretend to be someone else for a while; like an imaginary friend, almost.

There is a *real* Scarlett Scott out there, though. A real, flesh-and-blood person, with an entire personality and life that's probably nothing like the one I've been imagining for her.

She's not a prize-winning painter; she's a journalist.

My heart contracts painfully as a second realization comes hot on the heels of this first one:

It wasn't a "date".

Neither of my encounters with Jack Buchanan were "dates". They were business meetings. Ones designed to butter me — Scarlett — up and persuade me — Scarlett — to write a glowing review of Jack's whisky.

Which means Jack was absolutely right in what he told me: it turns out he really *isn't* the man I thought he was.

Chapter 18

The next morning is my day off work, so as soon as I wake up, I pull out my laptop and type Scarlett's name into the search engine.

Sure enough, it's all there in front of me: Scarlett Scott, food and drinks writer for *Culture Focus* magazine, specializing in restaurant reviews and... whisky.

Of *course* the woman I've been pretending to be would be an expert in the one thing I can't stand.

I don't know why I didn't think of looking her up before; I guess because it would have spoiled the happy little daydream I was having about her and her life — which was also my life as long as I was pretending to be her. There's nothing like a dash of reality to spoil your day, is there?

Now that I've looked up the real Scarlett, though, everything suddenly makes a lot more sense. Like the pile of magazines by Jack's bed, for instance; Scarlett's magazine, which he must have been reading so he could talk to her about her work — only he never actually got round to it because instead of *reviewing* his whisky, she just spat it all over him. And by "she" I mean me, obviously. *I* did that. Accidentally, of course, but even so, this is one hell of mess, even by my standards.

"Oh my God, what am I going to do?"

I push the laptop away and lock eyes with Jude Paw, who's lying on the bottom of my bed, clearly feeling affronted by my presence in his favorite sleeping spot. Even he, however, can tell that this is not the moment to mess with me, so he stands up and comes over to grudgingly put his head in my lap.

"What am I going to do, Jude?" I say again, stroking his silky ears. "He said he'd call me. What if he does? Do I answer it? Do I ignore it? What if he asks to see me? Do I go? Do I not? Do I tell him I'm not Scarlett? Because he's only going to call me because he thinks I'm her, and that I'm going to write an article about his stupid distillery, right?"

Jude stares at me with disgust, as if he's already regretting his rare show of tolerance for me.

"Emerald? Are you up there?"

I freeze in horror as Mum's voice drifts up the stairs. I've been doing my best to avoid her for the past few days, because she won't stop asking about Ben, the state of financial ruin he's left me in, and what I plan to do about it.

"Mony a mickle maks a muckle, Emerald," she told me when she caught me sneaking up to bed last night. And, okay, I might have absolutely no idea what she meant by that, but I *do* know she's not going to let this drop until Ben's been brought "bang to rights", as she puts it. Which is a problem, because my deadbeat ex and the money he stole from me is the very last thing I want to think about. Mum's more interested in Ben right now than I ever was, and her insistence that I Do Something about him is, quite frankly, exhausting.

I know she's right, though. I know I desperately need to Do Something about Ben and my missing money, and I will. I really will. I'll just do it tomorrow, is all. For now, I really need to clear my head, so I jump out of bed, pull on some clothes, then head downstairs, Jude Paw hot on my heels.

"Just taking the dog for a walk!" I call breezily to mum as I pass the kitchen doorway, not giving her a chance to reply. Then I grab Jude's leash, snap it quickly onto his collar, and am out the door and headed in the direction of the loch before she has a chance to stop me.

My hastily concocted plan is to head to my usual secluded spot by the water, where I can sit and stare moodily at the waves until everything starts to make sense again. I haven't gone more than a few steps, though, before I realize the flaw in this plan: Jude Paw, who is *not* one for walking, apparently.

"Are you sure you're even a dog?" I ask impatiently as he minces gingerly over the dew-soaked grass outside the cottage, looking thoroughly disgusted to be here. "Aren't you lot supposed to actually enjoy this?"

Jude just glares at me balefully, then sits down and refuses to take another step until I finally give in and pick him up. Tucking him under my arm, like a small, furry clutch bag, I stride purposefully down the hill towards the water. There's no way I'm going to go all the way around to my favorite spot with the dog's spindly legs digging into my sides like this, so, instead I head for the nearest bank, where there's a small gaggle of absurdly large swans, which, on closer inspection, turn out to be swan-shaped pedalos.

Okay. This is new.

I stifle a sigh of annoyance as I flop down in the long grass by the lochside, placing Jude Paw beside me. The pedalos are moored in the water, presumably waiting for some unsuspecting tourists to pay over the odds for a ride on one, and although there's no one around this early in the morning, I have a horrible feeling it won't be too long before someone turns up to interrupt the solitude and stop me wallowing in my misery, like I'd planned.

Sure enough, I've only been analyzing my almost-kiss with Jack yesterday for ten minutes or so, when the crunch of footsteps on the pebbled shore of the loch alert me to the fact that I'm not alone. Irritated, I turn around just in time to see...

No.

It can't be.

It seriously *can't* be.

It is, though.

Jack Buchanan is walking along the shore towards me, his eyes fixed on the phone in his hand. He's wearing joggers and a t-shirt — a t-shirt which I can't help but notice is clinging to some spectacularly defined muscles — so I'm guessing he's out for a morning run. Which just so happened to bring him right into my path.

Again.

Shit, shit, shit.

I can't let him see me. I absolutely *cannot* let him see me until I've had a chance to work out what on earth I'm going to say to him when I finally work up the courage to speak to him. And also because I'm *mortified*; I mean, let's not beat about the bush here. The last time I saw him I was clutching a feather duster and calling him a cad for running out on our "date"... which actually turns out to have been just a business meeting. Or a magazine interview. Whatever. Regardless of what it was, the fact that I then proceeded to more or less throw myself at him means that Jack now knows I like him. He *must* do. And, from what he said to his friend on the stairs, he's prepared to string me along to get his precious press coverage. Which actually *does* make him a cad after all, doesn't it?

I'm not going to get into that with him again, though. No, this time I really *will* keep my dignity intact in front of Jack Buchanan, and I'm going to do it by... by climbing into this swan-shaped pedalo and hoping he doesn't see me there.

Yes.

That'll do it.

Taking advantage of the way Jack still appears to be glued to his phone as usual, I quickly tuck Jude Paw back under my arm and get silently to my feet. Getting across the pebbled beach without making a noise — and with a toy poodle clutched in my arms — is a bit tricky, sure, but I somehow manage it, before gritting my teeth and wading out to the nearest pedalo, still keeping one eye on Jack.

The water is freezing; as in, the kind of cold that makes your heart rise into your throat, as if it's trying to get away from the pain in your legs. I'm still wearing my trainers, and there's no time to take them off, so I splash as silently as I can through the shallow water, before climbing gratefully onto the pedalo, where I crouch down in my seat, grateful for the huge "wings" on either side of me, which I'm hoping will totally obscure me from view.

"Emerald?"

Or, you know, *not.*

I hold my breath as I crouch lower in the boat, hoping he'll think he made a mistake and there's no one actually here. If I just stay *really* quiet...

"WOOF!"

With a clatter of paws on plastic, Jude Paw jumps up onto the seat beside me and starts barking his stupid head off. This is the last time I try to take him anywhere, I swear it.

Risking a quick glance over the side of the swan's wings, I

see Jack standing by the shore, almost level with me, his hand shading his eyes as he looks out in my direction. I quickly duck back down in my seat, but it's too late; even if he hadn't seen me, there's absolutely no way he could've missed Jude, whose barks have now reached a crescendo. Well, there's nothing for it; squaring my shoulders determinedly, I sit up, and, without looking back at the shore, place my feet on the pedals in front of me. It's easy enough to reach over the side of the pedalo to untie it from the buoy it's attached to, and, as soon as that's done, I press down hard on the pedals, propelling me, Jude and our giant swan out towards the center of the loch.

"Emerald, wait!"

I can hear Jack calling my name, and I'm vaguely aware that, even if I do manage to get out of this without having to face him, I'm probably going to get arrested for pedalo theft now. Which is really not something I'd ever expected to be able to say about myself.

This is not good.

This is *really* not good.

In fact, I don't think "catastrophe" is too strong a word for what's currently happening on this loch, and if you do, well, I can only assume you've never tried to dog-nap a poodle, while sitting on the back of an over-sized swan, have you? And good for you, if so.

To the casual observer, I probably look straight-up *insane* right now. The casual observer, however, doesn't know just what lengths I'm willing to go to in order to avoid Jack Buchanan; or how humiliated I feel every time I think about how I called him a "cad" for not liking me enough.

The memory of our conversation at his house — I actually thought for a second that he was going to kiss me! — helps

159

spur me on, and, within a few minutes I realize I've made pretty good progress. I'm never going to make it all the way to the middle of the loch — it's much too wide for that — but I'm surely a good long way from Jack by now, so I allow myself to pause for a moment to catch my breath.

The pedalo rocks dangerously from side to side as we come to a stop, making Jude finally stop barking as he scurries into my lap. As the noise abates, I risk a quick glance back towards the shore, and, yup, Jack's still there — and still waving at me with so much enthusiasm that I can't possibly continue to just pretend I haven't seen him, without making myself seem even stranger than I already have.

Why me, God? Why do these things always happen to me?

Luckily for me, though, I'm far enough away from him now that I'm at least not going to have to actually *talk* to him, so I do my best to feign a look of surprise as I raise my arm and wave back, with what I hope is my best, "Why, goodness me, I didn't see you there!" look.

And that, naturally, is the exact moment Jude Paw chooses to jump headfirst into the freezing waters of Loch Keld.

Chapter 19

I have no idea why he did it.

God knows, Jude has never been the most active of animals, even at the best of times — Mum was just talking last week about how she'd like to get one of those "doggie strollers" for him, so she can push him around like a baby — but considering that the stupid animal wouldn't even walk over the wet grass this morning, why he'd suddenly decide to go for a swim is absolutely beyond me.

Not that I have much time to ponder it, mind you. Jude hits the water with a yelp of regret, and immediately goes under, before surfacing a moment later, his eyes almost bulging out of his head with shock.

Didn't exactly think this through, Paw, did you?

Even in summer, the water in the loch is freezing, with freakishly strong currents that can pull a person out before they know what hit them. For a dog as small as Jude Paw, that's going to happen even faster than it usually would, so, before I have a chance to think about what I'm doing, I stand up and plunge in after him.

The water is so cold it takes my breath away. Literally, I mean. As in, for one endless moment, the breath is knocked out of my body, and time seems to stand still.

Is my life about to flash in front of me, then? Because it's going to look a bit like one of those 'hilarious out-takes' reels, if so, and I'm not particularly keen to see it.

I may have been living in London for the past ten years, but you don't grow up in the Highlands without knowing that Cold Water Shock can kill you, and although I'm a fairly strong swimmer, by the time I reach Jude and grab hold of him, I'm starting to panic.

Turning back towards the pedalo, I see it's already much further away than I'd thought it was, and I start paddling frantically towards it with one hand, while the other clutches Jude Paw to my chest. There's no time to think about what's happening. All I can do is swim for my life, and I'm only managing to stay calm because I absolutely refuse to believe this is happening to me.

I *know* how dangerous the loch can be. I know how easily it can overcome even the strongest swimmers; which is why McTavish and I used to sometimes sneak down here as kids to practice "saving" each other, just in case we ever needed to. As I struggle against the current, I desperately wrack my brain, trying to remember some of McTavish's words of advice on the subject, but, annoyingly, all that comes to mind is, "A nod's as guid as a wink tae a blind horse," and I don't *think* that one has anything to do with water safety, somehow.

My breath is coming in short, ragged gasps now. My lungs feel like they're filled with ice, and although I'm still doing my best to pull myself forward, my arms and legs are starting to grow heavy with the pain of the cold.

This is it. This is how I'm going to die. Five meters from a plastic swan, and with a toy poodle attached to me. What an interesting obituary that's *going to make.*

"Emerald! Emerald, hold on, I'm on my way!"

The shout jerks me out of my stupor, and I struggle around in the water to see Jack swimming towards me, his taught, muscled arms slicing decisively through the waves.

Jack. I'd forgotten about Jack.

Thankfully, though, Jack hadn't forgotten about me. Within a few seconds he's beside me, one arm looping firmly around my waist as he takes Jude Paw from my arms and turns us back around in the direction of the pedalo. I'm so grateful to see him — to see anyone who might be able to get me out of this mess — that I almost start crying. I'm too cold even for tears, though, so, instead, I settle for a strangled sob, which could just as easily have come from the dog as from me.

With Jack supporting my weight, my limbs feel less heavy. The pedalo still seems impossibly far away, though, and getting to it suddenly feels like an absolutely impossible task. Almost as if he senses this, Jack shifts Jude into his other arm, and swims around until he's facing me.

"Emerald," he says, his eyes locked intently on my face. "Emerald, look at me."

I look. His wet hair is slicked back, making the blue of his eyes even more vivid. Under other circumstances, I might be glad of the excuse to gaze into their depths, but I'm so weary it's all I can do to keep my own eyes open.

"Emerald, I need you to concentrate," Jack says, pulling me closer towards him. His expression is serious, but his tone is so soothing that my heart rate slows ever so slightly.

"It's just a few meters to the boat," Jack says reassuringly. "You can do this, okay? I'm right here; I won't let you go, I promise. But I'm going to need you to help me out here so I can get you and the dog back to the boat. Now, I want you to

163

grab hold of me tight, okay?"

I just nod, wordlessly. Later, I'll probably think of 101 *Titanic*-related jokes I could be making at this moment, but for now I concentrate on breathing as Jack strikes out towards the pedalo, my frozen hands clinging to his t-shirt as he pulls me along behind him.

It probably only takes a matter of seconds, but it feels like forever until Jude and I are safely back aboard our over-sized swan, with a soaking-wet Jack sitting beside me.

"Right," he says cheerfully, placing his bare feet on the pedals. "Let's get you back to shore, then, and you can tell me exactly what you thought you were doing throwing yourself into the loch like that."

Shit.

* * *

Back on dry land, Jack crouches down to pull on his trainers, which are still lying on the shore, beside his phone, and a hastily discarded sweatshirt, which he hands me without speaking. Unlike me, he obviously took the time to discard some of his heavier clothes before jumping into the water. Also unlike me, though, I suppose he at least had the advantage of knowing he was going for a swim, whereas I blithely thought Jude and I were just going for a quick pedal, to get out of Jack's way.

Stupid. Why on earth would you do something so stupid, Emerald?

Ben's back inside my head again. This time, though, it's hard not to see his point. Why *did* I think stealing a pedalo would be preferable to just talking to the man beside me? I know it seemed to make sense at the time, but right now it makes no sense at all, and my cheeks burn with shame as I meekly accept the sweatshirt and wrap it around Jude, who's trembling so hard his entire body is shaking.

"Come on," Jack says, straightening up. "We need to get you two warmed up. Your place is closest, I think?"

I blink up at him in horror. He's right, of course; Mum and Dad's house is, indeed, much closer than Jack's, which we'd have to go all the way around the loch to reach, this particular bank being blocked by the craggy rocks at the foot of the Tor.

Jack's not talking about *my* house, though; he's talking about Scarlett's, which, although not particularly close — Loch Keld is one of the largest sea lochs in Scotland — is nevertheless far closer than Buchanan House.

"I, um, I think must have I dropped my keys in the water," I mutter through lips which are still numb from the cold. "I don't have them."

Jack gives me a single long, hard stare, then silently picks up his phone and dials a number, while I stand there beside him, my teeth chattering.

"Okay," he says, hanging up. "One of my staff will bring a car around, with blankets for us all. Come on; we just need to walk up to the road to meet him."

Even the short walk to the road is much longer than I'd like it to be, given my current state, but the exercise helps get the blood flowing through my frozen limbs again, and, before long I'm sitting in the back of Jack's car — one of them — wrapped in a plaid blanket, and feeling thoroughly sorry for myself.

It's just a short drive to the house, and by the time we get there, even Jude Paw has stopped shivering, and just sits there glaring at me as if this whole misadventure of ours wasn't totally his fault.

"Don't look at me like that," I whisper as Jack lets us into the house through a back door which leads directly into a large kitchen. "You're the one who decided to jump into the loch, remember?"

The kitchen is large and sunny, with a huge wooden table in the center and a highly polished range under one window. The cupboards and appliances all look brand new, but the polished wooden floorboards are obviously original to the house, as is the massive fireplace at one end of it, complete with a log fire, which is crackling away merrily.

"Wait here for a second," he says shortly, disappearing through the door to the house. I race immediately to the fire and sink down gratefully in front of it with Jude on my lap.

"Here, put these on," says Jack, reappearing with an armful of clothes which he puts on the rug in front of me. He's changed into a fresh set of joggers and a different sweatshirt, and, aside from his wet hair, looks almost as if nothing remotely unusual has happened.

"Er, I'll just... I'll be out here while you get changed," he says, flushing slightly as he sees me stare at the clothes in my hands in confusion. He almost falls out of the door in his haste to leave, and I get wearily to my feet, too tired and cold to care much that I'm about to strip off my soaking wet clothes in Jack Buchanan's kitchen. The clothes he's given me — yet another set of joggers and an oversized sweatshirt which feels suspiciously like cashmere — are obviously his, and are much too large for me, but I pull them on anyway, and quickly roll up the legs and sleeves so I'm not tripping over them. Then I sink back onto the thick rug in front of the fire and use the blanket from the car to rub Jude Paw's fur dry.

By the time Jack reappears, Jude is snoozing peacefully by the fire, and even I'm starting to feel vaguely human again.

"I made you a coffee," Jack says, handing me a steaming hot mug. "I didn't know how you like it, so—"

"That's great, thank you," I tell him, accepting the mug gratefully, and wondering if he has a second kitchen hidden away somewhere that he used to make this.

"I have a coffee machine in my office," he tells me, sensing the unspoken question. "Comes in handy when I have to fish damsels in distress out of the loch."

"Um, yeah, about that..." I say, flushing again as I take a gulp of my coffee. It's very strong and very sweet, and, right now, it's pretty much the best thing I've ever tasted. "I'm so, so sorry. I can't thank you enough for coming in after us. Honestly, I've no idea why he jumped in like that." I nod towards Jude, who's now snoring loudly by the fire. "It's really not like him. If I'd thought he'd do something like that I'd never have brought him anywhere near the water, trust me."

"I didn't know you had a dog?" Jack says, looking at him curiously. "I didn't see him when I was at your house."

"Oh! Um, no, I don't," I say, hastily making up a lie on the spot. "He's... I'm pet sitting. For a friend."

"The guy with the tractor?"

Jack's expression is inscrutable as always, but there's a weight behind his words that makes me pause before answering him.

"The guy with the tractor? McTavish, you mean?"

"If that's his name. I've seen you around town with him a few times. On his tractor."

I stare at him, confused. It's true that McTavish has gotten

167

into the habit of picking me up from work lately. And it's also true that I've been letting him; partly because he's a lot more reliable than Frankie, who always seems to have some kind of cleaning emergency to attend to, but also because he's one of the only people in town who's still willing to talk to me. You can't beat that kind of loyalty.

"He looks like a... close friend."

This time there's no mistaking Jack's tone. He isn't just making polite conversation about me and McTavish. He's asking about him for a reason. And I have a sneaking suspicion that it's not just a sudden interest in tractors.

Is he really interested in *me*, though? Or is he still just thinking about that article he wants Scarlett to write for him, and wondering if McTavish is going to get in the way of it?

"He is a good friend," I say carefully, watching Jack's face. "I've known him for a long time."

"Oh. So, like a childhood sweetheart, then? I thought it might be something like that when I saw you together."

"Jack Buchanan, are you *jealous*?" I say teasingly. "Of *McTavish*?"

I can't lie, I'm delighted by this development. Insane though it is that Jack actually thinks there's some huge romance going on between me and McTavish, the fact that he's even *thought* about it is *huge*. For a second I wish I could text Frankie and tell her that Jack Buchanan is, like, *totally into me*; then I remember exactly why I can't, and all that hope that's been rising in my chest comes crashing back down again, making my stomach lurch.

"I'm not jealous," Jack protests, taking a seat opposite me on the floor. "I don't get jealous. I'm just *interested*, that's all."

On the rug next to me, Jude Paw opens one eye, then closes it again. I reach out and stroke his wiry fur while I work up the courage to ask the question that's hovering dangerously in the air between us. I really shouldn't go there. I know that.

But I just *have* to.

"Really?" I say softly, raising my eyes to meet his. "And is that because you're interested in *me*, or is it just because you're interested in the article you want me to write about you?"

Chapter 20

There's a long pause, during which Jude Paw suddenly stands up, gives himself a quick shake, then pads over to curl up in Jack's lap, from which position he sits there staring at me like he's just won a bet or something.

Traitor.

"Obviously I want you to write the article," Jack says at last, looking confused. "I mean, that's the whole reason Finn put us in touch in the first place, isn't it?"

I have no idea why Finn set "us" up — I have no idea who Finn even *is*, in fact — so I just shrug non-committally, and stare into my coffee cup so I don't have to look him in the eye. Jack's just given me exactly the answer I expected him to give me, and yet I can't help but feel utterly crushed by it.

I have to hand it to him, though, he's good. Good at pretending to like someone just to get them to do something for you. Good at making me feel like he might be interested in me, when all he really cares about is his stupid distillery. He's even good at making coffee.

It figures.

"Thanks for the coffee," I say abruptly, getting to my feet. "And for, well, saving my life earlier. I, er, owe you one. Well, two, really." I nod towards Jude. "I owe you two, I guess. Anyway, I won't keep you..."

I'm being weird, I know. And I'm definitely going to have to revisit my pitiful attempt at a "thank you" at some point, because whether he likes me or not, the guy *did* just jump into a freezing cold loch to pull me and my parents' idiot poodle out of it. I really do owe him for that. Right now, though, I just want to get out of here. I want to go home, crawl into bed, and pull my disappointment around me like a blanket. I want to luxuriate in it, with Taylor Swift songs and re-runs of *Friends*. Also, I really want to get out of these clothes, because Jack's borrowed joggers may be bone dry, but my underwear is still filled with lake water, and that is every bit as unpleasant as it sounds. Trust me.

"Emerald, wait!"

Before I can turn to leave, Jack is standing beside me, having dislodged an indignant Jude Paw, who stalks back to his spot in front of the fire in high dudgeon.

"Look, I phrased that badly," Jack says, running a hand through his hair, in that agitated way of his. "Of course the article is important to me. It's my business, and I'd be lying if I said some decent coverage wouldn't help with the launch."

I nod stiffly.

"I understand," I say politely. I try to step away, but Jack takes a step forward at the same time, which leaves us standing practically nose-to-nose.

Awkward.

"I don't think you do understand," he says softly, making no attempt to move further away from me. "The thing is, Emerald, the article isn't the only thing I'm interested in."

"It's not?"

171

"No, it's not." He grins devilishly. "There's also this whole Gala Day thing you mentioned the other day."

It takes me a moment to realize he's joking, but, as soon as I do, relief washes over me, followed quickly by its old friend, elation.

"The Gala Day?" I ask, smiling. "That's what you want to talk to me about?"

"Not really," Jack admits, moving closer again. "Although, with that said, I did have an idea about that..."

"I don't care about the Gala Day," I interrupt impatiently. "What's the other thing you're interested in? Tell me!"

"I'll tell you if you promise to come to my masquerade ball," he says, taking another step towards me. "You never did reply to my invitation, you know."

He does his best to look wounded by this, and it's all I can do not to leap forward and plant my lips on his. He's standing so close now that it would be the easiest thing in the world to just raise myself up on my tip-toes, like I did yesterday, and...

"I'm sorry," I say softly, tilting my face towards Jack's until our lips are almost touching. "I forgot."

"So, will you come?"

He leans forward almost imperceptibly. My heart is doing something strange inside my chest. I really, really need him to kiss me now. I might have to insist on it, in fact. It would be cruel to leave me hanging like this.

"Sure," I murmur, trying to rise a little higher on my toes. Damn, but he's tall. "Whatever you like."

"And the hiking party? And the ball? You can't leave me to deal with all that schmoozing on my own, can you?"

It should feel awkward, standing this close to someone; so close I can almost count every one of the dark lashes framing

172

his eyes, which have darkened to a deep, navy blue as he looks into mine. If it was anyone else, it *would* be awkward. But Jack's looking at me in a way that keeps me standing there, my eyes locked onto his. He's looking at me as if he actually *sees* me. Me. Emerald. Or, you know, *Scarlett.* Whatever. I can't think about that now. Because his lips are almost touching mine. I have only the vaguest recollection of him mentioning a hiking party, and I *definitely* can't go to the masquerade ball. But those are problems for Future Emerald to deal with.

"Sure," I say again, my arms finding their way around his neck. "I can even help you with the schmoozing, if you like. Practice makes perfect, you know."

His hands are on my waist now. I can smell the sweet, musky scent of his skin, and I breathe it in, feeling it go to my head like champagne bubbles as Jack's lips meet mine.

It's not exactly a kiss.

It's just a feather-light touch; so light that I barely have time to register it before it's over. It lasts a nanosecond, and yet I can still feel it on my lips, like a tattoo, even when it's over.

I don't want it to be over.

I don't want this moment to ever *be over.*

It's not quite a kiss, but it holds the promise of the *real* kiss to come, and I tighten my arms around Jack's neck as he lowers his face to mine once more, pulling me close, and sending shivers down my spine which most definitely aren't from the freezing water I've just been swimming in.

If he kisses me again, that dip in the loch will have been worth every sub-zero second, I swear.

But he doesn't kiss me again. Because, at the exact moment our lips are about to touch, the sudden slam of a door from somewhere down the hallway startles us into springing apart,

173

as if we're about to be caught doing something we shouldn't. Which actually isn't too far from the truth, I suppose.

Dammit.

Whoever slammed that door has just earned their position at the very top of my list of enemies. I take a step towards him, hoping Jack will just ignore it, but instead, he looks at his watch, frowning.

"Shit," he says, his face thunderous. "That'll be my assistant, Elaine. I totally forgot I'd asked her to come round this morning. Tell you what, though, just give me a second and I'll bring her to meet you. She can help out with the arrangements for the competition."

He gives my waist a quick squeeze, then disappears into the hall before he can see the look of dismay on my face.

Elaine can't see me.

I can't see Elaine.

Because, the last time Elaine and I met, I was wearing my Highland Maids cleaning uniform and being shown around this very house with Frankie, while doing my best to avoid Jack. I guess there's an outside chance Elaine might not recognize me, but, let's face it, luck hasn't exactly been on my side lately, has it? And if she realizes I'm the cleaner who she sent up to Jack's room a few days ago...

No. I can't let this happen. I just can't.

From the other side of the door, I can hear the low murmur of voices as Jack talks to Elaine; no doubt telling her all about his amazing idea to raise funds for the Gala Day at his house party. And let's just hope Elaine is a whole lot more enthralled by that plan than I was, because while she's standing in the hallway talking to Jack, she's not walking into the kitchen to blow my cover.

I stand rooted to the spot, listening intently. The voices don't seem to be coming any closer, and there's no time to waste, so, without taking my eyes off the door to the hall, I quickly creep forward, pick up Jude Paw from the rug, and make my way to the back door of the house, which I ease open as quietly as I can.

And, once I'm on the other side of it, I run.

Chapter 21

"*Where did you go? :(*"

I'm back in my room, having successfully run the gauntlet of the hallway, and somehow managed to avoid Mum and her questions, when my phone pings with a message from Jack. He's added a sad-face emoji, which makes me smile. He's always so serious and buttoned up that it's good to see he has a lighter side, too. He just keeps it really well hidden, is all.

Did that *really* just happen, though?

And did I *seriously* just run away from it?

"*So sorry,*" I type back quickly. "*I remembered I had to get the dog back to his owners; I had to run. Rain check?*"

I sit on the edge of my bed watching the three dots that indicate he's typing something back to me, and it's only when the phone pings again that I realize I've been holding my breath.

"*Rain check. Although I hope it doesn't rain for this so-called party I'm supposed to be throwing. Everyone's arriving the day after tomorrow for the first event. Will you come?*"

I consider my response to this carefully. This is the point where I should come clean, obviously. I should tell him who I am before this... whatever this is... goes any further. I could do it now, by text, then I could switch off my phone and just pretend none of this ever happened. The problem is, I don't *want* it to have never happened. And, if I'm being totally honest, I would very much like it to happen again. So, instead, I try to buy some time with the first excuse that comes to mind.

"*I don't have anything to wear to a house party,*" I type, cringing even as I write it. It's a poor excuse, although I suppose it *is* true; being forced to mingle with Jack's rich friends while wearing the clothes I clean people's houses in would be a bit too 'Jane Eyre', even for me.

"You could wear that white dress you spilled your drink all over," comes the reply, almost instantly. "It was very... distracting."

I smile to myself, feeling almost giddy with happiness. This is quite possibly the best conversation I've ever had in my life. Before I can reply, another message pops up:

"*The first event is an outdoor one, anyway. Some kind of hiking party, apparently. So you can wear anything you like. Wear my old joggers, if you like. You look better in them than me, anyway. Although not as good as you did in that dress.*"

This time, my smile isn't quite as bright. It figures he'd like me best in someone else's clothes. Clothes I could never afford for myself. Clothes that I—

Oh, my God.

I pause, my fingers frozen in the act of typing out a reply to Jack as my mind stutters out the end of that thought.

Clothes that I took from Scarlett's closet and have yet to return. Clothes that probably cost more than I make in a week, and which are currently buried amongst the heap of clean laundry on my floor that I haven't bothered to put away yet.

I stand up so quickly I give myself a head rush. My flirting with Jack is going to have to wait. Right now, I have to get to Scarlett's house before she does.

* * *

Fortunately for me, Frankie's so busy planning her next cleaning mission to Jack's house — which thankfully doesn't include me this time, as it's my day off — that she barely even spares me an eye-roll when I turn up at the office to ask for Scarlett's key.

"I left some of the cleaning stuff inside," I tell her, crossing my fingers behind my back as she rummages in a drawer for it. "I'll just pop back and get it; it'll only take ten minutes."

In a rare stroke of good luck, Mum managed to get what was left of the Coke stain out of Scarlett's dress, using something she referred to as a 'cleaning hack' she saw on Instagram.

"It was that Ada Valentine," she told me, holding the dress up to the light to admire her handiwork. "D'ye no follow her, Emerald? Och, she's a braw lassie, so she is. And the things she knows! She's the one I got the recipe for the mint chicken for, remember?"

I've no idea what mum's talking about, as usual, but whoever this Ada Valentine is, I'll be forever grateful to her for helping Mum get this dress looking as good as new again. God only knows what kind of trouble I'd be in right now if I'd actually managed to ruin the thing.

Back at the house, I carefully hang the dress back in Scarlett's wardrobe, and stow the sandals I wore that night underneath it, feeling a bit like Cinderella when the clock strikes midnight.

Goodbye beautiful clothes. It was nice knowing you, even if it was just for a few hours.

With that done, I bend down and pull the bag containing my own clothes out from under Scarlett's bed. It's as I'm straightening back up again, silently congratulating myself for remembering I'd left them there, that something on the bedside table catches my eye.

Culture Focus: the magazine Scarlett writes for, according to Google.

Curious, I pick it up and quickly leaf through it. There's only one article by Scarlett, and it's a very dull breakdown of Scotland's best distilleries, but as I scan through the text, I can totally see why Jack would want to be mentioned in something like this. None of the other distilleries listed have anything like the backstory Jack's has — or the setting. Scarlett could get a fantastic story out of it for her magazine; if only she were actually here to write it, obviously.

Instead of Scarlett, though, there's just me, and as I stand there, idly flicking through the glossy pages of the magazine, an idea slowly starts to form. Flicking back to the first few pages, I find what I'm looking for: the index page, complete with the names of all the magazine staff, including the editor — one Alex McNeil, apparently. Each name has an email address underneath it, and I pull out my phone and quickly snap a photo of the page. Before I can put the phone back in my pocket, though, it rings in my hand, an unknown number on the display.

"Ben?"

He's the only person I can think of who'd be calling me from a number I don't recognize, and I'm only a tiny bit surprised by the wave of disappointment that engulfs me at the thought of my ex-boyfriend getting back in touch with me. I should *want* to hear from Ben. I should want to know where he is, and what the hell he did with my money. But the relief I feel when I realize it's not him says it all, really.

"Emerald? It's Brian here. Brian from the bank?"

"Oh, hi!" I say, a little too enthusiastically. "Are you calling about my missing money? Did you find out what happened to it?"

"Och, no, there's nothing we can do about that," Brian says dismissively. "I was just calling to ask if ye'd heard from your ex yet? Did ye manage to track him down? Was it the Mafia right enough?"

"Brian, are you sure you're calling on bank business?" I ask suspiciously as I make my way out of Scarlett's bedroom and back downstairs. "Because it doesn't really sound like it to me."

"No, I'm on my lunch break," Brian says, unperturbed. "I was just interested. So, did ye find him? And did ye manage to get out of that hideous little town ye were stuck in?"

There's a loud crunching sound, as if he's eating a bag of crisps while he's speaking to me. This is most unprofessional. Then again, he's one of the few people I can actually talk to about my messy life without them instantly trying to "fix" me somehow. And it's not like I'm in any position to call someone else "unprofessional" is it? Not while I'm letting myself out of the house of the client whose identity I've been casually assuming for the last few days, anyway. Compared to me, Brian is practically angelic.

"No, I haven't heard from him," I admit, locking Scarlett's front door behind me. "I haven't really tried, though, to be honest."

"Emerald!" Brian's gasp of horror can probably be heard as far away as Fort William. "Ye have to get on that! Ye must be desperate to get out of the Highlands by now! All those midges! And the weather!"

It's obvious that Brian is from the city. He probably thinks Heather Bay is practically in the Arctic circle.

"It's not that bad," I say, defensively. "I can't even remember the last time I saw a midge."

I tug my sleeve down over my wrist, as if Brian will somehow be able to look down the phone line and see the cluster of bites currently decorating my arms. The funny thing is, though, Heather Bay may be miles from civilization, and polluted by midges every summer. But now that I really think about it, what I just told Brian is true. It's *not that bad.* Or, at least, it's not as bad as I was expecting it to be, coming home. Sure, I've not exactly been welcomed back into the bosom of the community, but no one has actively shunned me either; well, not other than Jude Paw, anyway. I've yet to be paraded down the High Street with someone ringing a bell behind me and shouting, "Shame, Shame!" And then, of course, there's the small matter of a certain sexy landowner who just so happens to live here.

"Do you really want to hear about this?" I ask doubtfully, as I head down the drive, towards the nearest bus stop. "It's a bit of a long story. And I'm not sure how it ends yet."

"Emerald, I'm about to blow yer mind here," says Brian drily, "But it's not actually all that exciting working for a bank. This is the most interesting thing that's happened all year. So, come on; don't leave me hangin' here."

"Well," I say, tucking the phone comfortably under my ear. "It all started with a cleaning job—"

* * *

I promised Brian I'd go to the police station to file a report on Ben ASAP, so I take the bus from Scarlett's house to the town center, only to find everything closed.

"Did ye forget it's Wednesday, Emerald? Young Dougie has his afternoon off. And so does everyone else."

I turn round from the locked door of the station to find McTavish standing behind me, having silently materialized there in a way that's really quite impressive for a man who travels everywhere on a tractor.

"Of course they do," I say, petulantly. "Because what would be the point of opening shops and other businesses at the height of the tourist season, after all?"

"Exactly," nods McTavish, completely missing my point. "What are ye up to?"

"I'm not up to anything now," I say, still annoyed. I'd forgotten everything in Heather Bay closes for a half-day on a Wednesday, and I really want to take back everything I just said to Brian-from-the-bank about the place being 'not so bad'. "I *was* going to speak to the police—"

"About yer stolen money?" McTavish interrupts. "Aye, Shona was telling me ye're no further forward with that."

"Shona? How on earth does Shona know?" I ask, but before he can answer someone clears their throat behind us, and we turn to see Bella McGowan making her way towards us in her purple Docs.

"Hello you two," she says briskly, stopping beside us. "Did ye forget it's a half-day, Emerald? Ach, well, I suppose ye'll just have to come back to mine, then. There's something I

182

want to talk to ye about."

Chapter 22

Ten minutes later, McTavish and I are squashed together on Bella's sofa while she buzzes around us, offering plates filled, not just with scones, but what seems to be every variety of cake imaginable.

"This is braw," says McTavish, accepting a generous helping of sweet treats from our host. "I'm that hungry I could eat the scabby heid aff a bairn."

I put my own plate back down on the coffee table in front of me, my appetite suddenly gone.

"I'm glad I bumped into ye, Emerald," Bella says as she takes a seat opposite us. "I wondered if ye'd had a chance to think about joining the Gala Day committee we talked about?"

"I have, actually," I say, leaning forward, eager to finally be able to deliver some good news for once. "I don't think I can be on the committee itself, Bella," I tell her apologetically. "But I did speak to Jack Buchanan about it, and—"

"Ye spoke to Jack Buchanan?" McTavish interrupts, his mouth still full of cake. "What were ye doing wi' that big galoot?"

"Cleaning his house," I say frostily. "I'm a cleaner, remember?"

"Aye, right," is McTavish's only comment. Ignoring him, I turn back to Bella.

"So, as I was saying," I continue, "I mentioned to Jack—"

McTavish gives a loud snort.

"I mentioned to Jack," I go on, glaring at him, "That you were looking to raise funds for it, and we thought he could possibly sponsor it. Or his distillery could. He's having a masquerade ball soon to launch his new business. I was thinking that could be a good time to announce the sponsorship? You never know, you might be able to get some other people on board, too."

I'm thinking on my feet here, which isn't generally my strong point. I haven't actually raised the possibility of making an announcement at the ball with Jack. In fact, I haven't really discussed the sponsorship idea with him in any depth at all. Future Emerald will deal with all of that, though. Somehow.

"Emerald, this is wonderful," Bella says. Her eyes are shining as she picks a plate off the table. "Absolutely wonderful. You've really come through for us. Here, have another cake. Ooops, sorry, Alfonso has had them all. He's a good eater, is our Alfonso."

She bustles off to the kitchen to get some more, and McTavish looks at me speculatively.

"Are ye sure ye want to be gettin' involved with all o' this, Emerald?" he says at last. "Will it not be a bit... triggering for ye, after what happened?"

I shrug, refusing to meet his gaze. The truth is, the last thing I want to do is to get involved with Heather Bay and its Gala Day. But I *have* to; and not just because it provided a convenient excuse for me being in Jack's house that day, but because, for the first time since The Thing happened, I can see a way to start to make amends.

"It's the least I can do, *Alfonso*," I say at last. "I know it won't make up for what happened—"

"What happened was an accident," he says firmly. "It could've happened to anyone."

It's the same thing Bella told me at our last meeting, and I give McTavish the same answer I gave her.

"Yeah, but it happened to *me*," I say resignedly. "And my life's been a complete mess ever since. I mean, look at me, McTavish. I'm almost thirty, and I'm living with my parents and doing a job my best friend gave me out of sheer pity. I'm a complete failure. And I just want to try and make up for it."

"Failin' means yer playin'," McTavish says gently. It's one of his few sayings that actually makes sense to me. Even if I'm failing right now, at least I'm taking part. At least I'm *trying.* And if I try hard enough, I might just be able to get my life back on track.

As if on cue, the door to the kitchen creaks open and Bella reappears. Instead of the plate of scones I was expecting, however, she's carrying the same wooden box I remember from my last visit; the one I steadfastly refused to open.

I resist the urge to hide behind McTavish as Bella places the box reverently on the table in front of us.

"Come on then, lass," she says, beaming at me. "Open it up. There's something in there I think ye'll like."

I very much doubt this, somehow. Unless this unassuming looking box contains something that's going to allow me to rewind time and be honest with Jack right from the very start — and some of the money Ben stole from me would be nice too — then it's probably not going to help me much. And we all know how much trouble Pandora unleashed by opening a box, light? All the same, Bella and McTavish are both watching me expectantly, and I don't want to disappoint them, so, with a small sigh of resignation, I lean forward and cautiously lift the wooden lid.

Inside, I find a small pile of photos which I don't even bother to look at, because I'm too distracted by the object sitting on top of them.

It's a tiara.

A beautiful, vintage tiara.

My tiara.

Or, okay, not *mine*, exactly; it's the tiara used to crown the Queen of Heather Bay Gala Day every year — an item that's been in the possession of the village since the event started, back in the 1920s. It's not real, of course; the "diamonds" that make up the centerpiece are fake, and the silver paint that covers the base of the tiara has started to flake away in some parts. The sight of it, however, still has the power to bring a lump to my throat; a lump of longing and regret for everything this item has come to symbolize for me.

"I didn't even get to wear it," I say, shaking my head as Bella lifts it up and offers it to me. "I was never even crowned Queen because of... well, you know."

"Ach, ye'll always be our Gala Queen, won't she, Alfonso?" Bella says briskly, refusing to allow me to become too maudlin.

"Aye, that's right, Bella," McTavish agrees. "The last ever Queen of Heather Bay."

"Well, maybe not, if this thing with Jack Buchanan and his masquerade ball works out," Bella says, eyeing me hopefully. "And I ken ye didn't get to wear this at the Gala, Emerald, but I was thinking maybe ye'd like to wear it to the ball? I'm assuming ye're invited, seeing as you and Mr. Buchanan seem to get along so well?"

McTavish snorts loudly, and I pointedly turn my back on him as I finally accept the tiara from Bella, holding it as carefully as if it were my firstborn child.

"I have been invited," I admit, turning the tiara around in my hands and admiring the way the stones in it catch the light. "I don't think I'm going to go, though. I, er... I don't have anything to wear to something like that."

I can't possibly tell Bella and McTavish the real reason I'm not going to Jack's ball, so I give them the same excuse I gave Jack earlier this morning. Unluckily for me, though, Bella overcomes it just as easily as Jack does.

"Well, if that's all that's stopping ye," she says, getting to her feet, "I have just the thing. Come with me."

McTavish and I exchange confused glances as we follow her down the hallway of the little bungalow to what Bella refers to as "the back bedroom". McTavish, I can tell, is secretly hoping for more scones, but, instead, the door opens to reveal rail after rail of dresses, all squashed in together, in every color imaginable.

"I've been collecting these since I became Chair of the Gala Committee," says Bella proudly, ushering us both into the room, where we stand together on the one square of carpet not occupied by dress rails. "I don't have the costumes from every single Gala — but I've got a lot of them, from the 1950s onwards. Not including the last year, obviously."

She pauses, awkwardly — we all know I'm the reason the costumes from that final pageant no longer exist — and I clear my throat to cover my embarrassment as I step forward to run my hand along the closest rail.

"This is amazing, Bella," I say, taking in the riot of color and styles in front of me. Fashion has never really been my thing — that was always much more Lexie's bag — but even I can see how much time and care Bella has put into amassing this collection. Most of the dresses are prom-style — formal, floor-length ballgowns, which I assume came from the various Gala Queens and their attendants — but there's a mixture of other styles, too, presumably chosen by the attendees, as something special to wear for Heather Bay's big day.

I clear my throat again, this time to get rid of the lump of sadness that's formed there as I look as these relics of a bygone age, which seem to stare accusingly back at me, The Last Queen of Heather Bay, as McTavish called me. These clothes were once precious to the people who wore them; chosen with excitement and worn with joy. But now they're stuck here in Bella's spare bedroom, doomed never to enjoy another Gala — and it's all because of me.

"This is beautiful," I say, pulling out an emerald green gown, and determinedly ignoring the tears that are threatening to spill from my eyes at any second. McTavish has long since lost interest in the clothes and has wandered back towards the kitchen in search of more scones, but Bella steps forward and holds the gown up against me.

"Aye," she says, her eyes shining with pleasure. "That's perfect, so it is. Matches yer eyes. Try it on, lass. Try on any of them, in fact. Ye're welcome to borrow as many as ye like. Now, where's that Alfonso got to?"

She heads off to the kitchen, leaving me alone with the dresses and my guilt. I'm just about to put the green dress back on its hanger and follow them to the kitchen, when a sudden change of heart makes me walk over to the mirror in the corner of the room instead.

I hold the dress up against me and look at my reflection. Bella was right; the dress is perfect. The green of the taffeta fabric makes my eyes light up, and my skin look porcelain, rather than just pasty. Even my hair looks sleeker, somehow, as if it's scared to show itself up in front of the beauty that is The Dress.

In this dress, I don't just look better than I usually do, in my old jeans and sweaters. I look like a totally different person. And I know who she is, too. She's the me who exists in my head. The me no one else has ever seen. She's Scarlett Scott.

And she's going to the ball.

* * *

"You're like my Fairy Godmother, Bella," I say as I climb back onto McTavish's tractor, clutching a bag full of clothes, plus the tiara, which Bella insists on giving me. "You're amazing. Thank you so much."

"Och, dinnae mention it," she says, looking pleased. "Ye've had a face like a wet weekend ever since ye came back to the Bay, and I ken from Shona that ye dinnae have the money to buy yerself something nice, so maybe these will help cheer ye up. Ye'll be like a whole new Emerald in these. Just wait and see."

"I liked the old Emerald just fine," McTavish says stiffly as we pull away from the bungalow. "Ye dinnae need fancy new clothes. Ye're just fine as ye are."

I'm not, though.

The truth is, I'm far from "fine" as I am, and I never will

be, unless I can somehow find a way to change my life for the better. I know the clothes in the bag I'm carrying aren't going to do it, but helping Bella with her Gala Day plans would at least be start; as would coming clean to Jack, and seeing if we can start over.

I'm going to do that tomorrow, on the first day of the house party. Right now, though, there's one more thing I can do to make amends for some of the lies I've told, so as soon as McTavish has dropped me off at Mum and Dad's house, I go upstairs, open up my laptop, and start writing.

I write about the distillery, and the jobs it will bring to the town. I write about Jack's grandfather, and the legacy he wanted to leave to Heather Bay. And finally, I write about the town itself, and how it's *not so bad.*

When I'm done, I sign up for a free email account using the name Scarlett Scott, and I write a message to the editor whose name was listed in the front of her magazine.

"This is a bit different from the kind of thing I usually write," I say. "But I hope you like it, anyway." Before I can think twice about it, I quickly attach the photo I took of the view from the distillery over the loch; the one with the sunset that looks like a painting.

Then I hit 'send'.

Chapter 23

The words "hiking" and "party" do not belong in the same sentence, as far as I'm concerned, and yet, when I double-check the text Jack sent me yesterday, I see that's exactly how he described today's event.

He can't mean we'll be actually *hiking*, can he?

Not like we hike in the Highlands, I mean?

No, he must just mean we'll be *strolling*, I expect. Or taking a pleasant turn around the garden, like in Regency times. At least, that's what Shona McLaren told Mum when she bumped into her at the butcher's yesterday afternoon, and if anyone would know, it would be Shona.

"It's a garden party, basically," Mum told me importantly as she bustled around the kitchen preparing another one of her chicken dishes. "A really posh one, though. Shona says absolutely no expense has been spared. Apparently the caterers have been flown in from that London to make the canapés. Heather Bay's food's not good enough for the likes of Jack Buchanan, it seems.

She sniffed in offense at this, before opening the oven door to reveal another neon chicken.

"Orange chicken," she said proudly. "Seeing as you liked the mint one so much, I thought I'd branch out. As I was saying, Shona says everyone who's anyone will be there; the cream of Highland society. Shona says—"

I never did find out what else Shona McLaren had to say on the matter, though, because the woman herself chose that moment to call Mum to talk some more about it, and I took the opportunity to escape to my room with some of the extra scones Bella snuck into my bag earlier. I was happy to know the event I'd chosen to tell Jack the truth about my identity at was going to be a garden party, not a "hike" as he'd called it — and I was happier still when I woke the next morning to an uncharacteristically blue sky.

Sunshine. Canapés. Relationship-shattering confessions. What a *Dear Diary* kind of day this is going to be, for sure.

"Ye will be careful, Emerald, won't ye?" Dad says, looking concerned as he drops me off at the entrance to the estate. "We don't know anything about this Buchanan lad. We dinnae want ye gettin' involved with another Ben."

"You know quite a lot about him from Shona," I point out. "And one thing you can definitely be sure of is that Jack Buchanan isn't likely to try to con me out of my life's savings. Anyway, I'm not "involved" with him. I'm just here on Gala Day business for Bella, like I told you."

Dad looks suspicious, but he simply nods and waves, before driving off, with Jude Paw riding shotgun as usual, leaving me to make my way down the long driveway to Jack's house. My stomach churns with nerves as I walk. I've been awake more or less all night, wondering how on earth to break my "I'm Not Scarlett" bombshell to Jack, and I'm still no closer to knowing the answer to that one.

I am, however, dressed for the occasion, in a white vintage

sundress I found in Bella's collection, which I've paired with an over-sized sunhat I bought for a trip to Tenerife when I was seventeen. On my feet, I'm wearing a pair of pale pink flats with a huge bow on each toe; beautiful, but also completely practical for all the strolling Shona has assured Mum I'll be doing.

For once in my life, I actually feel like I might fit in at this event. Like I'm finally becoming the kind of woman who can show up at a garden party — or anywhere, really — and be perfectly at home there. I'm becoming Scarlett, in other words. And also, if Jack *does* listen to my confession, then throw me unceremoniously out of his house, at least I'll be well-dressed for it.

The thought comforts me as I reach the end of the path and crunch my way across the circular driveway, which leads me around to the back of the house, where the guests have started to assemble for the party.

Think about Scarlett, I tell myself firmly. *The imaginary one, not the real one. That's who you are. You are clever. You are confident. You are absolutely not going to make a fool of yourself.*

With my head held high and my shoulders back, I stride confidently towards the hum of voices.

It's definitely not a garden party.

I repeat: NOT a garden party.

I can tell as much as soon as I round the corner of the house, and make my way past the first lot of guests, who are grouped outside, next to a huge glass conservatory which houses the swimming pool.

I knew *there would be a swimming pool.*

What I didn't know, however, was that Jack really *was* being completely literal when he called this a "hiking" party. For once, it seems Shona McLaren's intel was wrong; every single person I pass is dressed in walking gear of some description, ranging from leggings and trainers to hiking boots and those long sticks serious walkers sometimes carry around with them to prove how much better they are than you at hiking.

I am the only person dressed for a garden party — probably because I'm the only person who was expecting one — and as people turn to stare curiously at me as I pass, I'm just grateful to realize I don't recognize any of them. Jack's house-guests are a wide mix of ages and looks; the one thing they all have in common, though, is that they all have that unmistakable gloss of wealth and success — and they all appear to be looking down their noses at me, in my borrowed dress and unsuitable shoes.

I will kill Shona McLaren the next time I see her, I swear to God.

There's no sign of Jack so far, so I hover nervously on the outskirts of the group, wondering if I should just turn around and go home while I have the chance. I managed to persuade Frankie to let me swap shifts with one of the twins just so I could come to this... *thing*... which means if I go home now I'll have the rest of the day to just lie on my childhood bed and regret all the poor life choices that led me to this point.

Or I could, you know, just hold my head up and get on with it.

I'm not here to have fun, after all. Or even to wow everyone with my pretty-but-now-exceptionally-impractical choice of footwear. No, I'm here to tell Jack who I really am, and then leave. (Although I'm obviously hoping he's going to ask me to stay.) So that's what I'm going to do.

First, though, I'm just going to nip to the loo. Because let's face it, "who I actually am" is normally someone with messy

195

hair and lipstick on her teeth, and that's not quite the message I'm hoping to get across when I finally see Jack.

Keeping my eyes on firmly on the ground to reduce the possibility of me having to talk to anyone, I sneak past the other guests and tentatively push the conservatory door open. The room is warm and steamy, with exotic-looking plants dotted around the edge of the pool, and a selection of padded sun-loungers in one corner. It would be bliss to relax here with a book, I think enviously as I tiptoe towards a door on the other side of the room. I didn't see this part of the house when I was here with Frankie, but I'm hoping that the door will lead to somewhere with a bathroom, where I can freshen up before seeing Jack. My hopes, however, are in vain, because no sooner have I pushed the door open than I see a familiar figure standing in the corridor beyond it.

Jack is leaning carelessly against the wall, looking every inch the Laird of the Manor. I'm so busy admiring him, in fact, that it takes me a few seconds to realize he's not alone.

He's with Lexie.

Lexie Steele, in sleek black Lycra, with a pair of sunglasses pushed up into her blonde hair, looking glamorous even in workout gear. All of a sudden, I feel even more out of place in my white cotton sundress and big straw hat. Like an 18th century milkmaid or something, who's just wandered into an upscale cocktail party.

Should I go home and change?

*Should I go home and, I don't know, **die**?*

And what's Lexie doing here, anyway? With her hand on Jack's... oh my God, is she stroking his arm?

I stand there in the shadows, watching in horror as Lexie places her hand on Jack's forearm, standing far too close to him as she giggles coquettishly at something he's just said. Her head is tilted up towards his, as if she's expecting him to kiss her (To be fair, Lexie's only about 5'4", and she's wearing trainers rather than heels today. But even so...), and Jack's smiling down at her, like he didn't almost kiss me just two days ago. Like it's totally fine for Lexie to have her hand on his arm like that. Like he's actually *enjoying* it.

Flirting. Lexie is blatantly flirting with Jack — and I don't think I've ever hated anyone more in my entire life.

I'm going to have to update my list of mortal enemies as soon as I get home. And I know who's going to be going straight to the number one spot.

I know I don't have the right to feel indignant that Jack is flirting with someone else — it's not like he's my boyfriend, after all. He's not my *anything*, really. And yet, I find I *am* indignant. And really quite *mad*, if I'm being honest.

Is that what he does, then? Just goes around flirting with different women, one after the other? I should have known. Because men as handsome as Jack Buchanan know they can have anyone they want, don't they? *Handsome is as handsome does*, as Mum would say. And "a pretty face suits the dish-cloot", according to McTavish. Whatever that means.

Well, Jack is definitely handsome and Lexie is nothing if not a pretty face. (I've no idea what a "dishcloot" is, but I'm sure it's nice, too.) It figures they'd eventually find each other.

I thought Jack was better than that, though. I mean, I know I'm not the best judge of character; the disastrous end to my relationship with Ben is ample proof of that. All the same, though, I really thought Jack was different. I didn't have him pegged as a player. But if that's what he is, then I guess he won't mind me joining the game.

"Jack!" I exclaim brightly, marching over to where he and Lexie are standing, my brightest smile plastered on my face. "There you are! I was wondering where you'd got to!"

Okay, I didn't actually plan on being quite so perky. It's almost as if the spirit of Imaginary Scarlett has inhabited my body, though. And it turns out that Imaginary Scarlett is not the type of woman to appreciate being played.

"Emerald?"

Jack's face registers surprise, and then something I'd like to think might be pleasure, but it's hard to tell with him, sometimes. Lexie, meanwhile, doesn't even bother to hide her disappointment as I stand between the two of them, forcing her to remove her hand from Jack's arm.

Game on, Lexie. Your move.

Lexie, of course, rises to the occasion, as only Lexie Steele can.

"Oh my God, Emerald, what *are* you wearing?" she says, with a tinkly laugh. My jaw is already painful from the strength with which I'm currently clenching it. This is going to be a *really* long day. "Did you come in fancy dress? Are you supposed to be a shepherdess or something? Because Jack here was just telling me about his plans to reintroduce wolves to the Highlands, so I guess we might be needing your services to keep the sheep safe from them."

Round one to Lexie, then.

And... did she say *wolves*?

My eyes flick quickly in Jack's direction, but his face is once again as impassive as ever, and he shows no surprise at all at Lexie's comment.

Might as well go with it, I suppose.

"If I'm a shepherdess, does that make you the big bad wolf,

Lexie?" I say sweetly, smiling innocently at them both.

Lexie's fake grin drops a notch.

Round two to me.

"You know it," she says, recovering quickly, and giving me a wink. "Better watch out, Emerald; my teeth can be sharp, you know."

Okay, that's it. I'm going to have to kill her.

Fortunately for Lexie, Jack chooses this moment to intervene.

"I take it you two know each other?" he says, looking confused.

"Oh yes," Lexie says, her smile back in place. "Emerald and I go way back. We went to school together. We hadn't seen each other for a while, though, until Emerald turned up to clean my... OUCH! Emerald, watch it!"

Lexie bends down to rub the toe I just stamped on, and the breath leaves my body as I realize how close I just came to having my double identity exposed. I think my *soul* might have left my body too, actually; it's the only explanation for the way the world seems to be tilting around me as I force myself to continue standing there, when I all I want to do is turn and run.

"Alexandra, what on earth are you doing?"

I'm so certain Lexie's about to blow my cover that when I turn around to see her mother striding towards us, I'm almost grateful to see her.

Almost.

Today, Samantha Steele ("Call me Sam, please," she titters, holding out her hand to Jack, and looking up at him in exactly the same way her daughter was doing just a few minutes ago) is wearing tight black jeans tucked into a highly polished pair of riding boots, and an oyster silk shirt, which is open at the neck to reveal her slightly crepey décolletage. She must be pushing 60 by now, but it's obvious that Call-Me-Sam intends to grow old disgracefully; as evidenced by the way she's now batting her heavily mascara-d eyes at Jack, while reaching up with one red-taloned hand to groom her peroxide blonde hair.

"You've done quite a job with this place, Mr. Buchanan," she purrs, completely ignoring Lexie, who seems to almost shrink in the presence of her mother. "Such an improvement. I'm looking forward to seeing the distillery next. Purely professional interest, of course. We have to keep abreast of the competition, don't we? I hear the views are worth seeing alone."

I resist the urge to snicker at her unfortunate use of the word "abreast" given the whole "cleavage" situation she has going on there, and glance curiously at Jack, who returns my gaze with a "save me" look, which I ignore. If he's going to flirt with Lexie, then I'm sure he'll be able to handle Samantha, too.

Or maybe not, on second thoughts.

"Emerald liked the view," he says, replies, looking like he'd rather eat his own feet than participate in this conversation. "Why don't you show them the photo you took, Emerald?"

I glare at him, wondering why on earth he's dragging me into this conversation, before reluctantly fishing my phone out of my bag and scrolling through the camera roll until I find the photo of the sunset I took that night.

"Very nice," Call-Me-Sam says, in a tone of voice that suggests that this is not the type of woman who appreciates a good sunset. She probably hates puppies, too.

"Ours might not have the views," Samantha continues,

managing to make it sound like nice views are some kind of newfangled fad that will never take on. "But we do have decades of history behind us to make up for it."

"So does The '39," replies Jack, with the confidence of a man who knows he doesn't have anything to prove. "As I'm sure you're aware. My grandfather made his first blend around the same time your — it must have been your father, I take it? — made his."

Samantha Steele's mouth sets in a hard line at this blatant reminder that she's an entire generation older than the man she's attempting to flirt with. Fortunately for her, Lexie — who still hasn't quite recovered from the revelation that I've been to Jack's distillery and she hasn't — jumps in to save her.

"Here, Emerald, take a photo of the three of us," she demands, handing me her phone imperiously.

"And one for me, too."

Call-Me-Sam places her own phone in my hand, then the two of them drape themselves around Jack, whose eyes plead silently for my help as he stands there like a statue, teeth gritted with distaste. Clearly not a big fan of photos, then.

"Say cheese," I grin cheerfully, juggling the two phones as Jack continues to glare at me.

I take Lexie's photo first, then swipe up on Samantha's phone, which opens to a camera roll filled almost entirely with selfies. Only two photos at the very bottom of the page don't contain close-ups of the woman's duck-faced pout — they're just boring shots of whisky stills, as far as I can tell — and I cringe inwardly as I obediently raise the phone and snap a few more photos to add to her gallery.

Who even needs that many photos of their own face?

"Our grandfathers were great friends, Mum was telling me,"

Lexie is saying to Jack as I hand the two phones back. "Mum says there was even some talk of them becoming partners at one point?"

"Yes; and maybe you and Jack here — I can call you Jack, can't I? — will be partners one day too," Samantha says, clearly wishing it was her, and not her daughter, who was destined to be "partners" with Jack Buchanan.

"I feel a bit sick," I announce bluntly, not wanting to listen to any more of this. "I think I'm going to go and get some air."

"I'll come with you," Jack says immediately, seizing at the excuse. "The hike's about to start, anyway."

Lexie opens her mouth to say something else, but Jack's already steering me away from them and back towards the swimming pool room. As we reach the door, I can't resist a quick look back, and am just in time to see the smiles fall from Lexie and her mother's face simultaneously.

"Go after him, you stupid girl," I hear Samantha hiss to her daughter as we go.

I'm going to take that as round three to me, then.

Chapter 24

As soon as we're back outside the house, Jack and I stop and look at each other warily.

"Are you really feeling sick?" he asks, his brow creasing with concern.

"Only of those two," I admit, nodding in the direction of Lexie and her mum, who've just emerged from the conservatory. Samantha's face is thunderous, and Lexie looks like she's shrunk even more, somehow.

Dammit. Now I feel sorry for her.

"Me too," Jack says, grinning in relief. "Okay, I think I've done enough schmoozing for one day. Let's get this show on the road."

* * *

I had assumed everyone in the hiking party would walk together, like some strange, many-headed beast, but although we start off that way, before long, Jack catches my eye, silently beckoning me towards him.

"Come on," he mutters," guiding me away from the rest of

the group. "Let's get away from this lot."

"Your guests, you mean?" I ask innocently, as we strike out across the lawn, headed in a completely different direction from everyone else. "The ones you invited here for the weekend? The ones who're expecting the Laird of the Manor to entertain them? *That* lot?"

"I'm not the Laird of the Manor," he replies easily, refusing to take the bait. "Or, at least, I don't think of myself that way. And I'm not a one-man entertainment committee, either. That's what I pay other people for."

"Wow, you really weren't kidding when you said you weren't a people person, were you?" I comment, following him across the immaculately mown lawn towards the line of trees beyond the house. "Are you really planning to avoid your guests? For the entire weekend?"

"As much as I can," Jack replies, grimacing. "I'm sure Elaine and John have it in hand, anyway. They're good at this kind of thing. I'm not. I like to stick to my lane."

"Which is... whisky?" I venture curiously. "Or something else?"

"Apps," Jack replies, glancing at me. "The whisky's just a sideline, really; a passion project, I suppose. I spend most of my time glued to my laptop, coding. I'd much rather be doing that than... well, all of *this*."

He nods towards the retreating backs of the rest of the hiking party, who are, luckily for him, too far away now to realize their host is busy explaining how much he wishes he didn't have to see them.

"Hey!" I protest, nudging him in the side. "If you weren't doing this, you wouldn't have the pleasure of my company, you know."

"Well," Jack says, so quietly that I have to lean closer to hear him. "That *would* be a tragedy. You're one of the very few people whose company I don't mind."

It's the very faintest of faint praise, but it still makes my cheeks burn with delight. With every moment I spend with him, I can feel my resolve to tell him the truth slowly slipping away. I don't want to spoil this. Not while he's being nice to me. Or to Scarlett, anyway. Because, let's face it, Scarlett is the one he likes. She's the one with the confidence to tease him about his misanthropic ways and to poke him in the ribs to get his attention. I, meanwhile, am the one who turned up to his hiking party looking like I'm in fancy dress, and who's now having to style it out, and pretend that this is what I always wear to hike in.

Seeing as I'm still being Scarlett right now, I figure I may as well risk another Scarlett-esque question.

"So, is whisky-making your only, er, passion project?" I ask, picking my way cautiously across the uneven ground. We've left the sweeping lawn of the house now and are in the forest beyond it, which is bad news for me and my stupid shoes. "There's no... *person* you're passionate about, too, perhaps?"

I wince in horror at my own words. Maybe I *shouldn't* keep channeling Imaginary Scarlett right now, after all? Jack, however, doesn't seem to notice my embarrassment.

"A person?" he says, frowning slightly. "A woman, you mean?"

Lexie is what I mean. I'm not going to say it, though. That would just make me look jealous and insecure, and as un-Scarlett-like as it's possible to be.

"Like Lexie, maybe?" I say, instantly wanting to kick myself. "You two seemed very friendly back at the house."

For a moment, Jack doesn't reply, and we walk on in silence, the words hanging in the air between us.

"Were you jealous?" he asks at last, not looking at me. "Because if I didn't know better, I'd say you were jealous."

"No," I retort immediately. "Don't be ridiculous. Of course I wasn't jealous."

I add a quick eye-roll, just for good measure. I'm fooling no one, though. Not even myself.

"Oh," says Jack, looking wounded. "That's a shame. I was hoping you were."

His mouth twitches upwards in his approximation of a smile, and I grin tentatively back at him, almost light-headed with relief.

He still likes me. It's going to be okay.

Well, as long as I keep pretending I'm Scarlett, obviously.

"I don't even know Lexie," Jack goes on, slowing down slightly to allow me to catch up with him. "She basically ambushed me; just came waltzing over and started talking to me as if we already knew each other. I just went along with it to be polite. I was so relieved when you turned up to rescue me."

He shrugs as if this is no big deal, but it's exactly the kind of thing *I* would have done in his place — it's exactly the kind of thing I *have* done, actually — and the realization almost makes me stop in my tracks.

Jack isn't perfect. He's the sort of person who pretends to know someone just to avoid having to ask them who they are, and who has to be rescued from awkward social situations. He's...

"Oh my God," I say, actually stopping in my tracks this time. "Are you *shy?*"

Now it's Jack's turn to protest.

"Of course not," he says, pouting slightly. "I'm not remotely shy. I'm just not a people person. I already told you that. That's why I like coding. I know where I am with code. I understand it. I don't understand most people. That's why I try my best to avoid them most of the time."

I start walking again as I turn this information over in my mind. It's all just an act, I realize now. Jack isn't grumpy, and he isn't rude; or not on purpose, anyway. He's probably not actually *shy*, either. He's just someone who isn't particularly comfortable around other people. Someone who'd rather be alone with his computers and his plans than at the center of the house party of the century.

He is not who everyone thinks he is. In fact, in some ways, he's just as much of an impostor as I am.

Or, you know... maybe not.

As we slowly walk up the gentle slope of Westward Tor, I realize I know this place. The trees are taller and the heather is thicker, but this will always be me and Frankie's childhood stomping ground. It's a happy memory, but it doesn't last long. Without warning, I'm jolted back to the last time I sat on the summit looking down on the black acrid smoke rising from the village and knowing beyond doubt that I could never go back.

Some people burn their bridges; I burned my village hall — which amounts to the same thing, really.

But now here I am; right back where I started, with every-thing feeling so painfully familiar, it's almost as if I never left.

Jack, however, is a city boy, born and raised, and he's looking more than a little lost.

"Jack, where are we actually *going*?" I ask suddenly. As far as I can tell, we've been walking pretty aimlessly so far, but it suddenly occurs to me that Jack — or whoever organized this walk — must have had some *actual* destination in mind.

"The waterfall," he replies distractedly running his hand through his hair. "There's supposed to be a waterfall near here. My grandfather wrote about it in his letters to my grandmother, before they were married. It was where he proposed to her in the end, I believe. I've always wanted to see it."

I look at him thoughtfully, trying not to think about the fact that he was planning to take me to the location of his grandfather's romantic proposal. That doesn't mean anything, right? I mean, he was planning to take *everyone* at this stupid party there, not just me. It's just unfortunate that he didn't plan a little more thoroughly, because here's the thing: there *is* a waterfall on the Buchanan estate — I know it well. It's not anywhere near where we are now, though. The waterfall is up in the hills, as you'd expect. We, on the other hand, are currently looking down into the glen. There are no waterfalls here. Just a lot of sheep, and a couple of old ruined cottages that I used to pretend were the remains of fairy castles.

I bite my lip as I ponder what to do next. *I* know we're walking in completely the wrong direction. Scarlett, however, wouldn't. Because Scarlett Scott didn't spend her youth trespassing on Jack's land, did she? Emerald shouldn't have, either. But I did; and now I have a dilemma. Do I tell Jack we're hopelessly off track, and risk him asking how I know? Or do I just go along with him and risk getting both of us lost?

While I'm busy weighing up the pros and cons of these two options, Jack makes the decision for me.

"Come on," he says decisively, putting one foot on the wall

in front of us. "We'll go this way. I'm sure it's just beyond that hill."

"Isn't that a farmer's field we have to cross, though?" I ask, pretending I don't know perfectly well that it is. As if to prove it, right at that moment the farmer himself comes trundling into view on a quad bike, a very woolly sheep trotting obediently behind him. Even from this distance — and, well, also because of the sheep, obviously — I can see that it's Jimmy, my old nemesis from the Fort William bus, and his faithful sidekick, Edna.

Fantastic. Just fantastic.

"It's fine," says Jack, climbing over the wall, and waiting for me to follow. "According to the map, this is a public right of way. And it's Scotland, anyway; we have the right to roam, you know. We'll just stop to ask the farmer if it's okay first."

"And then he'll shoot us," I reply, climbing over the wall to join him.

"It's Scotland," says Jack again, looking faintly amused at my naivete. "People don't shoot each other here."

"They do if they're mad," I point out, thinking of at least two people I know personally (And by "personally", I mean, "Through Mum's friend, Shona"), who've been shot. Mc-Tavish was almost one of them, actually, but, to be fair, he didn't *know* the pellet gun was loaded when he pointed it at his own foot. And I'm pretty sure one of the other people Shona told me about was "shot" during a paintball game, now I come to think of it.

Maybe Jack is right. Maybe Jimmy won't shoot us. He probably won't even *have* a gun.

We trudge slowly over the field to where Jimmy is sitting waiting for us on his quad bike, and yup, he totally has a gun.

"See, I told you so!" I hiss under my breath.

Jack doesn't hear me, though; he's switched into full 'Laird' mode as he strides ahead of me, offering his hand to Jimmy, who looks at it suspiciously, before wiping his own hand on his trousers before leaning down to shake Jack's.

Fortunately for me, Jimmy is much too impressed to be speaking to the *actual* Jack Buchanan to be thinking about shooting us. Instead, he spends the next few minutes giving us a series of very complicated directions to the waterfall ("Och, ye dinnae ken yer arse fae yer elbow," he says. "Ye're miles away fae yon waterfall. Miles."), and telling us which fields have "beasts" in them (By "beasts" I know he means "cows", but it's clear from Jack's startled expression that he's assuming the beasts in question to be the mythical sort. Like dragons or something. I'm not going to put him right, either.), and which do not.

"Well, thanks very much," Jack says at last, when Jimmy finally stops talking. "We'll be sure to avoid the, er, *beasts*. If we can."

Jimmy nods, but I can tell there's something else he wants to get off his chest, and I can also tell that it's going to be about me. Sure enough...

"Interesting choice of footwear you have there," he says, except he says it in a tone which makes it abundantly clear that what he *really* means is, "What an absolute idiot you are!"

"They are, aren't they?" Jack replies drily. "And also very practical, too, I'm assured."

"Aye, right!" says Jimmy, snorting. Then he turns his back and drove away, Edna still trotting behind him.

"But they *are* practical," I say in a small voice, once Jack and I have trudged on for a few minutes in silence. "I've walked all this way in them, haven't I?"

Jack says nothing to this. It would appear I've finally exhausted his patience with my shoes, so we continue on until we reach the gate Jimmy had indicated we should pass through in order to reach the waterfall.

There's just one problem.

The gate is locked.

As in, there's a giant chain wrapped firmly around it, hugging the gate like a lover. This is not a gate that wants to be opened; that much is clear.

"Well, let's just climb over the fence," Jack says decisively. "It's only waist high. Should be easy enough, even in those shoes."

"Fine," I sigh, choosing to ignore the random jibe. "You go first."

Jack places his hand on the wooden stump of the gate, in the manner of a man about to conquer a great obstacle. As he climbs up and over the wire fence next to it, I can tell he's pretending to be Edmund Hillary; or maybe Leonardo DiCaprio in that movie with the bear. As he reaches the other side, he just manages to resist shouting that he's the king of the world, in fact, if I can just mix my movie metaphors for a moment.

Now it's my turn; not just to climb the fence, but to show Jack once and for all that I am a woman of substance. That, despite my stupid shoes, and — well, everything else he's seen of me so far — I, too, can be a capable, outdoorsy type, able to adapt to whatever situation I find myself in, and—

"AAAAARGH!"

I place both my hands on top of the fence and instantly jerk backwards in shock. Literally, I mean. Because that's what happens when you touch an electric fence, apparently, and this is how I find that out.

When I tell Mum and Dad the story later, I recall a loud bang (There wasn't one, according to Jack), a flash of light (nope), and a surreal slowing down of time (Er, no.), during which I lock eyes with Jack, seeing my own shock reflected in his face.

Oh, and I also scream really loudly. Loud enough to make all the beasts in the neighboring field turn to watch me with interest.

Unfortunately for me, though, the beasts aren't the only ones to hear my cries of distress. No sooner has Jack opened up the gate (Because, of course, *that's* the moment he decided it was worth unwrapping that infernal chain...) there comes the noise of a quad bike engine, and our old friend Jimmy appears over the crest of the hill, like the cavalry riding to the rescue.

"Whatever you do," I hiss to Jack in the moments before he reaches us, "Do not tell him I touched the electric fence. DO NOT TELL HIM. Because he's already judged me by my clothes; let's not allow my actions to confirm his opinion that I'm the type of idiot who touches an electric fence, while wearing silly shoes."

"But you did touch an electric fence..." begins Jack. I was just about to point out that *he* obviously hadn't realized it was electric either, and that it was just pure luck that he hadn't touched it with his bare skin, like I had, when Jimmy is upon us, wanting to know what happened. "Screams!" he said dramatically. "I heard screams!"

I turn to him, and try to look interested, and yet mystified, in a "Goodness, I wonder what it could've been?" kind of way, but it's no use.

"It was Emerald," Jack announces loudly. "She touched the electric fence."

Jimmy looks at me with undisguised amusement.

"She never did!" he says.

"She did!" confirms Jack.

"She never did!" repeats Jimmy.

"She did!" agrees Jack.

If Edna had been there, I'm sure she'd have chipped in too. Edna, however, is still some way away, struggling to keep up with Jimmy's quad bike, so I stop the two of them in their tracks by confirming to Jimmy that yes, it was true; I'm not only wearing shoes with bows on them, I'm also going around touching electric fences.

"Ach, I thought one of the beasts had maybe frightened you," says Jimmy, clearly disappointed that this was not the case.

"AS IF I'd be scared of a beast!" I reply hotly, but it's too late; Jimmy has already turned around and ridden off. "She never did!" I'm sure I hear him say as he goes.

Chapter 25

I t's possible that I might have *slightly* over-estimated the practicality of these shoes.

By the time we reach the waterfall, my feet hurt, my hair is in ragged knots, and the wind has picked up, leaving me shivering in my impractical cotton dress.

"Here," says Jack, unzipping the hoodie he's wearing and pulling it off. "Put this on. You look freezing."

"But then *you'll* be freezing," I protest weakly, but he just stands there holding it out to me until I finally give in and slip gratefully into it.

"There," he says, turning me towards him and zipping it up for me. "That's better."

"It is," I say, smiling up at him. "Thank you. You're a true gentleman."

I'm expecting him to release me as soon as he's done up the zipper, but he just stands there, his hands still on the hoodie, which he pulls a little tighter around me, wrapping me up in its warmth.

"A gentleman?" he says, his eyes twinkling. "I thought I was a complete cad?"

The hoodie smells like him, and being wrapped in it feels a bit like getting a giant hug from him.

I would really like to get a giant hug from him right now.

"I'm sorry about that," I say sheepishly. "And for coming round unannounced like that. And for falling into the loch, and forcing you to come and save me."

And for pretending to be a sassy food and drink journalist, when I'm actually just her cleaner.

"Anyway, I'm sorry for all of that," I finish lamely. "I don't think you're a cad. I think you're... well, I think you're quite nice, really. When you're not being grumpy and trying to avoid people, anyway."

"Quite nice?" he replies, teasingly. "You're going to embarrass me with all this effusive praise, Miss Scott."

Shit.

I completely forgot I was supposed to be telling him I'm not Scarlett. I should have done it by now. I really did mean to, I swear. I just got distracted by Lexie, and by Jack... and by Edna, and the stupid electric fence. And if I tell him *now*, well, that just means we'll have to walk all the way home together, with him hating me.

I swallow nervously.

"Anyway," I say, taking a reluctant step back, and out of his reach. "We must be close to the waterfall by now, surely? I think I can hear it..."

I know I can hear it. Because it's just around the next bend in the trail we're on. I need to get Jack *moving* again, though, before he tries to kiss me, still thinking I'm Scarlett.

At least, I *think* he was about to kiss me.

I hesitate for a second, wondering if it's at all possible for me to change my mind, hit the rewind moment, and go back to that moment. I wonder if I could just *live* in that moment, actually. But it's too late, Jack turns away, looking confused, and starts walking in the direction of the water, not speaking.

"So, um, was it true what Lexie said, back at the house?" I ask, desperate to break the uncomfortable silence that's fallen, and seizing on the first topic I can think of. "Are you *really* planning to put wolves out here? Like, *real* wolves?"

"Yup." His face hasn't quite lost the look of confusion, but at least he's talking to me again. "It's something I've been thinking about for years. Another passion project, if you like."

"You're passionate about wolves?"

I *really* want to make a joke about Lexie here, but I have a feeling it won't go down well, so I leave it be.

"About conservation," he says, turning to look at me over his shoulder as we walk. The confused look is gone now, I'm relieved to see, and his expression is animated. "Re-wilding is just one aspect of it, but it has so many benefits, especially here in the Highlands. Reforestation, biodiversity..."

"Scaring people shitless..." I continue for him.

Jack chuckles.

"It's not dangerous if it's done properly," he tells me. "I've been working closely with a local conservation group in Fort William, and we're pretty close to getting something set up. It's really exciting, actually."

He turns to look at me again, and I can tell by the way his entire face lights up as he talks that he really is as passionate about this as he says he is. It's quite endearing, actually. Or it would be, if it wasn't, well, *wolves* we were talking about. Why can't he have a normal hobby, I wonder? Like... I don't know, yoga. Or cross-stitch. People seem to love yoga and cross-stitch. But nope, leave it to me to fall for someone who wants to live with the wolves.

"Trust you to like wolves more than people," I say teasingly.

"I'm not sure all the sheep around here will approve, though. Or the farmers, for that matter."

I'm thinking of Jimmy and Edna, obviously. I really can't imagine Jimmy allowing a pack of wolves amongst his "beasts", somehow.

"Don't worry, we've been consulting the local farmers," Jack reassures me. "Like I say, as long as it's done properly, there should be no risk to livestock."

I doubt that very much, but we're about to round the bend that leads to the waterfall, and I want to see the look on his face when he sees it for the first time, so I keep the thought to myself.

"Whoa!"

The waterfall isn't big enough or impressive enough to make it onto any of the tourist itineraries for the area — or even to have its own name — but, from the way Jack's looking at it, you'd think it was Niagara Falls.

Find someone who looks at you the way Jack Buchanan looks at water rolling down some rocks in the Highlands, I guess.

"Emerald, this is amazing! Look at it!"

Jack reaches into his pocket. I assume he's getting his phone, to take some photos of the fall, but, instead, he pulls out his wallet, and carefully withdraws a faded old photo which he's tucked inside it.

"Here, look at this," he says, beckoning me forward. He holds the photo up, almost reverently, and I see it's been taken right on this spot, many decades before. In it, a couple in 1930s clothes stand beaming before the falls, his arm around her waist.

"My grandmother was pregnant with my dad when this was taken," Jack tells me, smoothing out a crease in one corner of

217

the fragile paper. "Isn't it strange to think of them standing here, in the exact same spot we are, all those years ago?"

I nod silently, not quite trusting myself to speak. The couple in the photo look so young, their faces alight with happiness and hope. I almost wish I didn't know the sad ending of their story; how none of the dreams they must have had for their lives together would come true.

"I think it's wonderful that you're honoring your grandfather's dream," I say, touching him lightly on the hand. "I didn't know them, obviously, but I...I think it would've meant a lot to them."

I squeeze his hand, hoping I haven't said too much. But he looks down at me, and his expression is soft and wistful.

"My grandmother was very old by the time I was born," he tells me. "She moved to the city after the war. She said she just couldn't bear to come back here without him. That's why the house was boarded up. But she did give me this photo. She said this was the place she felt closest to him when he was off fighting. So, yes, I think you're right. I think she'd be happy to know that something of him lived on here. Did I tell you this waterfall is the source of the water for the distillery?"

He tucks the photo carefully back into his wallet, and turns to look at the falls again, and I stand next to him, dutifully looking at the view as if I've never seen it before. But there's a lump in my throat as I stand there. I want to continue this conversation; to hear more about his family, and his life before he came back here. The things that drive him. But it feels wrong to get any closer now — to encourage him to share things about himself with me, while I'm still lying to him by being Scarlett. And until I can work up the courage to tell Jack the truth, this is still very much a 'What Would Scarlett Do?'

kind of a situation.

What Scarlett would do, of course, would be to gasp and smile, as if all of this is brand new to her; and, in a strange kind of way, it almost feels like it *is*. It's a long time since I last visited this place, after all, and I guess coming here with Frankie and McTavish wasn't *quite* the same experience as being here with Jack. Last time I was here, I seem to remember complaining a lot about how cold I was. Well, I'm cold now, too. That's kind of a given in the Highlands. Now that I'm looking at the place through Scarlett's eyes, though — and through Jack's — it looks entirely different.

Now, the water comes cascading down the hillside, sending rainbows into the mist above us, before pooling in the rocks below. The air smells like pine cones and, when Jack turns to look at me, his eyes shining with the sheer joy of being here, I can see tiny droplets of water caught in his dark lashes.

"Beautiful, isn't it?" he asks, grinning, and I nod instantly.

"Gorgeous," I agree. "Absolutely stunning."

And the scenery isn't bad either.

Jack takes one more photo, then holds out his hand to pull me out onto the little wooden viewing platform that clings to the edge of the cliff, offering the best possible view of the fall. I hesitate for just a second — God knows when this thing was last maintained, and the very last thing I need is to be plunged into icy cold water again — then slip my hand into his, hoping my palms aren't quite as sweaty as they feel.

I'm expecting him to let me go when we reach the edge of the platform, but, instead, he just stands there looking out, my hand still tucked safely in his, as my heart hammers in my chest. We're standing in what has to be some of the freshest air in Scotland, and yet, all of a sudden, there's not nearly enough of it, because I just can't seem to breathe properly. What air there is feels heavy with expectation and charged with the *what-is-he-going-to-do-next* of it all.

This is perfect. Utterly perfect, in every imaginable way.

It's just a shame it's not actually real.

Because it's not, is it? I mean, here I am, in this romantic-setting, with this gorgeous man, who, despite our slightly rocky start, seems to actually *like* me. Except he doesn't. He can't, because, the truth is, he doesn't actually *know* me. He knows Scarlett. He *likes* Scarlett. And I'm not her.

My eyes fill with tears as I realize what I'm going to have to do. I'm going to have to spoil this perfect moment; to ruin this perfect day. I'm going to have to tell Jack I'm not who he thinks I am, and I'm going to have to do it ... um, just as soon as he stops looking at his phone.

Which, I mean, *seriously?* Not this *again*, surely? Not me about to confess, but being thwarted by Jack and that infernal phone of his, which never seems to be far from his hand?

Right now, one of his hands is still clasping mine, while the other one holds his phone at eye level, scrolling quickly through a message.

"Sorry," he murmurs, presumably sensing my disapproval. "I was trying to turn it off so it wouldn't disturb us, but then this came in..." He trails off as he continues to scan the message, and I'm about to turn away in disappointment when he suddenly looks up at me, that rare smile of his lighting up his face.

"You didn't tell me you'd filed your article on the distillery?" he says, dropping my hand in his excitement.

"I... oh. Yeah. That."

Shit. I'd forgotten about that stupid article I wrote and

submitted under Scarlett's name. But how on earth does Jack know about it?

"This is from your editor," he says, answering my unasked question. "Telling me the article is going to be in the next issue of the magazine!"

"My... my editor? How do you know him?"

I swallow nervously, trying to buy myself some thinking time.

"Her, you mean?"

"Her?" I swallow again.

"Yes, Alex McNeil? Your editor? Your *female* editor?"

"Oh, yeah, that's what I said," I blurt hurriedly. "So, um, what did she say? And why's she messaging you, anyway?"

"Oh, she contacted me yesterday to set up a time to send a photographer up to take some photos for the article," he says distractedly. "I wrote back and told her not to worry, because it wasn't ready yet, but she's just sent me a copy of it. Hang on, let me just take a quick look..."

I smile nervously as I start inching my way back from the edge of the viewing platform, just in case my legs — which have started trembling uncontrollably — give way and send me plummeting to my death. Well, given my track record for accidents, I can't be too careful.

My heart feels like a butterfly that's caught in my chest, and it struggles to get free as Jack quickly scans the article. When I wrote it, I was just trying to do something good for once — something to help with his distillery plans. I didn't really think about the possibility of it actually being *published,* and I certainly didn't imagine I'd have to stand here like an idiot while the subject of my glowing praise read the damn thing right in front of me.

This is bad.

This is really, really bad.

"Emerald, this is good."

I blink in confusion as Jack finally lowers his phone and looks up at me.

"This is *great*, in fact. It's..."

He pauses, looking right into my eyes, and somewhere in the back of my head, Taylor Swift starts singing. It's *that* kind of a look. Intense. Meaningful. You could even say *smoldering*, if you didn't mind sounding like you were in a Mills and Boon romance.

"... it's fantastic," he finishes at last. "Really fantastic, Emerald. You really captured what I'm trying to do here with the distillery, for the community. And the bit about my grandfather..."

He pauses, seeing to struggle with his emotions for a moment.

"Well," he finishes, regaining his composure. "It's just... it's just fantastic. I can't thank you enough."

He can, though. Because, before I can figure out what to say in reply to that, his hands are in my hair, his lips are on mine, and he's kissing me: at long, long last.

It's nothing like I imagined it.

It's not, for instance, a tentative first-kiss; sweet, and a little bit shy. And it's not a chaste, dry kiss, like you might expect from someone as serious as Jack is most of the time. No, this is the kind of kiss you get from someone who's been waiting his entire life just to kiss you. It's an all-consuming, leave-you-breathless kind of kiss that makes me feel almost like I'm floating. Then I realize I actually *am* floating — well, sort of. Jack's hands are around my waist, and he's picked me up until my face is level with his. He holds me close to his body, as easily as if I were a doll, and I loop my arms around his neck and sink into his embrace. I'm not thinking about Scarlett now, or about Ben, or Frankie, or anything, in fact, other than Jack, and the way his lips feel against mine. The way his tongue darts experimentally against my mouth, parting my lips and making me pull him even closer, completely ignoring the mist from the waterfall, which is dampening our skin and probably turning my hair into a frizzy mess.

It's nothing like I imagined it. It's so much better; and it goes on and on, until every nerve-ending in my body is alive. Especially the ones on my right thigh, actually, which are literally *buzzing* with... *oh.*

"Sorry," I say, pulling my lips reluctantly from Jack's as I reach into the pocket of my dress to silence my phone, which is buzzing away merrily. Before I can switch it off, though, I catch sight of the name on the display, and my heart drops right out of my body.

It's Frankie.

Calling, I assume, to ask where the hell I am, given that my shift was supposed to start over an hour ago now.

"Oh my God," I gasp, horrified. "I need to go. I... I forgot something."

"You forgot something? What?"

Jack's brow is creased with confusion. He thinks it's just an excuse, I can tell. But this situation is very, very real, and if I don't get back to Heather Bay right now, Frankie's going to kill me.

"It's just... something with a friend," I say, my eyes pleading with him to just accept this. Don't question it. Just help me, please. "I promised her I'd be there, and I'm not, and, oh God, please, can we just—?"

I turn and start jogging back up the trail we just came down, and, after a few seconds, I hear the snap of twigs underfoot as Jack follows me.

"Okay, stay calm," he says from behind me. "I'm just going to call Elaine and get her to send someone out in the Land Rover to get us. I'll have you back in town as soon as I can. I'm sure your friend won't be too upset once you explain."

I turn to smile gratefully at him, but the mask is back down again, the dimples and smiles replaced by his usual, carefully neutral expression.

I've lost him again.

Sexy, dimpled, smiling Jack is gone; serious, moody Jack is back.

And neither of them know who I really am.

Chapter 26

J ack was right: Frankie isn't upset with me. She's absolutely livid.

"Do you have any idea how hard it was to persuade the twins to swap shifts with you?" she says when I finally get back to the office. "And then you can't even be bothered to turn up?"

"Frankie, I'm so, so sorry," I gasp, rushing to the supply cupboard to get one of the spare vacuum cleaners. I didn't dare go home first to collect Bessie or change my clothes, so I've rocked up here empty-handed, still wearing the cotton sundress, and shoes I can now barely stand up in.

It would be fair to say that this is *not* my finest hour as an employee; and I say that as someone who once spent three hours locked in a stationery cupboard without anyone noticing she was gone.

"I promise I'll make it up to you," I say, pulling a Highland Maids sweatshirt on over the top of my dress, and scraping my hair back into an "I mean business" bun. "I'll work a double shift now, and tomorrow if you like. And I'll—"

"Forget it, Emerald," Frankie interjects, looking weary. "I've already had to send someone else to the job. You might as well just go home. Or wherever it is you need to be that's more important than what I'm paying you for."

She's using her "I'm not angry, I'm disappointed tone," and I can't blame her. She didn't have to give me this job, after all. She probably didn't even *want* to, given my track record. But she did it anyway, just to help me. Just because she loves me, and always has my back. And this is how I repay her: by not having hers.

"Frankie," I say, going over to her, "I really am sorry. I didn't mean to let you down. It's just, I went out to the waterfall and, well, I got a bit lost, so—"

"You got *lost?*" She snorts in disbelief. "In Heather Bay? Are you trying to tell me those ten years in London have made you completely forget where you came from, Emerald? Is that it?"

"No! No, it's not that at all!" I reply, wounded. "It's just—"

It's just that I was with Jack Buchanan, and I was pretending to be someone else, because if I tell him who I really am, there's a very good chance your business will get the blame for my stupidity, and I can't let that happen.

I let my words trail off, and just stand there, wondering how on earth I managed to go from the high of kissing Jack Buchanan to this lowest of all lows, in the time it took me to put on my sweatshirt.

"Really?" says Frankie drily when she realizes I have nothing else to say. "Because you could've fooled me, Emerald. How long have you been back in the Bay? Weeks, no? And how often have you come to see me, other than at work? How much time have you spent with McTavish? With your old friends? "

"I've seen McTavish," I protest weakly. "He drives me home sometimes. And we had scones at Bella's once."

"Ach, that's right, stupid me," Frankie says, smacking herself on the forehead. "You've been letting McTavish do you the honor of giving you a lift home from work! That's a true friend, right enough."

Okay, I might be wrong here, but I *think* she's being sarcastic.

"There were the scones too, though..." I start to say, but Frankie interrupts me once again, and, to my horror, as she draws closer, I'm sure I can see tears in her eyes.

No. Surely not? Frankie *never* cries. Have I made my badass best friend *cry*?

"Och, give over, Emerald," she says, wiping her eyes roughly with the back of her hand. "You just happened to be there at the same time as him, that's all. And I bet whatever you were both doing at Bella's, it was all about you. Well, am I right?"

She has both hands on her hips now as she stares me down. She reminds me of Mum, actually.

I open my mouth to answer her, then close it with a snap as I realize she's right. I feel a blush start at my toes and work its way up my body as I remember how the conversation that day was all about me. Me and my lost money, me and my guilt, me, me, *me*. I'd never thought about it like that, but suddenly I'm so ashamed I want to cry.

"Did you know McTavish has had to start working as a taxi driver, because the farm's not making enough money?" Frankie continues, refusing to drop her gaze. "Did you know he had to sell some of his land to be able to afford the fees of his mum's nursing home? Did you know I signed up for that Internet dating? Or that Maggie Quinn's expecting twins?"

Now, in fairness to me, I have absolutely no idea who Maggie Quinn is. I *should* know all the other things she's just told me, though. There's no excuse. Not even one involving a dashing Laird and a secret double life.

"No, I didnae think so," Frankie says shortly. "I bet you

know all about Lexie Steele and what she's been up to, though. That's all you've talked about since you got back. Lexie, Ben, and how you're going to get out of this shitty little town you hate so much. Well, guess what, Emerald? Some of us still live here. And we actually *like* it, so sorry it's not good enough for you anymore."

She pauses for breath and we stand there facing each other, my face bright red and her eyes still suspiciously wet. She's my best friend in the world; the one who's been there for me ever since we met at playgroup when we were four years old. Right now, though, she feels like a stranger, and I know I have no one to blame but myself. Again.

"Frankie, I don't know what to say," I croak tearfully. "I'm just... I'm so sorry. I know you're right. I know I've been a mess since I got back. I've let you down, but I will make it up to you, I swear. I know I've not been the best of friends—" I pause to allow the eye roll she sends in my direction at this — "But I can change. I *will* change. I'll be Emerald 2... Emerald 3.0. I will, you'll see."

"But I don't want you to change," Frankie says sadly. "I just want Emerald back. The real one, I mean. Not this Emerald two-point-whatever, or whoever it is you've been trying to be since you got back. Just you. That's all."

She turns and picks her bag off the desk behind her.

"Och, I don't know," she says thoughtfully. "Maybe yer mam was right when she told you not to move to London. It's changed you, Emerald, and not for the better. I feel like I don't even know you anymore."

I chew my bottom lip, not knowing what to say to this. I've been trying my best to change, that much is true. Trying to do better, to *be* better. I've been trying to be someone else, just so I could escape the person I already was — the one who messed up so badly she felt like she didn't have any option but to change.

But maybe I really was better the way I was.

Frankie seems to think so, at least. So does Bella, and McTavish. And yet, here I am, letting my best friend down because I was off pretending to be someone else, in a bid to impress the Laird.

"I'm sorry," I say again, and it sounds totally inadequate, even to me.

"Look, I've got to go," Frankie says, slinging her bag over her shoulder. "Just promise me you'll have a think about what I've said, Emerald. And don't forget to put Bessie back in the cupboard before you leave."

I nod miserably.

"I will, Frankie," I say. "I promise. But, wait. I thought *my* hoover was Bessie? Who's this other Bessie, then?"

"They're all called Bessie, Emerald," Frankie tells me, her expression pained. "D'you think I have time to go around naming all of my vacuum cleaners?"

And then, with a flip of her curly hair, she's gone, the effect of her exit spoiled somewhat by the fact that she has to come back again a few seconds later for her car keys. But at least she tried.

* * *

Once Frankie's gone, I sit down at her desk and stare into space, my mind struggling to process everything that's happened today. Was it really just this morning I set off for Jack's house, determined to come clean to him? And now here I am, even deeper into the deception and having somehow managed to piss Frankie off into the bargain.

Frankie.

My heart contracts with pain at the thought of my friend. I've been so selfish since I got back; so caught up in my own problems that I haven't even stopped to consider anyone else's. Even now, though, I have to admit that I really wish I had someone I could talk to about what just happened with Jack. Frankie preferably, but McTavish would do, too. Hell, I'd even settle for a quick catch-up with Brian-from-the-bank, if I wasn't sure he'd have long-since finished his shift by now.

I give myself a quick shake, trying to clear my head. I promised Frankie I'd think about what she said to me, but instead my head keeps wandering back to Jack and that kiss.

Oh, that kiss.

In many ways, it was the perfect kiss. A knee-shakingly, heart-stoppingly hot kiss.

But... was it for real, I wonder now?

Did he kiss me because he *wanted* to kiss me, or did he just get carried away by the excitement of that stupid article I wrote? And if he did want to kiss me, did he want to kiss *me*, Emerald? Or did he really want to kiss Scarlett; the person he *thinks* I am?

Whoever he wanted to kiss, he'll be furious when he finds out she's been lying to him, won't he?

Ex-boyfriend Ben has picked a really bad moment to make his return as the Voice Inside My Head. For once, though, Ben's voice isn't just kicking me while I'm down. He's speaking the truth. And it's really time I faced it.

With a sigh that comes from the soles of my feet, I push myself up out of the chair and head to the door, stopping to check the rota Frankie's pinned to the wall on the way. She's got me down for three cleaning jobs tomorrow, starting first thing. My relief at the fact that she hasn't just scrubbed my name off the rota altogether, however, fades to nothing when I look at the name of my final client of the day.

It's Lexie Steele.

Chapter 27

L exie's house is a mess.

Dishes piled high in the sink, because the dishwasher hasn't been emptied. Clothes strewn across the bedroom floor. The bathroom counter is littered with lotions and potions, most of which are missing their lids, and there's a pair of knickers hanging jauntily from a lampshade, which I am absolutely not going to be touching. Not even with my Marigolds on.

I grit my teeth as I get to work, starting with the kitchen. If I didn't know better, I'd swear Lexie has done this just to spite me; a Lexie-like payback for walking off with Jack yesterday (Was it *really* just yesterday?) and leaving her standing there with her awful mother. Then I remember the way Samantha Steele spoke to her daughter, and the look of dejection on Lexie's face as she came out of the house.

Not everything is about you, Emerald.

"Shut up, Ben," I mutter through gritted teeth as I make a start on the dishes in the sink. "I like you a lot more when you're totally absent from my life, you know."

Then again, Ben's total absence from my life right now is one of the reasons I'm in this mess, and that thought occupies my mind while I work my way through the bottom floor of

Lexie's house and head upstairs. I'm just wiping down the shower when the sound of the door opening makes me jump, and I pause for a second as the sound of voices filters up the stairs.

"Sorry about the mess," I hear Lexie say brightly to whoever she's with. "The cleaner's coming round today. She should be here now, in fact. Emerald, are you in here?"

Shit. The last thing I want to do is have to face Lexie again after yesterday, but there's nothing for it. She knows I'm here, and I've finished the cleaning anyway, so I peel off my rubber gloves, tuck my hair behind my ear, and reluctantly head downstairs.

Lexie's in the kitchen, boiling the kettle for a woman who's sitting at the table with her back to me.

"Oh, there you are, Emerald," she says, smiling at me as if our encounter yesterday didn't even happen. "Thanks for tidying up in here. I've been rushed off my feet."

I doubt that somehow. I know Lexie is technically employed by her family's distillery, but I'd be surprised if she actually spends much time there when she could be doing yoga and painting her nails instead. Not to mention snuggling up to Jack Buchanan every chance she gets. I know I'm not being fair to her, though, so I simply smile back as I start packing up my cleaning supplies, which I left down here.

"How d'you take your coffee, Scarlett?" Lexie asks, making me freeze in the act of picking up my box of cleaning products.

Scarlett? Did she say Scarlett?

No. It can't be. It just can't be. It's just a coincidence, that's all. There must be dozens of Scarletts in this part of the world. Hundreds, even.

Reassured, I straighten up and turn to leave the room, the

heavy box clutched to my chest.

"Oh, Highland Maids?" the woman at the table says in a London accent, catching sight of the logo on my sweatshirt. "How funny. That's the name of the firm I hired to clean my place, too!"

With a crash that makes everyone jump, the cleaning products I'm holding fall to the floor, sending a strong scent of disinfectant into the air a one of the bottles releases its contents onto the flagstone floor.

Well, at least that'll save me having to clean it again for a while, I suppose.

"Sorry!" I exclaim, grabbing my mop and frantically trying to stem the flow of liquids. "Sorry, sorry, sorry! I'm so sorry, Lexie!"

"Yeah, you might have mentioned that," Lexie replies, rolling her eyes. "Come on, Scarlett," she adds, handing the other woman a steaming mug of coffee. "Let's take these into the living room. We can discuss the article there."

Scarlett gets up from the table and obediently follows Lexie from the room, sending a sympathetic glance in my direction as she goes.

"Right then," I hear Lexie say from the room next door. "Let's get to work, shall we?"

The door closes, and I sit back on my heels, pushing the hair out of my eyes as my mind frantically scrabbles to catch up with what just happened.

Scarlett Scott.

Is a real person.

And, of course, I *knew* she was real. Of course I did.

I just didn't expect her to be here, in this house. Or in *any* house, really. If I'm totally honest, I haven't been thinking much about Scarlett Scott — the *real* one, I mean; not the one I made up in my own stupid head — at all while I've been pretending to be her. I don't know; I guess the fact that she wasn't actually living in Heather Bay made her seem like less of a threat somehow. And, without the threat of her coming back and exposing me as the impostor I am, I just allowed myself to believe I could go on like this forever. Or at least for as long as it took to work up the courage to tell Jack the truth.

But now here she is, in the flesh. And also in a really nice pair of boots, actually; they were pretty much all I was able to take in of her from my position on the floor as she walked past. That and her long hair (Brown? Black? I can't even remember now...) and nice smile.

Oh God, this is such a mess. And I'm not just talking about the cleaning products all over the floor.

I still haven't moved from the floor. I'd really like to just stay here; maybe rocking back and forth and moaning like the madwoman I am.

Instead, I find myself inching silently forward until my ear rests against the door, which separates the kitchen from the living room. The low murmur of voices is a little too indistinct for me to make out every single word, but after a few minutes spreadeagled against the wooden door, I'm fully up to speed.

Scarlett is, indeed, back in Heather Bay for good, it seems, having dealt with whatever kind of emergency it was that sent her back to London not long after moving in. Lexie, meanwhile, has obviously taken a leaf out of Jack's book and is trying to persuade her to write an article on her mother's distillery.

Nice one, Lexie. Or you could try getting some ideas of your own, maybe, instead of just copying Jack?

"It's the strangest thing," Scarlett is saying now from the

other side of the door. "I honestly feel like I must be going mad."

I lean in a little closer. Why does she think she's going mad?

"Could you have, I don't know, written it and just forgotten you did it?" Lexie asks. "Like, on autopilot or something?"

"Nah," Scarlett replies decisively. I imagine her shaking her head. "I'd definitely remember writing an entire article. And the weirdest thing is, it's not even my usual style. I wish it was, really: it's much better than what I usually come up with. Oops, I probably shouldn't be telling you that, considering I'm supposed to be writing about you now! Oh, I'm sure it's just a mistake. Alex must have just assigned it to someone else and then forgotten about it. It's the only explanation. There was even a photo with it and everything, though. Here, let me show you..."

There's a short silence — presumably for Scarlett to show Lexie the photo in question — and I feel a part of my soul shrivel up and die inside my body.

They're talking about the article on Jack's distillery. Of *course* they're talking about it. Did I really think Scarlett just wouldn't find out someone had submitted an article in her name? Her editor would have told her, obviously; probably as soon as it landed in her inbox.

I am such an idiot.

I'm going to have to leave town, I realize, removing my ear from the door so I don't have to listen to any more of this conversation. *Again.* I'm going to have to leave this town in disgrace *yet again.* It's the only way out of this. Let's face it, it's just pure luck that's allowed me to get this far without being caught out in my lie. It's only a matter of time before it catches up with me, and now that Scarlett's back — and desperate to know who's been writing articles in her name, it would seem — it's probably going to happen sooner, rather than later.

I have just enough money from my cleaning job to get the train to Edinburgh, I reckon, doing some quick calculations in my head. After that I guess I can maybe find a cheap hostel or something where I can stay until I find another job? I don't even care what it is. I just need to get away from Heather Bay before I make everyone hate me again, just like I did back when I was a teenager.

But... Jack.

He's been messaging me all day. Just random stuff from his day, plus a few photos of, well, *wolves.* Which he says he's getting ready to welcome any day now. He hasn't mentioned The Kiss, or even come close to it. But I can tell we're skirting around the edges of that conversation. Sooner or later, we're going to have to dive right in and talk about what happened and what it means. Only we're not, though, are we? Because I'm not going to be here. I can't be.

But I *want* to.

It's not just Jack, though. As I sit there in this mess of my own making — both literally and figuratively — I suddenly know, beyond doubt, that I don't want to leave Heather Bay. I don't want to leave Mum and Dad; or Frankie, or McTavish. Hell, I don't even want to leave Jude Paw, and he left a half-eaten sausage under my bed last week, which stayed there until the smell alerted me to its presence.

Not even *that*, however, is enough to make me want to leave. How can I, when things are just starting to hot up with Jack? How can I leave when I promised Bella I'd help her raise her funds for the Gala Day? When McTavish might need my support with all the stuff Frankie told me about last night?

When Frankie will *definitely* need me to help her sort out her online dating profile (There's absolutely no way she's going to know how to take a decent selfie, let alone write something that will show what a wonderful soul she is), and when... I scrabble frantically for another excuse... when Maggie Quinn, whoever she is, has yet to have her twins?

How?

It's not fair, I tell myself, looking desolately at the surrounding mess. *I didn't want to come back here, and now I don't want to leave. Who would've thought it?*

"Aaargh!"

I'm not totally sure how it happens, but one minute I'm sitting there on the floor, thinking deep thoughts about Heather Bay, and how I don't hate it quite as much as I thought I did, and the next I'm on my back, staring at the ceiling, with Lexie next to me, and a pile of papers scattered around us.

"What the...?"

"For fuck's sake, Emerald," Lexie shrieks, sitting up. "What on earth were you doing behind the door? You could have killed me?"

"Cleaning?" I venture cautiously, sitting up and carefully moving my head from side to side to make sure it's still attached to me. "I was cleaning the floor, remember? Sorry, I didn't know you were going to come in just then."

"You should have finished that ages ago," Lexie insists, her eyes blazing. "How was I to know you'd be down there? I practically somersaulted over the top of you."

She rubs her elbow furiously, and I try to suppress a smile. She's exaggerating, of course, but if anyone could do a front-flip over another person, it would be Lexie.

"Sorry," I say again, struggling to my feet. It seems to be

the only thing I can say to her today. "Let me pick this stuff up for you."

I stoop and start gathering up the papers she was carrying when she tripped over me. They're photos, I see now. Whisky stills, it looks like. It must be photos of her family's distillery. One of them has some kind of weird logo on it, like a wolf with its teeth bared, and I stifle another smile as I hand it back to her. Trust Lexie to want to use a wolf in her branding. I can't deny it suits her.

"Here, give me those." Before I can comment on the wolf, Lexie snatches the photos out of my hand and puts them on the kitchen table. "I'm sorting these out so Scarlett can use them in the article she's writing on the distillery," she tells me unnecessarily. "Mum's going to be so pleased when it comes out."

She looks round at me, almost as if she's searching for my approval too, but I just shrug. I don't care about Lexie's mum and her distillery. I don't care about Lexie at all. I just want to go home and be alone with Taylor Swift and my misery.

First, though, I have to finish cleaning this floor. Wearily, I pick my mop back up and start sullenly pushing cleaning fluid around with it, while Lexie shuffles through her photos at the table. After a few seconds, Scarlett appears to join her, and I watch her curiously out of the corner of my eye, worried that if she sees my face, my guilt will be written all over it, and my secret revealed.

I think I'm going to throw up.

"Okay, I think I have enough for now," Scarlett says, taking the photos Lexie offers her, and putting them into an expensive-looking leather handbag. "And if I have any other questions, I can ask you at this masquerade ball. You are going to that, aren't you?"

Hold that thought; I'm not going to throw up. I'm just going to die instead. It'll be much quicker, and a lot less painful, than listening to the rest of this conversation.

"I am," Lexie replies gleefully. "Mum's coming too. Everyone is, I think. We were a bit surprised to be invited, given what happened between my grandfather and his, but I guess he wants to look like he's playing nice with the rivals, you know? Keep your enemies close, and all that."

Enemies? Jack and Lexie's family are enemies? First I've heard.

"I suppose so." Scarlett laughs uncertainly. "I must say, I'm looking forward to meeting the mysterious Mr. Buchanan," she adds. "I'd done so much research on him for that article I was supposed to write. I'm just gutted someone else beat me to it. He's a very interesting man."

"He's a very, very *hot* man," Lexie replies, winking at her. "I'm looking forward to seeing him myself, if you know what I mean."

Scarlett chuckles, and the two of them head back into the living room, leaving me to the cleaning, which I abandon again as soon as the door closes behind them.

Well, that settles it, I suppose. I might not want to leave Heather Bay, but it looks like I'm going to have to, because there's no way *two* Scarlett Scotts can appear at the same event, can they? And I know there was never any real chance of me getting to go, just as there was never any chance of this situation I've gotten myself into working out for the best. All the same, I feel like a child who was just given the biggest, best ice-cream in the shop, only to drop it on the floor without tasting a single bite.

I *am* that child. And I know I can't have my ice-cream *and* eat it, but it's still hard to admit the truth that's been becoming more and obvious as the days have gone by:

This charade is over.

And Cinderella definitely isn't going to the ball.

Chapter 28

I *am* going to the ball, though.

Yes, I know it's a terrible idea.

Yes, I'm aware there's a huge risk of something going catastrophically wrong.

I know that. I'm not stupid.

(Well, I mean, I *am* stupid, obviously. I'm just not so stupid that I don't *know* I'm stupid. Which is important, I'm sure you'll agree.)

When I get back from Lexie's, though, I find McTavish waiting for me.

"Emerald, it's Alfonso. Now's your chance!" Mum hisses excitedly as she ushers me into the living room, where McTavish is sitting eye to eye with Jude Paw, who's either trying to intimidate him, or just hoping for a scrap from the plate of sandwiches McTavish is clutching awkwardly. "I've given him some of that lemon chicken I made last night on a sandwich, but that willnae hold him forever. Ye might have to use some o' yer feminine wiles."

I can almost feel myself grow smaller in sheer mortification at this, but Mum pushes me sharply forward and I stumble into the living room, only just managing to stop myself from literally falling at McTavish's feet — which I suspect is what

Mum intended.

So much for my feminine wiles, then.

"Hi, Emerald," McTavish says eagerly, gratefully putting the sandwiches down as he stands up to greet me.

"Would ye look at that, Archie," Mum says happily, nudging dad in the side. "What lovely manners Alfonso has, doesn't he? I'm just saying what lovely manners Alfonso has, Emerald," she repeats a little louder for my benefit.

"Mum!" I groan, feeling like I've managed to slip through some kind of time portal and emerge as my 14-year-old self. "Just give us a minute, would you?"

"Of course! Of course!" We'll away and... clean out the fish tank," Mum says, nudging Dad again. "Won't we, Archie?'

"Oh. Aye. That's right," Dad replies, obediently shuffling after her. They make a big show of leaving the room, but I can tell they're just standing outside the door, like the Bennets when Mr. Bingley came to propose to Jane. I groan again as I cross the room and take a seat next to McTavish, who just stops short of tugging his forelock as he sits back down beside me.

"What's up, McTavish?" I ask, hoping it's not something that's going to take up too much time, and that he's not *actually* here to propose to me, like Mum and Dad seem to think. I need to start packing. And figure out what I'm going to tell Frankie about me leaving. And, well, listening to some sad songs that will allow me to have a good old cry while I'm doing it.

McTavish, however, has other plans.

"Emerald Taylor," he says, unnecessarily formally, given that we've known each other our entire lives. "Will ye dae me the great honor of accompanying me to the ball tomorrow night? The one that galoot Buchanan's throwing," he adds, as if there are dozens of other balls happening in Heather Bay that we might go to instead.

"Wh...what?"

My heart sinks as I stare at him, mortified. I've always known McTavish had a soft spot for me, of course. I've known since we were kids and he used to threaten to beat up anyone who tried to catch me when we played tag. I just guess I never expected him to actually *act* on it, and, now that he has, I'm going to have to tell him the truth and risk hurting him. I really, really don't want to hurt him. I don't want to hurt anyone, obviously; not Jack, not Frankie — not even the annoying Finn McNeil, who I still can't help but blame for everything that's happened. I particularly don't want to hurt McTavish, though. He's just too good and too pure-hearted to have anything bad ever happen to him. It would be like kicking a kitten.

That's why Old Emerald would just have said yes, rather than risk upsetting him. She'd have gone to the ball with him, and, I don't know, probably ended up *marrying* him, because she couldn't work out how to end things. I once ended up having a 6 month relationship with a guy I didn't really like, just because I didn't want to hurt his feelings. It's the kind of thing I do.

But not this time, though.

This time, I'm done with pretending. I'm done with lying. I'm done with passively going along with things and telling myself I don't have a choice, when the truth is that I *always* have a choice. I just generally pick the wrong one.

And it's time for that to stop.

"Look, McTavish... Alfonso," I say gently, turning to face him, and trying to ignore Jude Paw, who's watching us like we're his favorite soap. "I'm flattered. I really am. But the truth is—" I take a deep breath as "the truth" prepares to leave my tongue, for the first time in weeks — "The truth is, I just don't see you that way. I'm sorry."

"What way?"

I'd expected McTavish to be wounded by what I've said, but he just looks puzzled. Okay, this is not going to plan.

"*You* know. *That* way."

I gesture vaguely with my hands, as if this will somehow help clear things up. McTavish and Jude continue to stare at me, though, both of their heads tilted to one side as they try to work out what I'm saying, and I realize I'm going to have to *use my words*, as Bella McGowan used to tell the village schoolchildren, instead.

"I just don't fancy you," I blurt out, more bluntly than I intended to. "I mean, I just see you as a friend," I hurriedly correct myself. "A really, really good friend, but *just* a friend. Do you know what I'm saying?"

My face is telephone box red now, and I can feel my palms starting to sweat. I am not cut out for this truthful life. In fact, I'm just wondering if I can backtrack and tell him I *will* go with him after all, when something strange happens.

McTavish starts laughing.

Yes, *laughing.*

As if this is funny, as opposed to being utterly *mortifying.*

The living room door opens just a crack, then instantly slams shut again as McTavish finally gets a hold of himself.

"Emerald, did ye... did ye think I was asking to take ye to the ball?" he asks, still chuckling.

"You literally *did* ask to take me to the ball," I reply indignantly. "You just did it!"

"No," McTavish says, wiping his eyes. "I mean, aye. I did.

But I meant for you to take *me*. Because Shona McLaren says you've got an invitation, and I dinnae. I thought I could be yer plus-one. Just to get me through the door, ye ken?"

"No, I don't 'ken'," I say shortly. "What on earth are you talking about, McTavish?"

"Well, ye see, it's embarrassin'," he says at last, having the grace to look like he's finally taking this a little more seriously.

"It can't possibly be as embarrassing as me thinking you were asking me out if you're not," I point out. "Which, just to clarify: you're not, are you? Asking me out, I mean?"

"No," McTavish protests, a little too vehemently for my liking. "Emerald, yer like a wee sister to me. I could never see ye like that."

We're the same age, but I let this slide.

"And anyway, ye ken fine I've always been in love with Mary McNamee," he adds, as if this settles the matter.

Mary McNamee? Are people ever going to stop just saying names at me and expecting me to know who the hell they're talking about?

I let this one slide, too.

"But what about all those cards you used to make me?" I ask, confused. "And the time you got Charlie Lawson in a headlock because he stole my packed lunch?"

"Och, I was just being nice," McTavish says bashfully. "Just trying to look after ye, ye ken? That's why I made sure ye were elected Gala Queen that time."

I pause in the act of picking up one of the sandwiches to inspect it. As expected, the chicken inside has a strange, radioactive yellow glow to it. I put it back down hurriedly as I turn to meet McTavish in the eye.

"You... you *what*?" I say at last. "You did... *what*?"

"The Gala Day," he says cheerfully. "I kent ye wanted to be

Queen, so I fixed it for ye. It was no trouble. I just volunteered to be the one to collect all the votes, then, when no one was watchin', I tipped them into my pocket and replaced them with ones with your name on them."

My heart hammers in my chest as I think back to that day. Everyone in the class had to write the name of the person they were voting in as Gala Queen on a piece of paper, all of which were collected and then counted by the Gala Committee. I can still remember the shock on everyone's face when my name was read out. Even the teacher couldn't hide her surprise. It just didn't feel real — and now I know why.

It wasn't.

None of it was real.

I was never supposed to be the Gala Queen that year. My name coming out of the hat wasn't just some random trick of fate, and it definitely wasn't a sign of my sudden popularity. It was all McTavish's doing. And now that I know, I'm not sure whether I want to laugh or cry.

The event that changed my life was the result of a random act of misguided kindness by my friend, who, of course, couldn't possibly have known the fateful chain of events he had just unleashed.

I thought Bella was my Fairy Godmother, but it turns out it was McTavish all along.

As for the rest, however... well, that was all my fault, wasn't it?

Because McTavish might have lit the fuse, but I was the one who burned down the Town Hall. And there's absolutely no point in me being mad at him about it now.

"So, I wasn't voted Queen?" I ask in a small voice.

"Well, no," McTavish admits, looking embarrassed. "It was

Lexie, really. I voted for ye, though. And so did Frankie."

Of course they did. Loyal to the last, the pair of them. And I've barely even asked them how they are since I've been back.

"You didn't tell me why you want to go to the ball?" I say softly, hoping to change the subject.

"Ach, that's the embarrassin' bit," he replies, staring at his feet. "Frankie will have told ye about my wee issue with cash flow, I'm sure?"

"She did. I was sorry to hear it," I say gravely.

"Well, ye ken what it's like to not have any money," Mc-Tavish nods. "The thing is, though, Emerald, I have a wee bit o' land I'm hoping to sell. It borders the Buchanan Estate, and I was hoping yer man over there might see his way to buying it from me."

"He's not my man," I say automatically. "But yeah, I guess he might. It's worth a shot, anyway."

"Well, that's where you come in," McTavish says. "See, there's no way someone like me's ever going to get close to the Laird. But you ken him. So I was hoping ye would bring me along to this ball o' his, and maybe when I'm there, I can find a way to talk to him? I did try once before. I went round to that distillery o' his in the tractor, but then I saw ye with him, so I just snuck away again."

So that's what he was doing at the distillery that night.

As bad as my day has been, and as dejected as I'm feeling right now, I can't help but suppress a smile at the thought of McTavish casually sidling up to Jack at a masquerade ball and striking up a conversation; probably about pigs or sheep, which, let's face it, are the things McTavish most often tends to strike up conversations about.

Not that I'll be there to see it.

The smile falls from my face as I realize I can't do what McTavish is asking me. Because I'm leaving. And never coming back. And this one tiny little favor — the only thing he's ever asked of me in his life — is going to have to be refused.

I chew thoughtfully on a nail as I ponder just how to break this to him. Before I can come to any decisions, though, my phone pings, and I glance down to see a message from Frankie:

> *Emerald, I know this is a big ask given how things are between us right now, but I really need your help. The twins have both come down with food poisoning, and they're supposed to be helping out at the ball tomorrow night. Apparently some extra guests have turned up, and Elaine needs us to clean the rooms while they're all at the party. Can you fill in? I wouldn't ask if I wasn't desperate. Fx*

I frown. Frankie did mention something about having to be on hand on the night of the ball itself for any last-minute cleaning duties. I wasn't really paying attention, to be honest, because she'd said she had it covered. Now, though, it looks like she doesn't.

"Emerald?"

McTavish is still waiting for my answer. Before I can give him it, my phone pings again. Jack, this time.

> *Hey, how're the feet after that walk? You are still coming tomorrow night, aren't you? Please tell me you are. I'm going to need you to save me from all this socializing...*

Even his name on my phone makes the blood rush to my head. This is so unfair. I feel like I'm somehow being tested. And I've never been particularly good under pressure. Before I can answer him either, though, there's yet another ping. Frankie again:

> *Please, Emerald, I'm desperate. I can't find anyone else to fill in. I'm counting on you! Fx*

"McTavish, what happened to your teeth?" I ask impulsively, putting the phone down again. "You never did tell me."

"They got knocked out during the fire at the town hall," he says easily, as if it's no big deal. "I made it out fine, but I went back in to make sure you were okay, and a bit of the stage fell on me. Ach, it's nothing," he adds, seeing the stricken look on my face. "They're just teeth. I was always an ugly bugger, anyway. So, what d'ye say about the ball? Will ye take me?"

I look down at the phone, with its three unanswered messages, then back up at McTavish, with his kind, blue denim eyes, and his hopeful expression. *I'm counting on you*, says Frankie's message. She's counting on me, and so is McTavish, who *literally* ran back into a burning building to look for me. Jack's counting on me too, apparently, although I'm under absolutely no illusions that he's not going to be able to cope without my presence. I know Frankie will really struggle without me, though. And McTavish won't be able to go at all.

My friends need me. I've been letting them down ever since I got back to Heather Bay, too consumed by my own drama to even think about anyone else. But, just like I told Frankie, I can change. I can fix this.

And all of a sudden, I know how to do it.

Chapter 29

And that's how I came to find myself standing in front of the mirror in my childhood bedroom, wearing the most beautiful dress I've ever seen, and feeling like the world's biggest fraud.

Which I kind of *am.*

"Ye look beautiful, love," Mum says from behind me, her voice strangely wobbly. "Doesn't she look beautiful, Archie?"

"Aye," says Dad, sniffing ostentatiously. "As pretty as a picture."

They're acting like this because after the conversation they overheard — sorry, eavesdropped on — between me and McTavish, they think this is the closest they're ever going to get to being parents of the bride. And they're probably right, given how disastrous my love life has turned out to be.

I have scrubbed up better than usual, though, I have to admit. The green dress I borrowed from Bella fits like it was made for me, and the masquerade mask I'm holding actually *was* made for me; by Mum, no less, using a tutorial she found on Ada Valentine's Instagram, apparently.

I'm wearing a pair of high, sparkly gold sandals I'm 89.7% sure I won't trip up in, and although my hair is as unruly as ever (Ada Valentine didn't have a tutorial for performing miracles, sadly), it still looks better than usual, because sitting on top of it is the pièce de résistance, in the shape of Bella's Gala Queen crown. Dad's already made several jokes about my "crowning glory", and I suspect there will be several more before the night is done.

I don't care, though, because, for what must be the first time in my life, the image of myself I see in the mirror actually looks exactly like the image I carry around in my head. My knees may be shaking, and I've had to top up my anti-antiperspirant twice already, but I at least *look* like the person I've always wanted to be. And I might look like Scarlett, but I *feel* 100% Emerald. And that's the way I'm going to stay.

Just to prove it, tucked inside the beaded evening bag Mum dug out for me from her own wardrobe is a letter to Jack, which I wrote — and then re-wrote — as soon as McTavish left last night. The letter explains everything. How I was trying on Scarlett's clothes when he knocked on the door; how I made the wrong decision to try to protect Frankie's business; how sorry I am that I didn't make the right one. I tried to keep it short — to just cover the basics and retain just a little bit of dignity — but, before I knew it, all the rest of the story had come tumbling out, too: Ben, and the Gala Day, and the fact that, no matter how hard I try, I never, ever seem to get things right.

Until now.

My plan, hastily conceived at 2am this morning, as Jude Paw snored softly on the end of my bed, is to give Jack the note as soon as I arrive — or as soon as I've introduced him to McTavish, anyway — so I can't chicken out later. Then I'll go and find Frankie, help her do whatever she needs, and then... that's as far as I've got in my planning, actually.

I don't know what comes after me giving Jack the note.

I *do* know that, come hell or high water, tonight is the night I start telling the truth.

And I'm only around 98% terrified about it.

"Emerald, Alfonso's here!"

I pick up the long skirt of my dress and make my way down the stairs, keeping all of my fingers crossed that McTavish isn't going to be waiting at the bottom holding a corsage, like we're in an American prom movie. Fortunately, though, although McTavish is, indeed, waiting nervously in the hall, flanked by a beaming Mum and Dad and a put-out looking Jude Paw, there's no corsage to be seen. There is, however, something even more amazing; because as he turns and smiles up at me, I notice he's smiling with a full set of teeth.

"McTavish, your teeth!" I exclaim as I reach the bottom of the stairs, grateful not to have tripped up on my dress, which was my other big fear for the evening. "What happened?"

"Got them fixed," he grins, looking proud as punch. "I've been meanin' to do it for a while, actually. I was just lucky Mike at the dentist could fit me in at short notice. Owed me a favor, so he did."

I don't want to ask what kind of favor Mike-the-dentist might owe McTavish, so I just put a hand on his harm and squeeze it reassuringly.

"Well, I think you look fantastic," I tell him, ignoring the loaded look Mum shoots at Dad. "I mean, you did anyway, obviously, but you look even more fantastic now."

He does, too. He's wearing the full Highland regalia, kilt and all, and his hair is neatly combed back, making his eyes stand out even more against his face, which is lightly tanned from all that time he spends outdoors. He's actually quite good-looking, I realize with surprise. How did I never notice that before?

There's no time to think about McTavish and his Clark Kent-style makeover, though, because, before I know it, Mum's ushering us out the door, Dad's beeping the car horn impatiently, and McTavish and I are rushing outside in a flurry of tartan and taffeta.

We're going to the ball.

And Cinderella herself could not possibly have felt more nervous.

* * *

Jack's house is lit up like the Magic Kingdom. The trees that line the road leading up to it are threaded with fairy lights, and when we reach the house itself, there are floodlights pointing up at the towers, making it look like Cinderella's Castle, only a bit more *Scottish*.

People are milling around in small groups, both inside the house, and out here on the lawn, all of them dressed to the nines, and looking like they're on a film set or something. It's all very 'Great Gatsby', just without the American accents. And, well, all the *death*, I hope. I can't really *count* on it under the circumstances, though, can I?

For once, the weather is on my side, and it's the perfect balmy, midsummer's night, the sun still high in the sky even though it's almost 7pm.

"Going to be a storm," Dad mutters darkly from the driver's seat as we pull up outside the house.

"Aye. A bad one, too," comments McTavish, unfolding himself from the passenger seat — for once it seems Jude Paw has been usurped — and coming to open my door for me. I say nothing. I know dad's an ex-fisherman and McTavish is a farmer, so they presumably know more about the weather than I do, but, to me, this evening seems perfect. Or at least it would be, if it wasn't for the whole "impostor-about-to-confess" thing.

There is that.

Swallowing down the nerves that have started to rise in my throat, I take the arm McTavish offers me, and raise my mask to my eyes before we climb the stairs to the front door, me handing my invitation to the be-suited gentleman — is that a *butler?* Does Jack seriously have a *butler?* — who steps forward to open it for us.

The butler (Nope, I still can't believe he has a *butler...*) takes the invitation and looks curiously at us both but doesn't comment. I breathe a sigh of relief as he ushers us forward into the giant lobby I remember from the day I came here to clean with Frankie. I'm past the first hurdle. The hired suit on the door has accepted me as Scarlett Scott, and has accepted McTavish as my plus-one, even though the invitation didn't *technically* say I could bring one.

I'm in.

Now I just have to find Jack, give him the note, find Frankie, do a quick spot of house-cleaning, and work out what the hell happens next.

First, though, I'm going to need a drink. A big one.

* * *

McTavish and I are standing awkwardly by one of the stair-cases, each clutching a glass of champagne (Which McTavish says tastes like "boiled pish". I don't ask him how he knows.), when I see him.

Jack comes walking down the staircase opposite the one we're standing next to, his ocean eyes scanning the crowd below him. In his black bow tie and dinner suit, he looks every inch the Laird of the Manor. Only I know he doesn't actually feel it, though, and my heart goes out to him as I see him hesitate for just a moment on the bottom step, before striding forward confidently, his hand outstretched as he starts welcoming his guests.

You would never even guess how much he hates all of this.

Unlike everyone else here, Jack hasn't bothered with a masquerade mask. Not that it would've mattered even if he had. I mean, it's not like those things *actually* hide your identity, is it? It's not like when Clark Kent puts his glasses back on, and suddenly no one can tell he's really Superman. If that kind of thing actually worked in real life, I wouldn't be feeling even a fraction as nervous as I am right now.

"They're not very good, these, are they?" I mutter to McTavish, waving my own mask in front of me on its stick. "Mum did a great job, don't get me wrong. But it's not much of a disguise, really. Especially when you have hair like mine to give me away."

It's true. I've already spotted Bella McGowan, Doreen from the post office, and I'm pretty sure that guy over there is a news anchor or something; he looks really familiar. One person I haven't yet seen, however, is Scarlett Scott, and the thought makes my heart beat even faster in my chest. She might not be here yet, but I know she'll be here soon. Which means I have to get to Jack before she does, otherwise... Well. I don't even need to finish that sentence, do I?

"Why would ye want to disguise yerself, though?" McTavish starts to say, but I'm not listening, because, in the time it took me to work out which channel I've seen the news anchor guy on, Jack has found a new friend, who's clinging to his arm and gazing up at him adoringly.

Lexie.

Why am I not surprised?

"Come on, McTavish," I say firmly, grabbing him by the sleeve of his jacket. "We're going in."

* * *

Lexie looks amazing.

Evil, of course — the woman is made of pure evil, after all — but still: amazing.

Her golden blonde hair is styled in a Grace Kelly wave, without a single lock out of place. Her lips are bright red, to match her strapless evening gown, and her eyeliner is winged; which I know because, although she is carrying a gold, jewel-encrusted eye mask, she's not bothering to wear it either. Well, would *you* cover your face if it looked like Lexie's? Exactly.

She looks like a 1950s movie star, and although the dress I'm wearing is probably from that era, next to Lexie I just feel old-fashioned and a little bit dull.

"Hello Emerald," she purrs, looking me up and down as she spots us approaching. "Alfonso."

McTavish and I nod in unison, like puppets, and I see Jack's eyes light up and then darken again as he turns to see us both

258

hovering behind him.

"Emerald, you made it!" He bobs forward, as if he's about to kiss me on the cheek, then he glances at McTavish and steps back again, his hands clasped firmly behind his back.

"You look beautiful," he says, sounding as if he's speaking at gunpoint. Also, he appears to be looking at McTavish, rather than me, as he says it. Which, okay, isn't *quite* the effect I was hoping this dress would have, but...

"*Really* beautiful," he says again, this time looking me in the eye and managing to sound a little more like he means it. This time, there's the faintest suggestion of a smile somewhere behind his eyes. Not an *actual* smile, of course, but like he's *thinking* about smiling, but hasn't fully committed to it yet.

I smile back uncertainly. All I can think about is the letter, and how I don't want to give it to him. I'm definitely not going to do it in front of the audience of Lexie and McTavish, though.

"Oh!" I say, remembering one of the reasons I'm here in the first place. "Jack, this is my friend McTavish. You might recall me mentioning him to you?"

I place heavy emphasis on the word "friend" and give Jack what I hope is a meaningful look, to remind him of our conversation about McTavish and I, and how we're not actually having the torrid romance Jack thought we were.

"Is there something in your eye, Emerald?" Lexie asks sweetly, as Jack shakes McTavish's hand with obvious reluctance. "You've got a really strange expression on your face."

I turn and bare my teeth at her in an approximation of a grin. *This is horrific. I'm going to have to do something.*

"Look, isn't that Jett Carter?" I say excitedly, pointing to a man standing just across the room. The poor guy looks nothing like the world's most famous actor — not even in a mask —

but the distraction he provides as the three people I'm with all turn to stare at him (Lexie's head moving fastest, I can't help but notice...) is just enough for me to pull the letter out of my bag and slip it into Jack's pocket.

There.

It's done.

There's no going back now. He's going to read it, and he's going to know exactly who I am. Then he's probably going to explode with anger and run off with Lexie, while declaring he never wants to see my stupid face again. Unless...

The second the letter leaves my possession, I know I need to get it back. All of a sudden, the letter seems like the coward's way out. I can't leave it like this. I can't leave *him* like this. I need to know if there's any possibility at all that he might actually like me for who I am, rather than for I've been pretending to be. It's a long shot, I know, but all the same...

As everyone turns away from the man who isn't Jett Carter, and Lexie makes her disappointment clear, I surreptitiously start inching my hand back towards Jack's pocket and that traitorous letter. The small movement, however, catches his attention, and he turns to look at me, his eyes meeting mine with an intensity that makes time stand still. For a long, delicious, moment, we just stand there gazing at each other, as if we're the only two people in the room, and Lexie and McTavish aren't standing right next to us, gently bickering about Jett Carter and his latest girlfriend.

The moment stretches on, and I realize I'm holding my breath in anticipation. Jack's eyebrow raises almost imper-ceptibly in an unspoken question, which I struggle to decode. Is he wondering if I've been thinking about the kiss? (Yes.) About him? (Oh yes.) About *us*? (Very much yes.) Or is he just wondering what my hand's doing next to his jacket pocket? Or maybe he's wondering...

"Isn't that your phone?" he asks, nodding towards my handbag, which, sure enough, is emitting a loud buzzing noise.

I really must start putting this thing on silent.

"Whoops!" I say, a blush creeping up my face as I reach quickly into the bag, pull out the phone, and glance quickly at the display.

Frankie.

I completely forgot about Frankie.

Chapter 30

"**W**hat the actual fuck, Emerald? What on earth are you wearing?"

As it turns out, I'm only running a couple of minutes late by the time I meet Frankie at the designated spot, just outside the front of the house. If she was thinking about scolding me for my lateness, though, it would've had to have waited until she stopped laughing at my outfit.

"Did you... did you think you had to dress like you were actually going to the ball?" she splutters at last, wiping her eyes. "Oh my God, only you, Emerald!"

"Haha, yeah, only me," I reply, smiling weakly. "What am I like?"

"Well, there's nothing we can do about it now," says Frankie, who is, of course, flying the Highland Maids flag in her branded uniform, which has been neatly ironed for the occasion. "Good job we've only got a couple of bedrooms to clean. Imagine if you had to do the whole house dressed like that?"

She starts laughing again, and I allow myself to relax slightly. At least she's still talking to me, then. After our last encounter, I wasn't so sure she would be.

"You okay?" she asks gruffly, as we turn and walk back towards the house.

"Yeah. You?" This is as close to a heart-to-heart about our last conversation as Frankie and I are going to get; big shows of emotion are really not her style — which is why her outburst the other night was so surprising to me.

"Yeah," she says now. "I was quite enjoying watching all the posh folk rock up to this do while I was waiting for you," she goes on, chuckling. "There was this one woman they wouldn't let in because she didn't have an invitation. She kept insisting someone must have taken it, because she was definitely supposed to be 'on the list'. Oh, look, there is she is!"

She points to where a tall, dark-haired woman is standing, talking furiously into a phone, while casting dirty looks at the guy on the door, who just shakes his head wearily at her. I blink as I suddenly realize who I'm looking at.

It's Scarlett.

And the reason she didn't get into the party was the fact that her invitation is currently in my evening bag.

"Just a second," I mutter to Frankie, "I have to do something."

Then, before I have a chance to think twice, I hold my mask up to my eyes, then dart across the driveway to where Scarlett is standing, pulling out the invitation as I go.

"Um, excuse me; I think you dropped this," I mumble self-consciously as I hand it to her. Scarlett looks down at the invitation in surprise, then back up at me.

"Thanks," she says, looking confused. "Sorry, have we met? I feel like I know you from somewhere?"

Before she can figure out where it is, I turn and run back to Frankie, who's too busy checking her phone to have noticed where I went.

"Come on," I say, tugging her sleeve. "Let's go around the back. I know the way."

* * *

I spend the next ninety minutes living my own personal hell as I dash between Frankie and McTavish, cleaning rooms with one, sipping champagne with the other, and doing my best not to let either of the two know what I'm up to.

Oh, and I'm also doing my best to avoid Jack, Lexie, Scarlett, and, well, anyone else who might possibly know me.

As parties go, it's not the best one I've ever been to, to be perfectly honest.

One thing it's proved to me once and for all, though, is that this whole "double life" thing is not for me. I just don't know how people do it. All those men you hear about who have a wife and kids in one town, and then a whole other family in another, neither of whom knows about each other? How are they pulling that off, I wonder? And can I maybe get some tips here? Because I'm not even two hours in yet, and I'm exhausted. *Exhausted.* Not just by the effort of keeping up the deception — which is hard enough — but also by the knowledge that Jack is right here, under the same roof I am, and with a ticking time-bomb in his pocket in the shape of my letter.

As I clean and chat and swap identities at the drop of a hat, I develop a weird kind of sixth sense, which allows me to know exactly where he is in the room at any given time; a skin-tingling awareness of his presence, almost as if he's tied to me with some kind of invisible thread. That's how I know when he starts thinking about coming over to talk to me again, and although I quickly hand my champagne glass to McTavish (I'm in "party guest" mode right now, while Frankie is upstairs, polishing one of the bath taps...) and try to make a run for it, I'm not quite fast enough. Before I know it, he's standing in front of me again, and when I try to move away, I realize my legs don't want to move.

He's going to say something about the letter. He must have read it by now, surely?

"I'm going to be making a speech soon, to launch the new brand," Jack says, tugging at his bow tie. It takes a second for my brain to catch up with this and register that the 'brand' he's talking about is The 39: a.k.a the reason we're all here.

So... I guess he hasn't read it, then?

"I was thinking you could then say something about the Gala Day fundraiser right after that?" he goes on, totally oblivious to the fact that my heart has just stopped beating at his words. "Elaine has got your Bella McGowan set up in the other room with a stack of paper and some pens, so she's ready to take the details of anyone who's interested in helping out. All you'd have to do is say a few words about the event and what it means to the town. You could—"

"No."

The word is out of my mouth before I even have time to think about it. Jack stops in the middle of his sentence and looks at me, frowning.

"No?"

"I mean... well, I mean 'no'," I tell him apologetically. "I can't... I don't do public speaking. I'm too shy." Jack raises an eyebrow at this but doesn't comment, so I blunder on.

"Anyway," I add, "I think it would be better if Bella does that. She's the chair of the committee, after all."

"Okay." He shrugs, as if none of this could possibly be of less interest to him. "Will you at least stick around, though? To give me some moral support? I don't normally 'do' public speaking either, you see."

"Sure." I smile at him reassuringly. His shirt is open at the neck, and he's still tugging irritably at his bow tie, which is dangerous for me, because that whole "open shirt, undone tie" look is a particular weakness of mine. His eyes meet mine, and something unfathomable passes between us. Something I would very much like to fathom, if I only had the time.

"Emerald, I—"

Whatever he's about to say is lost as a ringing sound fills the air and everyone looks around to where the man Jack referred to as his PR manager (Or "the man from the stairs," as I think of him) is standing on a small stage that's been erected at the far end of the room.

"If I could ask everyone to gather around, please," he calls, tinging a fork against his champagne glass again. "Mr. Buchanan would like to say a few words."

"Well, here goes nothing," mutters Jack, as all eyes in the room swivel around to look at him — and, by association, me — curiously.

"Jack!" I call out his name before I can stop myself, but, as he turns back to face me, I know I can't possibly tell him about the letter right now, with everyone watching. Instead, I take a step closer, then stand on my tiptoes to straighten his bow tie, while he stands there, looking slightly nonplussed, but nevertheless pleased.

"There you go," I say awkwardly, smoothing down his lapel.

"Now you're perfect."

You were always perfect.

"Oh, I forgot to tell you," he says over his shoulder as he walks away. "Finn's here! He got back from Glasgow this morning, apparently. He should be around here somewhere..."

And, with that, he turns and walks away, leaving me to the horrified realization that there's yet another person here tonight who could very easily blow my cover at any second.

I really should have left while I had the chance. Damn McTavish and Frankie for persuading me to come here.

Jack climbs up onto the stage, takes a microphone from the man beside him, and immediately launches into a short speech, welcoming everyone and thanking us all for coming to this party. He speaks easily and eloquently, like a man who's been charming audiences his entire life, despite his earlier protestations. He even manages to get a few laughs.

I, however, barely hear a word he says, because now I know the dreaded Finn McNeil — Scarlett's interfering cousin — is somewhere in the room, every nerve in my body is stretched taught, just waiting for him to pounce. As I stand there, a rigid smile on my face as I pretend to listen to Jack, I imagine eyes boring into the back of my skull, whispers filling the air, someone's breath on the back of my... actually, no, wait, there really *is* someone standing so close behind me that I can feel their breath on the back of my neck! I whip quickly around, but, to my relief, it's just Lexie, who smiles sweetly. For once, I'm actually glad to see her. Then she speaks.

"Hello, Scarlett," she says.

There's a loud gasp, which appears to be coming from me, and then the world seems to tilt on its axis, the floor beneath my feet tilting wildly under me, as if I'm on a ship on the high seas. The blood rushes to my head, and then drops instantly back down to my feet, like it's trying to escape the scene of a crime. *My* crime.

"Wh-what?"

A few of the people standing closest to us turn round to stare, and someone shushes us, annoyed at the interruption. Lexie shuffles forward until her lips are almost touching my ear. "Sorry, did I get that wrong?" she whispers, her eyes wide with faux-innocence. "It's just, I could swear you were calling yourself Scarlett these days?"

The words hang ominously in the air between us as I stare at her, horrified.

"How?" is all I manage to say. "How did you know?"

"Oh, that was easy enough," Lexie whispers, grinning poisonously. "Scarlett showed me a photo the other day that someone had sent to her magazine, along with an article that claimed to be by her. The thing is, though," she shuffles even closer, "Scarlett didn't actually write it. Can you imagine? Someone else wrote it, pretending to be her!"

She pulls back just enough to let me catch the mocking look in her eyes before continuing.

"When she showed me the photo," she says, still speaking so softly that only I can hear, "I felt like I'd seen it before. It was only this morning that I remembered where it was: on your phone, on the day of the hike."

I want to turn and run, but my legs won't move. It's like I'm stuck in one of those nightmares where you're trying to escape some unseen danger, but your legs feel like they're weighed down with lead. Instead, I just have to stand there, tears pricking at the back of my eyes, as Lexie goes on.

"I still wasn't 100% sure, of course," she says, thoughtfully.

"I mean, it seemed like a really bizarre thing to do, even for you, Emerald. But then I bumped into Scarlett again a few minutes ago, and she told me you'd walked up to her and handed her an invitation to this very party. One with her name on it. Imagine!"

I don't have to imagine, though. I know exactly what I've done. What I don't know — and desperately *need* to know — is what Lexie's going to do about it.

"Would you two shut up?"

The man directly in front of us turns and glares at us, and Lexie and I dutifully turn and face the front of the room, where Jack is still standing on the stage, addressing the room. He's talking now about his grandfather; how he was the one who had the idea to start a new distillery here in Heather Bay, and how he died before it came to fruition.

"He may not be here to see it," Jack says, "But I'd like to think he'd have been proud of the whisky we've created in his honor."

I think I'm probably the only person in the room who can hear the lump in his throat. It's hard to detect, but it's there, nevertheless, and, just for a second, an emotion other than terror forces its way to the front of my mind.

Pride. Even in spite of my current predicament, I'm so proud of him, and what he's achieved, that I want to burst into applause; to let him know how well he's done. Instead, I force myself to stand there quietly, Lexie's breath still damp on my skin, as Jack walks over to a large screen that's been set up to one side of the makeshift stage.

"Well," he says, with that boyish grin I love so much, "Here goes. Ladies and gentlemen, The 39!"

He presses a button in his hand, and a photo of the distillery appears on the screen, overlaid with a logo: a circle with the name of the blend around the edges and a stylized drawing of a wolf in the center.

A wolf.

A drawing of a wolf.

Now, where have I seen that before?

I frown, trying to remember. And, all of a sudden, it comes to me.

I guess Lexie isn't the only one with a good memory for a photo.

"Lexie," I say pleasantly, taking advantage of the applause which echoes through the room as the branding is unveiled. "Why did you have photos of Jack's whisky stills in your house the other day?"

There's a long silence from behind me, during which the applause finally dies down, and the breathing on my neck becomes suddenly ragged.

"Lexie?"

I turn, expecting to see her eyes blazing with defiance. Instead, though, they're filled with fear.

"Please, Emerald, don't tell anyone," she whispers desperately. "You can't tell anyone. Please, I'm begging you."

Well, well, well. How the tables have turned.

"What do you mean, Lexie?" I hiss, grabbing her by the elbow and dragging her to the back of the room, away from the crowd. "Are you saying it was you who sabotaged Jack's distillery? Did you do something to the stills? Is that why you had those photos?"

"Not me," Lexie stutters, all of her earlier bravado suddenly gone. "I swear it wasn't me who did it. You have to believe me, Emerald. I didn't do it. It was... It was..."

"Let me guess," I say, crossing my arms over my chest and

fixing her with a stare. "It was your mother, right? Trying her best to get rid of the competition, I suppose?"

I wait for her to reply, but she simply stares sullenly at her feet. Her beautiful face is pale beneath her makeup, the red lipstick standing out like a slash of crimson blood in the snow.

"Please don't tell anyone," she says again at last. "You can't tell anyone, Emerald. She'll be so furious with me."

"But, Lexie," I say, pushing my hair out of my eyes. "It's you who should be furious with her! She did this! Her! Not you. Although..." My words trail off as another thought hits me. "You might not have done it," I say in a low voice. "But you did know about it, didn't you?"

Lexie shakes her head slowly, but it's more of a confirmation than a denial.

"You knew, and you did nothing to stop it," I say, anger starting to rise. "Do you realize how serious this is, Lexie? Jack could've been seriously injured that night! So could his staff! Did you and your mum ever stop to think about that?"

It's as if Lexie is shrinking before my eyes, her confidence melting away like the Wicked Witch of the West when Dorothy throws the bucket of water over her. It's not a nice feeling, to be ruining someone like this. But I think of her words to me just a few minutes ago; the mocking satisfaction in her eyes as she told me how she'd worked out my secret. And, in that moment, I see red.

"I'm telling Jack," I say flatly. "Or the police. Or *someone.* I'm sorry, Lexie, but you can't just go around messing with people's lives like that and expect to get away with it."

"What, like you thought you'd get away with pretending to be Scarlett Scott?" Lexie hisses back, suddenly recovering some of her old spirit. "Because, let's face it, Emerald, it's not like you're some kind of angel here, are you? And if you tell Jack my secret, you better believe I'll be telling him yours."

On the stage, Jack is working his way through a few more slides, all showing suitably Scottish scenes; heather, and mountains, and stags... all, of course, accompanied by a bottle of Heather Bay's newest malt.

"My grandfather was proud to be a part of this community," Jack is saying now. "He loved Heather Bay, and everything it represented to him: family, and friendship, and, above all, home. And he wanted, more than anything, to give something back to the village he loved."

My mind whirs as I listen to his words. From just in front of the stage, Bella McGowan gives a whoop of approval. Next to her, McTavish is smiling from ear to ear, his cheeks ruddy from all the whisky he's already sampled. Not far from them both, I see that Frankie has snuck in, taking a break from her cleaning duties to nod along at Jack's words, her blonde curls bouncing their agreement.

I feel a hard lump rise in my throat as I look at them all. This is the community I turned my back on, all those years ago. The people I'm planning to turn my back on yet again, just as soon as this night is over. And, you know what?

It's really not so bad.

"I mean it, Emerald," Lexie murmurs from beside me. She's now fully recovered from her shock, I see, and she knows all too well that she's got me here. If I tell someone — *anyone* — that Lexie's mum was responsible for the break-in at the distillery, she'll immediately tell them I've been impersonating Scarlett, and that way we'll both lose. If I don't tell anyone, though, I'll be letting down my friends and my community yet again.

I'll be letting down Jack.

And I'm just not going to do it.

"To honor that wish," Jack is saying from the stage, "I'm happy to announce that The 39 will be sponsoring the Heather Bay Gala Day, which will return next year for the first time in a decade."

The room erupts in applause, and Jack grins down in surprise at the excitement he's just created. "I'd like to thank Bella McGowan here," he says, nodding to where Bella's spiky head can just be seen in the crowd, "for chairing the committee who've worked so hard to bring this much-loved event back to Heather Bay. I'd also like to—"

I tune out again as I turn to face Lexie, who's watching me with the air of a woman who knows she's won.

Well, not this time, bitch.

"I'm sorry, Lexie," I say bluntly. "But I have to tell him. You can do what you want to me. I really don't care anymore."

Lexie's eyes blaze with an intensity I've never seen from her.

"Is that right?" she says coldly, taking a step towards me. "I think you just might live to regret that, Emerald. I really do."

I can actually see the exact moment she decides to do it. It's written all over her obnoxiously pretty face, and, the next thing I know, her hand fastens around my wrist like a handcuff, and she starts dragging me towards the stage, almost pulling me off my high heels with the sudden movement.

"Coo-ee, Jack!" she calls brightly as she pulls me level with her. "Isn't there someone else you'd like to thank for her hard work? Everyone, let's have a round of applause for Scarlett Scott! And here she is!"

With a single sharp shove from behind, she propels me forward, right to the front of the stage, and all the back in time, to when I was eighteen years old, and about to be crowned

Queen of the Heather Bay Gala.

Chapter 31

Ten years earlier

The Gala Day smells like cut grass and cotton candy. Of toffee apples and late afternoon rain. It smells like dashed hopes and disappointment; and it also smells like stale tobacco smoke, thanks to Lexie Steele and the pack of cigarettes she'd stolen from her mum earlier that morning.

"Want one?"

I'm standing behind the makeshift stage that's been set up in the town hall, nervously twisting the fabric of my prom dress through my fingers as I wait for my big moment. I thought this was what I wanted; but now that it's actually happening, I'm so nervous I'd give anything to swap places with Lexie, who's been asked to help out backstage, but who's actually just been standing around smoking, as far as I can tell.

"Here, take one. It'll help calm your nerves. Trust me."

Lexie's standing beside me now, holding out the packet of cigarettes. The four short sentences she's just uttered to me count as the longest conversation I've ever had with her, and even though I haven't actually contributed to it yet, the fact that the most popular girl in the school is even talking to me is almost as exciting as the thought of being crowned Gala

275

Queen.

Which will be happening in just a few short minutes.

My stomach clenches with anxiety, emitting a low growling sound. I will literally die if Lexie heard that. No, I mean it. I will die. Literally.

"Here."

Ignoring the interruption from my traitorous belly, Lexie thrusts the cigarettes towards me again. I hesitate as I look down at the open pack. I really want her to like me. I want, more than anything — more even than I wanted to be Gala Queen — to be the kind of person Lexie Steele likes.

The problem is, I don't smoke.

I don't even **want** to smoke.

Mum has frequently told me she'll kill me if I ever take up smoking, and I have absolutely no doubt that she means it.

But Lexie's offering me a cigarette, and I'm not stupid: I know it's more than that. It's acceptance she's offering me. Belonging. And acceptance is the thing I crave the most so, with what I hope is an air of confidence, I take the cigarette she's offering me and put it in my mouth, leaning forward to let her light it.

Smoke instantly fills my lungs, making me cough. I'm choking. I think I'm probably dying, actually. It's okay, though, because Lexie's smiling at me. "Welcome to the club," her smile says. "Come on in."

With an effort of will that I didn't know I had in me, I straighten up, stifle the cough, and take another, hesitant puff of the cigarette. This time the smoke doesn't burn. It's not too bad, actually; and, even if it was, here I am, side-by-side with Lexie Steele, finally one of the cool girls.

Now that's definitely something to celebrate.

The moment, though, is all too short, because, before I can take another drag, there's a flurry of applause from the other side of the stage, and the disembodied voice of Bella McGowan echoes through the village hall, telling everyone it's time welcome Heather Bay's newest Gala Queen.

Me.

"Quick," Lexie says, pushing me hard in the back. "It's your moment, Emerald. They're waiting for you."

I don't want to go, but Lexie pushes me again, and my legs have no choice but to stumble their way forward. As I go, I twist round and hurriedly hand the cigarette to Lexie, who reaches out for it, before giving me one final push, which propels me through the backstage curtain and out onto the stage.

With my dress on fire.

Literally, I mean.

That's not just some bad metaphor for how hot I'm looking or something; I mean the skirt of my prom dress is **actually** in flames, smoke billowing from my backside in a way that would almost be comedic if it didn't mean my life was in mortal danger.

The applause that had started up as I appeared on stage quickly turns to screams of horror as everyone realizes the Gala Queen is here — and she's on fire.

It's quite an entrance, to be fair. I'm not sure there's ever been one quite like it. Leave it to me to bring the drama.

For a split second, I just stand there gawping down stupidly at my dress, and then suddenly Lexie's there behind me, tugging hard at the skirt, which dramatically parts company from the bodice with an obscenely loud ripping sound that I can hear even above the hubbub of noise from the over-excited audience. At some point in the future, I'll probably

277

want to thank Lexie for saving my life with her quick-thinking. Right now, though, I've just turned eighteen, I'm so self-conscious that I blush when anyone tries to talk to me... and I'm standing on a stage in front of everyone I know, wearing nothing but the top-half of my dress, and my favorite Flying Haggis underpants.

(Look, they're my lucky pants, okay? Of course I was going to be wearing them. It's not like I expected them to be on show to the entire town...)

The shocked silence that follows this sorry situation probably only lasts for a split second, but, for me, it rolls on indefinitely, and it doesn't take me long to work out that I'll be living inside this moment for the rest of my life. In it, I age by roughly 100 years. I go from being the hopeful young Gala Queen, to just some girl standing in front of everyone she knows in her not-very-nice underwear. I am Carrie on her prom night. I'm Neville Longbottom making a fool of himself again in front of the Slytherins. Most of all, though, I'm Emerald Taylor; and I'm never going to be able to show my face in this town again.

After what feels like a lifetime of standing there frozen on the stage, I finally break free of my trance, and turn to run backstage, safe in the knowledge that at least things can't possibly get any worse.

And that's when someone throws the bucket of water over me.

Cold water.

Freezing cold water, in fact.

"Sorry," Lexie gasps, as I scream in shock. "I just wanted to be sure the fire was out."

Okay, **now** *things can't get any worse.*

Sobbing so hard I can hardly see through my tears, I some-how manage to stumble my way back through the curtains behind the stage and into the dressing area, where I hastily grab my coat, throwing it on, and pulling it tightly around my body, as if it can somehow protect me from what just happened.

But it can't. Nothing can; and as I run blindly out into the street, my high heels almost tripping me up as I go, I just want to get as far away from this place as I possibly can.

It's not until much later that I find out what happened after I left. How a spark from my dress had landed on the curtains at the back of the stage, which had smoldered un-noticed for a while before going up in flames, which quickly spread to the wooden stage I'd just been standing on.

By the time the fire brigade arrived, called in from Glenroch, ten miles away, the fire had taken firm hold, and it raged on for hours, until all that was left was an empty shell; a bit like myself, now I come to think of it.

Or that's what I heard, anyway. By the time the fire took hold I was at the top of Westward Tor, looking down on the town, no longer sure whether the wetness on my cheeks came from my tears, or from the rain that had started to fall. I'd already made up my mind to leave; to take the University place I'd been offered in London, rather than one I'd have preferred, in Edinburgh, and to never, ever come back. I'd decided that before I even found out about the fire; but when I finally climbed down from that hill and made my way home, where I found Mum and Dad waiting for me with their "bad news" faces firmly in place, I knew there was no other option.

It was the cigarette, of course; the one Lexie gave me. I must have dropped it on my skirt as I turned to hand it to her.

But... did I, though?

Is that really what happened? Or is that just what I was told, hours after the fact, when Lexie had already given her statement to the police? Was I really the one responsible for the fire that burned down the village hall, and changed the course of my life forever?

Or was it...

Chapter 32

"**Y**OU."

I've somehow ended up on the stage at the masquerade ball, with Jack on one side of me, looking confused, and Lexie on the other, still holding my wrist with a grip so tight I can tell it's going to leave bruises.

"You," I say again, speaking through gritted teeth as I turn to glare at her. "You were the one who dropped the cigarette, weren't you? Did you do it deliberately? Or was it just some kind of 'accident'?"

Lexie doesn't even bother replying to that. Instead, she just stares back at me defiantly, then turns to address the audience in front of us, who are watching us with the kind of interest that suggests they all sense a drama about to unfold. Out of the corner of my eye, I see McTavish trying to work his way through the crowd, his expression serious. Behind him, Frankie's eyes are round 'Os' of shock.

This is really not the way I wanted Jack — who I don't even dare to look at — to find out I've been impersonating Scarlett Scott ever since I met him.

"What do you say, everyone?" Lexie calls out brightly. "Let's have a big cheer for Scarlett Scott" — she says the name in ALLCAPS — "who's responsible for bringing the Gala Day back to Heather Bay."

She holds my hand aloft in triumph, but instead of the cheers she asked for, there's a single beat of silence, and then a gruff voice I recognize as belonging to Jimmy the farmer pipes up from the back of the room.

"I hope tae God not," shouts Jimmy, who's obviously had a few too many over the course of the evening. "Because that's no whoever ye think it is, Lexie, hen. That's yon Emerald Taylor. The one who burned down the hall, ye ken?"

There's a general murmur of agreement at this, but I can't see the reactions of anyone around me, because I've got my eyes tight shut, like a toddler who thinks that if she can't see anyone, then no one can see her, either.

I wish.

"Emerald, what is this?" Jack's voice says in my ear. "What's going on here? Would someone like to explain it to me?"

I open my mouth, but before I can speak, another voice rings out, clear as a bell.

"I've no idea who that is on the stage," says the voice. "But *I'm* Scarlett Scott. And I don't know anything about a Gala Day. Lexie?"

"*I'm* Scarlett Scott," yells McTavish suddenly. I snap open my eyes to see him standing wild-eyed at the front of the stage. Oh my God, he's trying to do *Spartacus*. All I need now is for Frankie to declare that *she's* Scarlett Scott too, and then this evening truly will descend into farce.

"Can someone please tell me what's going on?" Jack snaps. He's having to shout in order to be heard above the buzz of gossip which has started to spread across the room as the partygoers try to figure out what's going on, and why three separate people are all claiming to be someone no one in Heather Bay has ever heard of.

Well, no one except Jack.

With an effort, I raise my eyes to meet his. Judging by his expression, I can tell he's still in the "confused" stage of the emotional journey he's about to go on. Pretty soon, though, that confusion is going to turn to anger, and the anger will probably stick around for a long time, I suspect. Possibly forever.

As for me, meanwhile, a strange sense of calm has descended now that my secret is out. The feeling won't last; I know that. My legs are already threatening to give up on their mission to continue holding me upright, in fact. Right now, though, my sense of outrage at Lexie and what she's done to me — both now and in the past — outweigh everything else. It's the one thing that's keeping me going. And it's also the thing that allows me to finally pull my hand from hers and clear my throat to speak.

"Jack, Lexie's mum was the person who sabotaged the distillery," I say, speaking as clearly and as calmly as I can. "You'll find the photos that will prove it in Lexie's house, but you'll have to get to them before she does, obviously."

A sudden memory comes to me of the day of the hike; me taking Samantha Steele's phone and seeing all of those selfies on the camera roll. Selfies and...

"There are also some photos on her mum's phone," I add, before turning my back to the audience, and speaking quietly, so only he can hear.

"Everything else you need to know is in the letter you'll find in your jacket," I tell him, my voice shaking. "And you're not going to want to speak to me again once you've read it, so I'll just tell you now that I'm sorry; for everything, but most of all, for letting you down. I didn't mean for any of this to happen. I really didn't. But it's happened now, and I just hope...I just hope you don't hate me, is all. Please try not to hate me. Every single word I said to you was the truth. It just wasn't the person you thought it was who was saying it."

My voice is shaking with emotion by the time I finish this short speech and prepare to climb down from the stage. Before I go, though, I realize there's one more thing I want to tell him.

"Your grandfather would be proud of you, Jack," I say softly, reaching up and touching him lightly on one cheek while he stands there looking utterly bamboozled by everything that's happening. "*I'm* proud of you. I just want you to know that."

My vision blurry with tears, I move reluctantly away from him. Part of me is secretly — okay, not-so-secretly — hoping that he'll reach out to stop me. That he'll take the letter out of his pocket and just rip it into pieces before my eyes, telling me he doesn't care what I've done, because he loves me anyway, and he always will.

But, of course, that's movie romances I'm thinking of, isn't it? Fairytale ones. And this is real life, where those things don't happen. Where, when you mess up, you have to live with the consequences.

Well, I guess I may as well make a start on that.

I take one last look at the scandalized faces all staring up at me from the foot of the stage, and my mind whirls back ten years, to that moment on the stage of the Heather Bay village hall. Same people, same looks of horror; just a different stage, and a wholly different accident.

I guess that's the next decade's worth of village gossip sorted, then. Shona McLaren is going to have a hell of a time trying to keep up with this one.

Climbing down from the stage, I make a beeline for Scarlett, who looks much calmer than you'd expect, under the circumstances. Or maybe it's just that she has absolutely no idea what's going on.

The crowd parts to let me through, and I do my best to block out the stares and the whispers that surround me as I walk straight up to the woman whose life I've been pretending to live, and look her right in the eye.

"I'm sorry, Scarlett," I say, wincing at the inadequacy of the words. "I know this probably doesn't make any sense right now, but it will, and when it does, I want you to know I'm sorry, and I'll make it up to you any way I can. I'll contact your editor as soon as I get home and tell her it was me who wrote that article, too."

Scarlett looks at me speculatively. I'm waiting for anger, but, for some reason, it doesn't come.

"You're right," she says at last, her London accent more pronounced than ever. "I have absolutely zero clue what's going on here, but I have to say, it's the most entertaining evening I've had in a while. And here was I thinking the Highlands were going to be sleepy!"

"No," I say wearily, shaking my head. "No, it's not sleepy. I'm really starting to wish it was, to be honest."

It's true. Never again will I complain about how boring my life is. Never again will I wish I was someone else, living a different life. I'm just not cut out for it; and as soon as all this is over, I'm going to go back to being plain old Emerald Taylor.

Whoever she is.

"Look," says Scarlett, rummaging in her evening bag. "I get that this is a bad time, but the journalist in me is sensing one hell of a story here, and I've been thinking about taking a bit of a break from the food and drink stuff, anyway. Between you and me..." she leans in conspiratorially, "I don't even like *whisky*, anyway."

I grin back at her uncertainly, her unexpected kindness suddenly making me want to cry.

I like her.

I wasn't really expecting to like her.

Shame bubbles up inside me, turning my skin tomato red ("That will clash horribly with your hair, Emerald," ex-boyfriend Ben says in my head. Trust him to choose this particular moment to make a comeback...), as Scarlett hands me a business card.

"Give me a call when you can," she says kindly, giving my hand a pat. "I have a feeling we have a lot to talk about."

I just nod in reply to this, not trusting myself to speak without crying. I really want to hug her, but it seems inappropriate, so, instead, I simply stuff the card she's given me into my bag and turn round to take one last look at Jack.

He's reading my letter.

All around him, the room is in chaos; Lexie's mum has appeared from nowhere and is screaming at her daughter, who has both of her hands over her ears, like a toddler who doesn't want to play anymore. Both Assistant Elaine and PR Man John are up on the stage beside Jack, seemingly competing for his attention. Even Old Jimmy has joined the fray and is surreptitiously opening one of the bottles of The 39, which are arranged on a table behind Jack, ready for their launch — which I've ruined.

In the midst of all of this, Jack stands completely motionless on the stage; the one still spot in the room, his eyes fixed on the paper in front of him. As I watch, he seems to reach the end of my ramblings, and finally looks up. As his eyes rake the crush of people in front of him, searching for someone — me, I assume — I cross my fingers tightly behind my back, willing him not to hate me, now he knows the truth.

The room is in an uproar. Someone jostles my elbow, almost knocking me over as they push past. A short distance away, I see Frankie determinedly trying to make her way towards me, elbowing people out of her way as she bulldozes through the crowd.

"Who the fuck is Scarlett Scott, anyway?" I hear someone yell above the general hubbub.

I ignore them all. For now, there's just me and Jack, alone in this crowd. When our eyes meet, it's as if someone has pressed the mute button on the world; the room, and everyone in it, falls away, leaving us alone together.

We're not really alone, though. We're not Darcy and Elizabeth, or Jane Eyre and Mr. Rochester. We're not even Maxim DeWinter and... the second Mrs. DeWinter. Which would have been slightly unsatisfying, sure — I never really rated their relationship — but still better than *this*.

Because Jack Buchanan is not looking at me the way a hero looks at his heroine. Not at all. Even from this distance, I can see the hurt blazing in his blue eyes as he glares across at me. The betrayal. The never-getting-over-this of it all. And, just in case I was in any doubt about that, he folds the letter once, then folds it again, turning it into a neat square, which he tucks into his breast pocket before turning and stalking away, Elaine and John hurrying after him.

He doesn't look back.

By now, Frankie has almost reached me, and I break free of

the trance I've been in to see McTavish hot on her heels.

"Right," Frankie says briskly, reaching for my hand. "I don't know what you've done this time, but let's get you the hell out of here. We can talk about it in the car."

We won't, though, because I just can't do it. I can't leave with Frankie and McTavish, and go back home to Mum and Dad's house, as if this was just some random "accident" of mine that we'll laugh about in years to come. "Remember the time oor Emerald pretended to be a journalist," Dad will chortle, and Mum will shake her head fondly, and follow up with the equally amusing tale of that one time I almost burned Heather Bay to the ground.

But no. This is not something I'm ready to talk about; not now, and probably not ever.

"Frankie, I'm sorry," I say, the sob I've been successfully holding down until now finally breaking free of my throat. "I'll explain everything, I promise, but right now I just need to be on my own."

"Okay then, Greta Garbo," Frankie says, sounding irritated as she lets me go. I only half hear her, though. Because, if Jack really isn't going to even speak to me — which is no more than I deserve, of course — then I just don't want to be here anymore.

It's time to go.

Chapter 33

The thunderstorm Dad and McTavish warned me about has crept up while I was inside the house, and the first fat droplets of rain start to fall as I stumble my way down the steps outside.

I don't know where I'm going, or what I'm going to do when I get there; I just know I need to not be here anymore.

And so I run.

And I run.

I keep running until I reach the familiar territory of the loch, which lies, dark and brooding, just beyond the sloping back lawn of the house, where I stop for a second to catch my breath. The sobs are coming more freely now as I remember how Jack jumped into the water near here to save me and Jude, when I stupidly tried to escape him on a pedalo.

Why did I want to escape him?

Why would I ever want to not be near him?

I can't think about that now, though, or I'll just lie down right here on the shore of the loch and cry, so I stop just for long enough to pull off my high-heeled sandals, which are threatening to break both of my ankles on the pebbled beach of the loch, and then I run for home.

I run blindly, and without thought, through the rain that's

steadily turning into a downpour. Mum and Dad's house is on the opposite bank of the loch, but there's no easy path to it. On this shore, the cliffs at the bottom of the Tor fall almost down to the beach, jagged and menacing against the rapidly darkening sky. I can either go over the hills or around them. The second option, however, means getting into the water itself, and I may not be thinking straight, but I'm not quite far gone enough for the suicide mission that would be trying to swim the loch at night.

My dress is soaked and my feet are already cut and bleeding from the stones I've had to stumble across to get this far — not that my spindly heels would've been much better, mind you — but, fortunately for me, I know this land so well I could quite literally find my way blindfolded.

Or so I thought, anyway.

The Highlands in summer are graced with long hours of daylight; the light never quite seems to leave the sky entirely, even once the sun has set. Tonight, though, the dark clouds which have descended like a blanket on Heather Glen have stolen the sun. If it was light enough to see clearly, I know the tops of the hills next to me would be wreathed in mist. As it is, though, the darkness is so impenetrable it's like a solid obstacle in my path. And for the first time since I left Jack's house, my over-riding emotion is no longer heartbreak.

It's fear.

You don't have to live in the Highlands for long to know how dangerous it can be up here; how the weather can change in the blink of an eye, and how the hills that look tame and friendly in the sunshine take on an altogether different personality in the dark.

I could actually die out here.

The thought hits me as if falling from the top of the mountains themselves. And once it lands, it's determined to stick around.

Of all the mistakes I've made and accidents I've had, this has to be the stupidest one yet.

Then, all of a sudden, my phone starts to ring inside my bag.

My phone! I can't believe I forgot I had it with me!

Pulling it out of my bag, I clamp it to my ear, almost dropping it in my excitement.

"Jack!" I yell into it, the wind instantly whipping my words away. "Jack, is that you?"

The line crackles ominously, then a faint voice comes through.

"Jack? No, it's Brian; Brian from the bank? Is that you, Emerald? Are ye OK?"

Disappointment courses through my body. I so much wanted it to be Jack on the other end of the line that it takes a second or two for me to register that, no matter who's calling me, they can help me get down from this hill.

"Brian, listen," I say urgently, struggling to stay upright on the uneven ground. "I'm at the bottom of Westward Tor, and I need to get home. It's too dark to see. I need you to call mountain rescue for me, okay? Brian? Brian, are you still there? Can you hear me?"

There's no answer; the line has gone dead.

Swallowing my disappointment, I pull the phone away from my ear and look at the signal strength without much hope. The reception's never great up here, even at the best of times, but my spirits rise slightly as I notice a single bar and an almost full-battery.

Yes! Is my luck finally about to change?

As if in answer to that question, the phone slips from my numb fingers and goes tumbling merrily down the hill below me. As I stand there speechless in the dark, I'm sure I hear it shatter on the rocks.

"No!"

I didn't even plan to shout anything — it's not like there's much point after all — but it feels strangely satisfying, so I shout again and again. "NONONONONO!"

I pause, hearing the faint echo of my own voice coming back to me.

I'm on my own, then. No phone, no help, no ... point in finishing that thought. Positive vibes only, as Frankie is fond of saying.

Frankie.

As I force my way forward through the dark, I think longingly of Frankie's warm van, which I could be sitting in right now. Of Mum and Dad's cozy kitchen, which only has a *view* of the mountains, rather than this up-close encounter with them.

The thought of home drives me forward. I might be scared, but I'm not far from the other side of the cliffs, after which it's a straight shot up the comparatively gentle slope of the hill which leads to home.

I can do this.

I am a strong, independent woman, who is absolutely done with having "accidents". This late-night walk will not be one of them.

That's when I hear the growl.

It's so low, and the rain so loud that at first I think I must be imagining it. But then the storm eases up for just a second, and, nope, there it is again: the unmistakable sound of an animal — an angry one, by the sounds of it.

Wolf.

As soon as I hear the third growl, I know what it is. My mind flashes frantically back to my conversation with Jack on our walk; the one where he talked about his plans to introduce wolves back to the Highlands. Re-wilding, he called it. *Insanity*, though, would be a much better word for it. Because if that's a wolf I can hear in the darkness beyond me, then it looks like everything that happened at the masquerade ball tonight is going to be the very least of my worries.

Assuming, that is, that I even live to tell the tale.

Taking a deep, shuddering breath to try and calm myself, I inch slowly forward, not wanting to alert the wolf to my movement. "It's not dangerous, if it's done right," Jack's voice says in my head, an echo of our previous conversation. He seemed so sure this plan of his was a good one, and yet, here I am, almost within sight of home... but with a snarling wolf on my tail.

I guess Jack didn't really expect soaking wet women to be out on the hills in the middle of the night.

At that moment, the first clap of thunder shatters the air, and something in me snaps.

With my heart in my mouth, I scramble forward, falling onto my hands and knees in my haste to get away from the wolf. Another thunderclap follows the first, and lightning flashes almost immediately.

Less than one second between the two. It means the storm is immediately overhead. I can only hope it's loud enough to swallow the sound of my screams as my hands make contact with the sharp shards of stone beneath them.

Blood. Can wolves smell blood? Because I feel like that's something they'd be able to do, and I feel suddenly sick to my stomach as I realize how much trouble I'm in.

As it turns out, I *can't* actually do this, after all.

Behind me, something warm and furry suddenly makes contact with the back of my leg, and panic takes over.

The hill is too steep and too treacherous in the rain to make running a possibility, but it's amazing how quickly you can move with an *actual* wolf on your heels, and I have never in my life been more motivated than I am at this moment.

I feel, rather than see, the wolf behind me as I struggle forward. I'm going in the wrong direction, I know — I need to be going *down* the hill, rather than up it — but turning around now would send me right into the jaws of the beast, so there's no choice but to continue climbing.

Up and up we go, towards the summit of the hill. If my brain was working rationally, I'm sure it would have something to say about the sheer absurdity of this situation ("Classic Emerald," Ben mutters in my head. I swear if I somehow get out of this alive, I will find that man and I will wring his neck, if it's the last thing I do.), but right now I'm moving on autopilot, my weary legs carrying me up this path I must have trodden a hundred times before. Although never with a wolf as a companion, it has to be said.

After what feels like an interminable amount of time, I finally see the stone that marks the summit of the hill. The clouds briefly part, allowing some light to filter through from the moon, and I pause briefly, looking down at the town below, its lights spread out across the glen like jewels on velvet.

I've seen it like this before, of course; the last time being the night of the Gala, when I climbed the hill to scream my frustration at the sky and vow to never come here again.

Such drama.

Such needless drama; especially given that the architect of

my downfall turns out not to be my own, stupid self, but Lexie. Lexie and her jealousy, setting in motion a chain of events, which have ended with me right back where I started — on top of this hill at midnight, with the town spread out before me, and my life once again destroyed.

"You win, Lexie," I mutter weakly, allowing myself to sink to my knees. The ground is muddy and wet, but I can't make myself care. My dress is already ruined. Everything is ruined, and all I want to do is just lie here in the dark and try to convince myself that none of this is actually happening.

So that's what I do.

The wolf has been silent for a while now. I might have somehow managed to shake it off, or it might just be sitting there in the shadows, waiting for the right moment to pounce. I don't know. What I do know is that I've reached the end of the trail: literally. There's nowhere to go now but back down. There's nowhere to shelter from the storm, and there's no one coming to save me, because no one knows where I am.

So I just lie there, rain pounding on my face, heart shattered into a million pieces, and wait to find out what comes next.

It's a light.

A bright, blinding light, shining right down on top of me, visible even through my closed eyelids.

Okay, I'm dead.

I must be.

It's the only explanation. And, let's face it, it's not an altogether unexpected one under the circumstances.

I lie there on the wet ground, considering this. For now, death doesn't appear to be expecting anything of me. It's not painful or scary; possibly because I've lost all sensation in my body at this point, but still. It's actually kind of comforting, really, which is not remotely what I thought it would be like. *Interesting.*

I squeeze my eyes tight against the light. I'd thought the wind had died down, but I can still feel it blowing over my body, which seems to be rising up into the... wait, am I *floating*?

I am floating.

I am rising up into the air, as if I'm as light as a feather.

Okay, this confirms it; I'm definitely dead.

A sob escapes my throat. I'm not sure I'm okay with this, actually. It might not be painful, but it's still *death*, and even though it smells sweet and kind of spicy, and with a slight musk to it that reminds me of.... My brain struggles with a sudden sensory memory before finally figuring it out.

Jack.

It reminds me of Jack.

My eyes snap open.

I expect to see nothing but white light, just like in the movies.

Instead, I find myself staring into the deep blue of the sea. Jack is holding me tightly in his arms, his brow furrowed with concern as he looks down intently at my face. Behind him, I see the dark, hulking shape of a helicopter perched on top of the hill, a searchlight shining from the front of it, and its whirring blades creating the wind I can feel on my skin.

Jack is saying something as he looks down at me, but the wind carries it away, and it doesn't matter, anyway.

He's here.

He's come to save me.

And as his lips meet mine in a perfect, rain-drenched kiss, there's suddenly nowhere on earth I'd rather be.

Epilogue

One year later

This year the Gala Day smells like whisky and roses. It smells like heather and sunshine, and those weird corn-dogs on sticks that everyone's suddenly obsessed with.

It also smells like Jack Buchanan's aftershave, which is at least 100% better than all of those things put together.

It would be fair to say that a lot has changed in the last twelve months.

One thing that hasn't changed, however, is the simple fact that there are no wolves in Heather Bay.

And there never were.

As Jack and I kissed on the hilltop that night in the storm, a small, furry shape suddenly propelled itself forward and onto my lap: a shape which, once the terror subsided enough for me to be able to focus, turned out to be not the ferocious wolf of my imaginings, but an extremely wet and very scared, miniature poodle.

"Jude just wouldnae settle," Dad said later, as we all huddled together around the kitchen fire, Jack's arm still wrapped firmly around my shoulder, as if he's afraid I'm going to rush off up the mountain again.

"At first we thought he was just bothered by the storm," Dad continued. "Dogs can sense them coming, ye ken? But he wouldnae stop barking at the door, and when yer maim finally opened it to show him there was no one there, he went running off into the night. I've never seen anything like it."

Mum thinks to this day that Jude's canine sixth sense alerted him to the fact that I was in danger and sent him rushing off to save me. I, meanwhile, think it's more likely that he sensed drama and wanted to be in the thick of it. Whatever the reason, though, I have taken his name off my list of mortal enemies and put it on my list of Very Good Boys, instead. And that's where it'll stay, no matter how many times he pees in my shoes.

So it wasn't a wolf stalking me on the hill that night; it wasn't me who lit the fire that burned down the village hall; and no one in Heather Glen hates me.

Well, no one but Lexie, obviously.

And, okay, her mum. Who really, *really* hates me, even though she only has herself to blame for everything that went down that night.

(I'm still not convinced about Edna the sheep either, to be honest, but she can't speak to defend herself, so I'm giving her the benefit of the doubt.)

In the end, Jack decided not to press charges against the Steeles for what they did at the distillery, deciding he'd rather try to move on and not have the distillery embroiled in a local scandal before it was even open for business.

"Unless you want to me to pursue it?" he said, his eyes locking onto mine as we sat by the bank of the loch one afternoon a few days after The Incident, as I'd already come to think of it. "They hurt you much more than they hurt me, after all. The distillery can be fixed; I'm not sure you can be."

"I'm already 'fixed'," I said firmly, nestling back into his arms. "I know the fire wasn't my fault now, and that's good enough for me. I don't have to carry the guilt around with anymore. I can start afresh. With you, I hope."

He leaned down and kissed me by way of answer, and it was a long time before I was able to formulate coherent thoughts again.

"Anyway," I told him, when we finally pulled apart, "I think the public humiliation they both went through at the ball is punishment enough. Trust one who knows."

I shivered, despite the warmth of the day. I knew only too well what it's like to be the most hated person in town; how life changing the weight of that guilt can be. I wouldn't wish it on my worst enemy. Not even Lexie.

(Maybe Samantha, though. Oh *come on*, I may have learned a lot from my impostor experience, but it hasn't turned me into a *saint*.)

Not that Lexie's even here to be hated *or* forgiven, mind you. In a move that couldn't help but remind me of myself, ten years earlier, she left town not long after the ball; literally just disappearing overnight, like one of those people you read about who just vanish one day, and are never seen again.

Like Ben, in fact.

Ben has still been neither seen nor heard of ever since he walked out of our flat, with a reminder to me to turn the lights off. Like Lexie, he's gone without a trace. When I finally told him the whole story, Jack immediately offered to pay off the debt Ben left me, but I turned him down. I don't want his money. I just want his trust; and Frankie's, too, which is why I went back to my job at Highland Maids shortly after my misadventure on the hillside, and have been working there ever since. In the last few months, I've been taking on more of the managerial duties to give Frankie a bit of a break.

Surprisingly, I actually quite enjoy it I think I might be cut out for managing more than I am for cleaning; there's just much less scope for accidents that way.

Not that I've been having many accidents lately, mind you. I think I might have given them up for good, actually. I did promise Jack I would, after all, during the lengthy heart-to-heart we had after the ball. The "no holds barred" one, with no miniature poodles to jump into the loch, no assistants to interrupt us, and definitely no feather dusters.

"I wasn't angry with you when I read the letter," Jack said, taking my hand in his. "Confused, yes; but I mostly just felt sorry for you — that you'd had to go through all of that with Ben, and the fire, and that you hadn't felt you could tell me the truth. I'd have understood, you know. I'd have helped you. That's why I came after you that night."

He did, too. It turns out he'd only left the room to call the police — not Young Dougie, but the detective from Glasgow who'd been investigating the incident at the distillery — and then he'd come running after me.

"When I found your shoes on the beach, I thought..."

He paused, shaking his head at the memory.

"That I'd jumped into the loch again?" I smiled up at him. "Well, I suppose it wouldn't have been the first time."

"Then I remembered what you'd said about the Tor, that night at the distillery," he went on. "About how you'd always go there to be alone with your thoughts. I knew that's where you'd be. Because if there's anyone in town mad enough to climb that hill in a thunderstorm, you'd be the one."

"I didn't actually intend to climb it," I protested, slapping him playfully on the arm. "It was the 'wolf' that drove me up there. I'm just glad you worked it out."

"Well, me and Brian," Jack said, grinning. "He did call Mountain Rescue, after all."

"And he'll never let anyone forget it," I agreed, thinking of how happy Brian had been to have even a small role in my drama. "Did I tell you he's thinking of coming up here for a holiday soon? He says he's heard so much about the place now he has to see it for himself."

We sat there for a long moment, looking out at the water. We must have told each other this story a hundred times now; how I thought I was dying — and how Jack thought I was too, when he finally reached me that night. We'll probably be telling it for the rest of our lives.

"The next time you decide to impersonate someone, try to make it someone who doesn't go rushing up hills," Jack said, dropping a soft kiss on top of my head.

"Trust me, I'm never doing that again," I assured him, my eyes suspiciously misty as I reached up to touch him lightly on the cheek. "I honestly didn't think you'd ever forgive me when you knew who I really was. I didn't think you could possibly love me the way I really am."

"Oh, but I can," he assured me, his voice soft. "I love you *because* of who you are. Just you. No one else. And you only really lied about your name. Everything else you said was the truth. Everything that actually mattered, anyway."

"Did you... did you just say you love me?" I said, wishing there was a way to stop the blush I could feel burning my cheeks. "Because you don't have to, you know. I wasn't saying that so that you'd—"

He silenced me with another kiss.

"I said it because I meant it," he said at last. "I don't say things I don't mean. And I reckon I'm a pretty good judge of character, too. So I might not have known your real name, or where you lived, but I knew who you were in here—" he touched me lightly on the forehead, "—as soon as I met you. I knew you were someone worth getting to know. And I was right, too."

"As soon as you met me?" I said teasingly. "Even when I was covered in Diet Coke and spraying whisky all over you?"

"Yup," he said smugly. "Even then. Like I said, I'm an excellent judge of character."

"I'm not," I replied ruefully, thinking of Ben, and Lexie, and all the other people I've trusted over the years, only for them to prove beyond doubt that I didn't know them at all. "I'm a terrible judge of character. I mean, when I first met you, I thought you were... well, an asshole, really."

"And that's what I like about you," he replied, bursting out laughing. "You're never afraid to say what you think, are you? Even when you're blatantly wrong."

"I was definitely wrong about you," I said shyly. "You're not an asshole. I mean, you *do* drive too fast; that much is true."

Jack nodded solemnly.

"Noted."

"But you're not an asshole," I went on. "You're the very best person I know, in fact. And I know a lot of people. And dogs. And sheep."

"Is that your way of saying you love me too," Jack asked, brushing the hair back from my forehead.

"It is," I admitted, leaning into his arms. "I do love you. And I don't say things I don't mean either - not any more — so you can trust me on that. I'm out of the impostor game for good. It's enough trouble just being me, without trying to be someone else at the same time."

"I quite agree," said Jack, his mouth twitching. "And you can believe me when I tell you that 'just you' is more than enough for me."

* * *

"Earth to Emerald! Are you even listening to me? I swear you spend half of your life in a daydream. I think it's getting ready to start."

Frankie's voice snaps me out of my thoughts. She's standing on one side of me on Heather Glen High Street, while Jack holds my hand on the other. In the distance, we can hear the distant sound of the pipe band which will lead the procession through the village, all the way to the recently refurbished town hall, where there will be more food and drinks — including Bella McGowan's famous scones, and Jack's second blend of The 39 — than even McTavish can handle.

There will be no crowning of the village Queen this year, though.

Once the full story had come out about how Lexie had started the fire deliberately, in a bid to humiliate me for stealing the role she wanted for herself, Bella and the rest of the committee quietly agreed not to subject any more of the local girls to the popularity contest the Gala had become. Instead, there's just going to be a huge party, with everyone welcome.

There will be no smoking allowed, needless to say.

As the sound of the band gets closer, and a buzz of excitement ripples through the crowd at the thought of the first

Heather Glen Gala in over a decade, I feel Jack's hand tighten around mine.

"Are you okay?" he whispers, his cheeks dimpling as he smiles down at me.

I nod, happily. I am very much okay. And as the lead piper comes into view at the end of the street, another realization hits me. There is no voice in my head anymore; not Ben's not Scarlett's, not Lexie's, not anyone's.

It's just me. Just Emerald.

And I wouldn't have it any other way.

Thank you

From the bottom of my heart,
thank you for reading my first novel.

I really hope you enjoyed it and can take a few
minutes out of your day to leave
a review on Amazon!

Want to know what happens next?

In December 2022 I'll be releasing Lexie's story as book 2 in
the Heather Bay series. Can she redeem herself, and break
free from her mother's influence?

In Spring 2023, meanwhile, you can follow Scarlett in her
pursuit of love (and a missing Ada Valentine). You never
know, you might even find out what really happened to
ex-boyfriend Ben...

About the Author

Amber Eve is an awkward Scottish redhead with a tendency to have "accidents". The character of Emerald Taylor is in no way based on her.

You can connect with me on:
- https://www.patreon.com/ambereveauthor
- https://twitter.com/foreveramber
- https://www.facebook.com/foreveramberUK
- https://www.instagram.com/foreveramberblog

Subscribe to my newsletter:
- https://mailchi.mp/cb43d14786a9/book-alerts

Also by Amber Eve

If you'd like to know what happened next to the residents of Heather Bay, catch up with them in these upcoming titles by Amber Eve:

The Accidental Actress - pre-order now
Lexie Steele was always the Main Character.

Until one day, she wasn't.

Leaving her Highland home town in disgrace, Lexie flees to L.A., to start over. Then a chance encounter with renowned actor Jett Carter gives her the chance to do just that, in the most unexpected way.

He needs a fake girlfriend.

She needs to show everyone back home that she's made a success of her life in spite of her past mistakes.

They could almost have been made for each other; but romances made in Hollywood aren't built to survive the realities of the Scottish Highlands — or are they?

The Accidental Investigator - available Spring 2023
Moving to the Scottish Highlands isn't quite what Scarlett Scott expected it to be. And when local influencer Ava Valentine goes missing, things start to get even more complicated...

Printed in Great Britain
by Amazon

11377601R00181